D1516815

BARKING WITH THE STARS

This Large Print Book carries the
Seal of Approval of N.A.V.H.

A PAMPERED PETS MYSTERY

BARKING WITH THE STARS

SPARKLE ABBEY

THORNDIKE PRESS
A part of Gale, a Cengage Company

Farmington Hills, Mich • San Francisco • New York • Waterville, Maine
Meriden, Conn • Mason, Ohio • Chicago

LIBRARY OF CONGRESS CIP DATA ON FILE.
CATALOGUING IN PUBLICATION FOR THIS BOOK
IS AVAILABLE FROM THE LIBRARY OF CONGRESS

ISBN-13: 978-1-4328-4974-0 (hardcover)

Published in 2018 by arrangement with BelleBooks, Inc.

Printed in Mexico
1 2 3 4 5 6 7 22 21 20 19 18

To the men and women who have served and are dealing with the effects of post-traumatic stress.

And to the loyal therapy dogs by their side in the day-to-day battles.

CHAPTER ONE

I should have known something was up by the way folks were looking at me. The sideways glances and the subtle turning away should have given me a clue. But the swirl of chatter, the yips and barks, and the swell of people and pets, surrounded me as soon as I walked in.

Still, I haven't always been a pet therapist, I was trained as a clinical psychologist, for Pete's sake. You'd think I'd have a little bit of insight.

But there'd been a fender bender in the southbound lanes of PCH and traffic had been backed up so I was running late. I'd skidded into the hotel in a big ole hurry, gotten directions, and raced to the volunteer check-in at greyhound speed. Then in such a tizzy over my tardiness, I just assumed that was the reason for the stares. I'd failed to catch that there might be something else going on.

"Oh, there you are." Rufus McGrill, the onsite organizer for the star-studded event, hurried up, his tablet at the ready, his face nearly as red as his hair. "People have been looking for you."

"I'm so sorry." I dug in my bag for my credentials which the volunteer packet I'd been given said I needed to be wearing at all times. "Traffic was awful." Ah, there it was. I slipped the lanyard over my head and adjusted the tag, which proclaimed, "Barking with the Stars Official Pet Liaison."

My friend Diana Knight had been the one who'd gotten me involved in the celebrity fundraiser which would benefit a group called Warriors for the Paws, but I have to tell you, convincing me had not taken a ton of arm twisting.

When Sunny Simone, the CEO of Warriors for the Paws, had told me that every day twenty-two veterans take their own lives, I'd felt sick. Twenty-two. What a shocking number. That's a suicide every sixty-five minutes. Her group matched trained therapy dogs with veterans who'd developed post-traumatic stress disorders from the horrors they'd experienced in combat zones. Too many soldiers came back with PTSD, and these dogs could be just what the doctor ordered for so many —

from waking their human from night terrors to helping the veterans remain calm in stressful situations to helping with episodes of depresssion. I'd checked them out and Warriors for the Paws was making a difference. I was in.

"Yoo-hoo, Caro."

Hearing my name, I looked for the source.

I spotted an arm waving from across the room. Diana Knight was so petite that I couldn't see the rest of her, but I recognized the blond hair and the flash of hot-pink nails. And, well, who could miss those diamonds?

Once Hollywood's darling in a series of classic romantic comedies in the fifties, Diana was a classic herself. Now, in her eighties, she had not slowed down one bit. As she parted the crowd and headed toward me, I could see she had her rescue puggle, Mr. Wiggles, tucked close to her. Diana's heart was as big as her fame, and she collected strays like she collected fans. I guess in a way you could say I was one of those strays.

"Oh, my." She stopped in front of me and took a deep breath. "What an unbelievable turnout of volunteers." Dressed to the nines, as always, she sported an icy-blue pantsuit with a brightly colored scarf thrown over her shoulders and wrapped around the pup like a sling. "Mr. Wiggles is glad to see you. Aren't you, buddy?" She picked up the pup's paw and wiggled it so it looked like he was waving at me. "Say good morning to Caro."

"Good morning." I gave the pup a nuzzle.

"Don't you look amazing, as always?" she continued. "Is that a new Stella McCartney?"

I nodded. Diana loved fashion and kept up with the latest designers. She hardly ever guessed wrong. I'd picked up the top recently and loved the dog-print motif.

"If I had your height and gorgeous red hair, I'd wear her, too." She continued without taking a breath, "Have you seen Armand and Elizabeth? They were looking for you. And that nice Rebecca Tyler was name-dropping your name all over the place and bragging about how wonderful you were during the Pet Intervention project."

Mr. Wiggles pushed against the scarf/sling and gave a little yip.

"The crowd is a little overwhelming for him. He's not used to not being able to run around at will." She placed him on the floor but kept her hand on his leash.

"But a crowd is great for the cause, though, right?" I smiled at Rufus who waited for Diana to finish, though I couldn't say he waited patiently. In fact, his red hair now stood upright, making it appear as if his forehead was on fire.

"You were saying . . ." I threw the conversation back in his direction.

"Sunny would like for you to take a look at the accommodations for our headliner, Purple, and her dog, Lavender. I know you've already been working with them. Anyway, Sunny said you had to approve the dressing room setup." He glanced down at the screen. "And then, if you could, check on . . . uhm . . . Babycakes?"

I nodded. "That's Shar Summer's Chinese Crested." Shar was a hit sensation on a popular television show about triplet sisters who perform magic. In reality, all three triplets were played by her. I'd known this type of event would be right up her alley.

"That's right." Rufus clutched the tablet to his chest.

"First, I have to check in with Kristen Karmania and her teacup Chihuahua. I promised I'd let her know when I got here."

"No." I wasn't sure who said it first, Diana or Rufus, but they both said it with force.

"What do you mean, no?" I looked from one to the other.

"Well . . ." Rufus stood poised like he wanted to make a run for it. "You see . . ." His voice trailed off and he looked down at his tablet.

"Oh, for Pete's sake, just tell her." Diana rolled her eyes. "KK and her band of bimbos have been led astray by your ex and have said to tell you your services are no longer needed. They don't even have the chutzpah to tell you in person."

"Geoff is here?" I wasn't as worried about being dumped as I was about my ex-husband. I should have expected it, but I hadn't heard from him recently so I'd wrongly assumed he had moved on. "That . . ." I couldn't think of a term for Geoffrey that I could say in polite company.

"I'm afraid, it's worse than that." Diana took my arm and steered me away from Rufus and the group of people who had slowly inched closer in an attempt to hear.

"You see, he has not only inserted himself into the Barking with the Stars event and ingratiated himself to some of the celebrities, but he's also been spreading rumors."

"What kind of rumors?" I didn't care so much about losing Kristen Karmania, or KK as the press referred to her. She hadn't been a client for long and in the short few weeks I'd been working with her, I'd had

12

my doubts about whether she really had any interest in following my advice. Chihuahuas can be high strung, but Scamp, her teacup, was Zen in comparison to KK herself.

"Well, hello there, Ms. Lamont. Do you care to comment on all the buzz?" Callum MacAvoy, ace reporter for the local television station and a constant thorn in my side, inserted himself between Diana and me.

I wasn't sure if he meant the event or the rumors being spread by my ex. Either way the answer was the same.

"No, I don't." I looked behind him and didn't see a camera crew so he wasn't really reporting on anything at all. Plain and simple, MacAvoy was on a fishing expedition.

"Excuse us." I scooped up Mr. Wiggles, linked my arm with Diana's, and moved us to a corner that seemed semi-private. "What is Geoff saying?"

"He's telling people, your clients, that you are taking some time off. That you're on the verge of a nervous breakdown since being held hostage by that crazy man you helped capture a while back, and you're going to give up your practice and move to England." Diana's voice quivered with disgust.

"What?" I couldn't wrap my head around

Diana's words. "I'm what?"

"There you are." Of course, his voice projected from across the room.

Speak of . . .

Though it was a sad cliché, "speak of the devil" was exactly what popped into my head as Geoffrey Carlisle, my ex-husband, slithered up and put his arm around my shoulders.

"Are you okay, my dear?" Gloriously handsome on the outside and rotten to the core on the inside, Geoff's fake worry might have sounded sincere. To someone who hadn't been emotionally destroyed by him. "I've been hearing the most awful things. Like you're losing it." He smiled but more at the nearby eavesdroppers than at me.

"I am about to lose it, but not in the way you mean." I kept my voice low. "Remove your arm from me. And don't touch me again."

He dropped his arm and took a step back. The man had movie-star looks and played them. His dark hair a perfect foil to his expensive custom-made charcoal suit — blue tie chosen to complement his vivid-blue eyes. Contacts.

"You look good, Carolina." His tone was pleasant but dripped with insincerity.

I glanced down at my jeans and the designer dog-print top. There was a time when Geoff's polish would have caused me to feel inadequate. Not anymore. I knew who I was and I liked my bohemian look.

Besides, my clothes were all washable, and when you're dealing with wound-up canines, that trumps fashion any day. Somehow, I didn't think his high-priced Tom Ford suit would fare so well when someone's puppy peed on it.

CHAPTER TWO

Down, girl. I walked away from Geoffrey without another word. I'd learned there was nothing to be gained from engaging with someone who wouldn't know the truth if it hit him upside the head. The last time we'd talked, I'd told him in no uncertain terms that I hoped we never crossed paths again. Ever. And I'd meant it.

Now, here he was. Smack dab in the middle of my world again and, from what Diana had shared, not only attempting to take over my clients, but this time he also seemed intent on trashing my reputation.

As I stomped back to the dressing rooms, I was pretty sure everyone I passed could see the steam coming out of my ears. I stopped and took a deep breath. I'd deal with the rumors and lies later, but first I needed to check on Babycakes. That was, if Shar Summers hadn't also fired me.

It was easy to find Shar. I simply followed

the trail of pink. The television star was looking over what would be her dressing room. I poked my head in the door. It was already awash in pink satin, pink pillows, and pink clothes.

She looked up from where she sat at a sparkly dressing table draped in pink beads. "Hello, Caro." She waved a hand decorated in multiple pink rings. "Come on in."

The petite star had her dog tucked under one arm, and with the other hand she was flipping through what I assumed were the program notes. The little Chinese Crested was high strung. And, in the sequined doggie coat and hat, looked more like a well-dressed alien than a canine.

"Did you need something?" I took a deep, calming breath. No need to bring my own unresolved Geoffrey-tension into the situation.

"I just wanted to know if there was something I should be doing with Baby. You know, to get her to be okay with this. I can't have her nipping at the other celebs or their pooches. I haven't had a problem with her lately but this will be a lot of people and a lot of puppy dogs."

"That's why I suggested you bring her today. So, she can get acclimated and once she's used to the place she won't be so nervous." I'd also thought maybe Shar wouldn't be so nervous as well. Nervous owner translates to nervous and unstable dog. But I hadn't said all that aloud.

"My angel-baby seems a-okay." She set aside the notes. "Right, girlie-wirlie?"

I knew from the baby-talk she was addressing the dog and not me. "Ri—"

"What the hell is this?" A voice screeched from the dressing room next door.

We all three froze.

"I said, What. The. Hell. Is. This?"

Each word was punctuated with something hitting the wall. More really bad words followed at the same volume, and Shar sat mid-sentence — her mouth open, blond curls frozen, her blue eyes wide. Babycakes began to shake.

"This is not what I asked for. I asked for pomegranate juice. POM-OH-GRAN-IT! Got it?"

The door opened and then slammed shut, rattling the sparkly pink beads draped on Shar's mirror. I opened the dressing room door and peeked out in time to see Purple, the event's headliner and biggest star, stomp down the hallway toward the exit.

"Wait!" A Keith-Urban-look-alike in faded jeans and spiky blond hair followed her. A roadie maybe? Or one of her musicians or

18

technical crew?

Purple didn't turn around, but raised a hand over her head and made a smoosh of dismissal. "Later."

"Come *on.*" The guy slapped his leg with the paper he held and retreated.

Rufus and his clipboard attempted to intercept Purple at the end of the hall, but she pushed him aside and continued.

"Wow, and I thought I was high maintenance." Shar had come up behind me. She played a bit of a ditz on her TV show, and sometimes I wasn't always sure it was acting, but in this case, she was spot on with her assessment.

"Wow, is right." I didn't know who Purple had been yelling at but whoever it was certainly had not deserved such an abusive dressing down.

"That's Diva with a capital D, or I guess P in this case." Shar giggled at her joke as she continued to stare down the hall where Purple had disappeared.

I was thinking a different word entirely, but my mama raised me better so I didn't say it aloud.

Purple was an amazing singer, but she was even more famous for wearing wigs that obscured her face. The wigs varied in style and color, though mostly a white blond with

19

some sort of bow or hair ornament and a vivid streak of purple down the right side. They always completely covered her facial features except for her mouth, thus creating an irresistible air of mystery.

No doubt about it, the look was very effective marketing. You couldn't argue with that. The singing sensation had become much more than a talented vocalist. The enigma she created with the mystery surrounding what she really looked like and why she covered her face was the stuff of legends. She'd topped the charts, filled stadiums, and was a much-sought-after late-night talk show guest.

And her fans. Well, they were something else. They bought her music, they followed her from venue to venue, they dressed like her, they collected Purple t-shirts, Purple dolls, Purple posters, Purple key chains, and Purple underwear. I swear I am not making that last one up.

Shar and I ducked back into her dressing room.

"How do you think she sees?" Shar tipped her head.

"I've wondered that myself." I'd been working with Purple and her dog, Lavender, at the house she'd just purchased in one of Laguna Beach's gated communities, and in the half-dozen or so times I'd been there, I'd never seen her without the wig. It seemed to me that always wearing a wig would be beyond uncomfortable, but you couldn't argue with the fame the image had created.

"Thanks for getting me involved with Barking with the Stars." Shar set Babycakes down carefully in her pink puppy stroller.

"I'm glad you were able to do it." I handed her the list of tips I was sharing with everyone. "It's such a great cause."

"There's something I need to tell you." Shar looked up from the paper, her blue eyes blinking furiously.

"What is it?" Shar and I had some history and her nervousness could mean a number of things.

"It's just that I don't know if you know it, but there are some online sites with bad reviews about you and your business," she said in a rush. "Some of the others were talking about it earlier. No one believes them, of course, but I thought you should know."

Geoffrey.

Apparently not content to simply spread lies about my mental health, he'd also taken advantage of other ways to trash me and my business. What a jerk.

"Thanks for letting me know." I unclenched my fists and concentrated on breathing normally. "I really appreciate it."

"I don't know what you can do, but thought you'd want to know." She went back to reading through the list.

Once I'd finished up with Shar and Babycakes, I moved on to my next celebrity check-in. I shared my tip sheet and then spent some time with Armand and Elizabeth Watts, who'd just had their first child.

I had been working with them for months. Their little Skye Terrier, Plucky, had initially had some difficulty in dealing with the idea that he was no longer the center of their world. But they had been great to work with and things were going well now. Armand, a superhero movie actor, and Elizabeth, a romcom darling, were the latest Hollywood "It" couple and the people-watching magazines followed their every move, so lending their support to Barking with the Stars would add even more press interest in the event.

As I was leaving their dressing room, I saw Rufus down the hallway chatting with Diana, and decided to check in. I knew she understood, but I'd sort of left Diana standing when I walked away from Geoffrey.

"How do you think things are going?" I asked.

Rufus's color seemed to have calmed, so I hoped that was a good indication his blood pressure had returned to normal and that things were going smoothly.

"Well, our celeb-who-shall-not-be-named has apparently calmed down." He tapped his tablet and looked around. "At least for now."

"I was going to check out her dressing room next, but I really wanted to do my assessment with her and the dog present. Maybe I'll stop by her place on my way home." Perhaps I could help in providing some calm or at least figure out what had her so on edge.

"Oh, she's not there." His smile seemed like more of a grimace. "We've put her up in the Starfish Suite here at the hotel."

"Really?" The woman had just purchased a fabulous house in Laguna Beach. The drive to the hotel was ten, maybe fifteen, minutes, tops. "Why would you need to do that?"

"She's having some remodeling work done on her house and the noise is, quote, driving her up a wall, unquote." He made air-quote hand gestures as he spoke.

"Then it makes it even easier for me to

stop by." I patted his arm. "Hang in there, Rufus. You're doing great. Besides, in a week this will all be over."

"Thanks, Caro." He smiled, this time a genuine smile. "You're right. Just so many egos in one place. Sometimes I wonder what we were thinking."

On my way back to the lobby, I ran in to Mandy, Purple's assistant, who was pushing a luggage cart through the courtyard and toward the westward wing of the complex.

"Can I get someone to help you with that?" I held the door for her to pass through. "I'm sure the hotel staff would be happy to assist." In fact, I was pretty sure they would be appalled that she was doing it herself.

"No, I'm good." Mandy was smaller than I was in stature, but she clearly worked out. She wasn't having any problem maneuvering the overloaded cart. "Thanks, though," she added as an afterthought.

I followed her to the next doorway and held it as well. "I'd heard you and Purple were setting up here for the duration."

"Yep, the noise the contractors were making in doing the demo work was awful." She stopped in front of the elevator and pushed the button.

"Listen, I was hoping to check in with

Purple and Lavender." I realized Mandy, much like Rufus, kept everything running. "Would now be a good time?"

"I can check." She pushed the button again. "It's been a stressful day."

I wanted to ask about the earlier incident but it was really none of my business. "I don't want to put you in a bad spot, so if she's not up to it, that's fine. I can come back. But it might be a good idea if I see how Lavender is doing. Especially after a day in all the chaos." The elevator had arrived and I held the door for her. "The problems she's had I understand have mostly been in hotels when you all were on the road."

"You're welcome to try." Mandy pushed the luggage rack into the elevator. "Follow me."

The elevator stopped on the sixth floor and we got off. Again, I held the door so she could push the cart through. As she turned it toward the hallway leading to the rooms, one of the boxes shifted and I reached forward to grab it.

"Holy Guacamole! Don't run me over." A voice from the other side of the cart sounded all too familiar.

"Betty?" I leaned around the cart to see Betty Foxx, who worked at my cousin

Melinda's pet boutique.

"Carmen, what are you doin' here?"

Betty never called me by my given name. I'd given up on figuring out whether it was due to not actually remembering it or if she was messing with me. Clearly her loyalties lay with my cousin, Melinda, so I was guessing the latter.

"I could ask the same of you," she shot back.

Betty, as usual, was dressed in what some might call satin pajamas but what she'd determined was fashion-forward day wear. This matched set was a hot pink with big white polka-dots. As always, the look was finished off with a single strand of pearls and eyebrows painted on with lipstick.

You heard that right. Lipstick eyebrows. In this case, neon pink.

On this foible as well, I'd given up on trying to figure out the logic.

"Well, I got this here bow. Made special for that big star Purple's dog." Betty held aloft what looked like a corsage box. "I gotta deliver it to her and when I went by the house, the lady there told me she was living here. Temporarily."

"I can take that." Mandy held out her hand.

"No way, Jose, lady." Betty shook her gray

curls and held the box out of reach.

"Purple is not seeing anyone right now," Mandy said firmly. "She's resting."

"Well, it looks like you and Carol are goin' that way so I'll just tag along." Betty shifted her white patent-leather pocketbook and crossed her arms. "I'll hang out until she's rested and ready to see me."

"Fine." Mandy seemed to know she wasn't going to win this one. "Follow me."

When we reached the Starfish Suite, Mandy took out a key card, swiped it, and opened the door. "You two wait here." She held up her hand.

I hated being lumped in with Betty, and the fact was I was still plenty upset with her and the problems she'd caused my cousin, Mel, and me over a family brooch. Mel and I had been on the outs for a while over our Grandma Tillie's brooch, and just when we were getting close to a truce, well, let's just say Betty stepped in and made things worse. And now neither of us had the brooch.

Mandy motioned us into the room.

Referring to the space as a "room" was a pretty big understatement. The suite was probably on par with my house in terms of square footage.

Purple was ensconced in a large royal-blue high-backed chair. She was draped in a black-and-white satin robe, and her Lhasa Apso, Lavender, sat on a small settee by her side. Although I'd met with the pop star many times, I was always disconcerted by being unable to make eye contact.

Her platinum-blond wig completely obscured the top half of her face and the usual vivid streak of purple accented the right side. What I could see of her face was smooth and flawless, her jawline delicate. Her lips, the deep hue of a classic red rose, were perfect.

In the short time I'd known her it always seemed to me Purple was forever on stage. Setting the perfect scene. Playing a part. As a psychologist, I found it fascinating. As a person, I found it concerning.

Mandy had pulled the luggage cart into the room and had begun taking the boxes off one by one. Her movements were swift and efficient, like the woman herself. Pick up a box, pull it off, drop it. One after another.

"Would you like something to drink?" Purple raised the crystal glass she held, her voice soft and nothing like the strident tone I'd overheard when I'd been in Shar's dressing room. "Perhaps some pomegranate juice? It's very good for you." She set the glass down on a small white satin-draped tray on her lap. More of the staging. "Mandy, would you get these lovely ladies something to drink?"

"No, thank you," Betty and I answered at once.

"Please have a seat." The singing sensation made a regal gesture in the direction of the couch.

Betty and I sat down side by side on the blue-and-white striped sofa. I looked over at Betty and her odd outfit and bizarre hot-pink eyebrows. Somehow it didn't seem quite as crazy in the presence of a pop star with a wig covering her most of her face.

"What's with the wig?" Betty asked, always to the point. "Can you see outta that?"

"You've brought the bow?" Purple ignored her question and held out her hand. Slim and elegant fingers tipped in a dark magenta.

Betty scooted forward and handed the box to her.

Purple opened it and held it out for us to see. A big purple hairbow with tufts of wide gold.

"Perfect." She stroked the shiny ribbon. "Look, Mandy. This will be perfect." She held it high over her head so her assistant could admire it.

"Very nice." Mandy had all the boxes unloaded from the cart and had begun to open them setting the contents on the large, glass conference table. The boxes appeared to contain awards and other memorabilia. I wondered why Purple would need those at the hotel. But then, I wondered about a lot of things in this situation.

"What's all this?" Betty had moved from the couch to where Mandy worked. She picked up a trophy that looked a bit like an Oscar but the figure was a woman whose face was obscured by hair. A Purple, maybe, instead of an Oscar. "Man, that's heavy." She almost dropped it.

"Put that down." Mandy's voice was sharp as she took the statuette from Betty and put it down carefully on the table.

"Fine." Betty, not to be deterred, moved on to another item. "Hey, this doll looks just like you. I guess it does anyway." She lifted up the doll's hair to peer at the face. "Why do you cover your face? I knew a lady once who had a bad accident and she kinda wore her hair over one side. That what happened to you?"

Again, with a glare Mandy removed the item from Betty's hand and placed it on the table.

"Betty." I gave the little senior a hard

stare. "Not appropriate."

She shrugged her narrow satin-clothed shoulders and moved on to another item. "Sorry. Just askin'."

"What do you think, Caro?" Purple held the bow out to me. "Would you try it on Lavender, please?"

I took the bow from her and turned it over in my hand. "Custom-made by Kim's Designs exclusively for the Bow Wow Boutique," the tag said. It was good quality and light enough it shouldn't be a problem for the dog.

I bent down and clipped it to Lavender's top knot. I stroked her back and she wiggled a little in answer. She didn't seem to mind the bow.

"After my parents were killed, my grandfather raised me." Purple's tone was suddenly very serious. "He was a decorated veteran of World War II and I always wear his Purple Heart close to my heart." She tugged on a chain that had been hidden by her robe collar. "That's why I wanted to do this event for the vets."

"I'm sure Warriors for the Paws appreciates your support." I was feeling a little softer toward her. "Your involvement will make such a difference in what they can accomplish."

Mandy unclipped the ribbon from the dog and placed it on the desk. "I'll put this with the rest of her things for the show." She went back to unpacking the boxes.

I wondered what it was like having someone as efficient as Mandy taking care of all the details of your life. There were days when I needed someone like her.

"What's this?" I could see Betty inching closer and closer to Purple but I wasn't sure what she was up to. She'd picked up a plastic bag from Mandy's cart.

"That is medication. Put it down." Mandy was out of patience with Betty. I understood. I'd been there myself from time to time.

"I'll attach my gramp's Purple Heart lapel pin to Lavender's bow," Purple continued, oblivious to Mandy's irritation, "and we'll both be honoring him when I go on stage for the finale."

Betty moved back toward the couch but very close to Purple, and as she did I saw something in her hand, and realized her intent. The scamp was going for Purple's wig.

"Betty!" I stepped forward to stop her.

As I did she tripped over my foot.

And ended up face first in Purple's lap.

Red liquid flew everywhere. Purple's white

wig was red.

The white on her black-and-white robe was red.

The dog was red.

"What happened?" Betty raised her head, the white satin drape from the tray Purple had been holding had landed on Betty's head. It covered the top of her face, a satin mirror of Purple's iconic look. She lifted it up and peeked out. Red juice dripped from her hair, her eyelashes, her nose.

"Are you okay?" I asked. She didn't appear to be injured but I wanted to be sure. "Is everyone all right?"

"What on earth?" Mandy had rushed over.

"I'm so sorry. Mrs. Foxx tripped over my foot." I had no idea why I was defending the elderly rabble-rouser. "Purple, are you okay?"

Mandy picked up the small camera which had flown out of Betty's hand and landed on the floor when she tripped.

"Take her and get out."

CHAPTER THREE

Betty and I stopped in the hotel restroom and cleaned her up so she could drive home. I offered to call Mel or Betty's daughter, but she'd insisted she was fine. As upset as I was with her, I did want to make sure she was okay.

Once Betty was off, I gathered up my bag and headed back to the lobby. And what a lobby it was. I hadn't had time to truly appreciate it in my earlier rush. The Ocean Mark P was the west coast installation of a pair of newly opened high-class resort hotels. The P was for Pacific. Its sister hotel on the Atlantic coast, Hilton Head's Ocean Mark A, had been open a couple of years.

Across the sand-colored stone promenade, Sunny Simone stood chatting with Rufus McGrill. The lanky redhead still clutched his ever-present notebook. I thought maybe it would be a good idea to give him a heads-up about Betty's close encounter of the pomegranate kind with Purple.

Heading in their direction, I paused a few seconds by the unique aquamarine fountain that graced the center of the lobby. The calming ebb and flow sounded like waves on Main Beach, and the sparkle of the water as it splashed down the crystal palm fronds reminded me of the spray of water when my pooch, Dogbert, shook off the salt water after a run on the beach.

Deep breath.

As I approached Sunny and Rufus, I noticed a big mountain of a man with dark skin, darker eyes, and a military posture who stood to one side holding the leash of a gorgeous black Lab. He was obviously waiting to speak to one of them as well. I stepped toward him to wait for them to finish their conversation.

Though I'm tall, this guy towered over me. The dog, who sported a working-dog vest, stayed close by his side. When I reached out a hand to introduce myself, the Lab stepped between us, but the man motioned to him with a hand sign as if to say, "It's okay."

I waited. It was difficult to not pet the Lab, but I knew that with therapy or service dogs, a stranger's touch, though well-intentioned, can often be an unwelcome distraction.

"Caro Lamont, pet liaison for the event." I indicated my name badge.

"Jonathan Trimble, I work with Warriors for the Paws." He took my hand. "And this is Whiskey." He indicated the Lab.

"What a handsome boy." As much as I wanted to, I still didn't pet him. "Do you work on the training side? I'm fascinated with the process and what type of a facility you have. I'd love to know more about it."

I glanced at Rufus and Sunny. Still talking.

"We do the majority of the training with the veteran in his or her home so not a lot is done there." He lifted a muscular arm and ran a hand over his bald head. "The work we do at the facility is mostly working with the dog to see if it's a good candidate. These are shelter dogs so we've got to know if there are any issues that would present problems." The deep timbre of his voice said drill sergeant but the good humor on his face belied that notion.

"I didn't realize you used shelter dogs. Do you choose certain breeds over others?" I was curious because some breeds are easier to train.

"We have good success with Labradors, Golden Retrievers, and German Shepherds, but we're willing to work with any breed." He shifted his position and again the Lab positioned himself between us. "Sometimes the veteran contacts us because he or she has a dog in mind, but in most cases, we're placing a shelter dog that's already been evaluated."

"When you work with the potential owner-trainer in their home, what kind of behaviors are you working on?" The idea of the veteran being involved in the training made a lot of sense to me.

"We're looking for bonding and the ability to recognize if the owner is in trouble."

"I've heard some groups use a PAT or a Puppy Aptitude Test. Do you do that?"

"Our dogs aren't all puppies but we use something similar. Our test screens for social attraction, willingness to follow, acceptance of dominance, as well as how sensitive the dog is to touch, sounds, and sights. And then finally, how stable the dog is."

"Wow, how many wash out?"

"Well . . ." He flashed a smile. "It's not so much winners and losers as it is making sure the dog is right for the person and the person is right for the dog."

"Right. Makes sense." I totally got that concept. In my line of work, I often dealt with pet incompatibility. A high-energy dog that needed a lot of exercise when the person didn't have the time or inclination to keep up the pace resulted in a badly behaved canine and a frustrated owner. I'd often wished I could have been involved in the selection part of the process, rather than at the problem stage.

His dog moved again to make sure he was between Jonathan and me. "He's making sure you have space, isn't he?"

"Whiskey senses my tension, ma'am." Jonathan patted the dog's head and the canine responded to the affection with an adoring look.

"I'm one of the Warriors for the Paws success stories. A couple of years ago I couldn't even leave my house to get groceries. Hell, most days I couldn't leave my chair. After two tours of duty in Iraq . . ." He stared off in the distance. "Let's just say, I didn't have a life. At least, not what most people would consider a life. Now, Whiskey and I go pretty much anywhere."

"Like here," I noted.

"My fifteen-year-old daughter is a huge fan of this Purple, the singer that's doing the event. I'm going to be able to bring her to the show. I can do things with her now." He swallowed hard.

His pain and struggle for composure was so raw, I felt it like a stab in my own chest.

"I'm glad you have him." I wanted to give the big guy a hug but I knew better. I fought the lump in my throat. "And, Jonathan, thank you for your service."

He went very still, looked down, and dropped a shaking hand lightly on Whiskey's head. When he looked back at me his dark eyes were full.

With a brief nod of acknowledgement, he straightened his shoulders and pointed. "Looks like Rufus is available."

"You go first." I could wait. I didn't look forward to the re-telling of the Betty disaster.

Rufus motioned to Jonathan and held out some papers. "If you'd look this over and then I can show you where we're planning to stage the dogs."

"Caro, I thought you'd left." Rufus spotted me.

"I had but ended up running in to Mandy, Purple's assistant." I paused. "And, well, things went downhill from there."

I filled Rufus in on the situation and had to give him credit that he kept a straight face through the whole story.

"Wow." He shook his head. "I don't even know what to say about that one."

"I just wanted you to be aware." I turned to go and then turned back. Jonathan Trimble had moved a few feet away to give us some privacy. "Nice to meet you, Jonathan. Thanks for answering my many questions."

"No problem." He gave a wave.

Back in my car, I checked my messages. The new client I'd tried to squeeze in today had cancelled, which actually worked out well. Liz Bennett had a Jack Russell named Domino and she'd pressured me a bit to fit them in. I'd only agreed because it was just an initial meeting to do an informal assessment of the pet and their family members. However, I really don't like to rush those first meetings, so no problem. We'd reschedule for another day and take our time.

I stopped by my office, grabbed some lunch, and had plenty of time to get to my next appointment — Nick and Bonnie Humphries and Rosie, their barking beagle. This was only a quick check-in as I'd been working with them for a while.

Leaving the appointment, I noted that I had missed a phone call from Sam, my . . . uhm.

Well, what was Sam? At thirty-three, I thought I was a little past having a boyfriend, but I wasn't comfortable with anything more. In spite of the assumption on everyone's part that Sam and I were on the fast track to matrimony, we were not having that conversation. Or rather, I wasn't. He, on the other hand, had been hinting at commitment.

I could hear my Grandma Tillie's voice in my head saying, "Caro, you gotta fish or cut bait."

Is that where we were? I wondered. Right now, he was away on a business trip in New York. Maybe this was a good time for me to figure out where my heart was on Sam and me.

I didn't have enough of a schedule gap before the next house call to return his call, so I'd have to do that when I got home. I added it to my list.

Yes, I'm a compulsive list maker. As a people therapist before I became a pet therapist, I knew my list making was a crutch in my attempt to feel in control of my life. But, hey, it's a crutch that works for me.

The rest of the day sped by with appointments. When I finally turned my car toward home it was with a sigh of relief.

As I pulled into my driveway, my cell phone rang. It was another cancellation. This time a client I'd had since I'd first opened my business in Laguna Beach. My heart sank. They'd made an excuse about travel, but I knew that wasn't it. With two cancellations and one outright your-services-are-no-longer-needed in twenty-four hours, Geoffrey's campaign to destroy my business seemed to be working.

I walked in the door thankful to be home. I needed to deal with the chaos Geoff had caused, but at the moment I just wanted to kick off my shoes, hold my pets, and forget about the day.

"Hope you guys had a better day than I did," I said to the fur crew.

They looked at me as if they understood. I grabbed Dogbert's leash, clipped it to his collar, and took him for a short take-care-of-business walk around the block. Once we had that handled and we were back home, it was clearly time to think about dinner. Thelma and Louise, my two felines, paced from the kitchen to their bowls like they hadn't been fed in this century.

"I know, girls, y'all are starving and I'm fixin' to get you some food." I reached into the pantry and grabbed the cat-food container. I'd tried a new brand and they seemed to be giving it their seal of approval.

I tried to reach Sam but got his voicemail. I left a message so he would know I called, but with not knowing his schedule and with the east coast/west coast time difference, it might be hard to catch him.

I searched to see what was available for my own dinner, settled on a chicken salad, and began assembling ingredients. Of course, as soon as I pulled the already grilled chicken out, all three fur kids were right by my side.

We made short work of dinner and cleanup, and I decided a nice long bath was in order. I walked through to my bedroom. My house wasn't big by Laguna Beach standards and was tiny by Texas standards, but I loved it. Loved the open layout, loved the neighborhood. Nothing like the house I grew up in, I'd chosen it because of the always soothing view of the Pacific and I'd decorated it with comfort in mind. Overstuffed furniture meant for you to sink into and an eclectic blend of other pieces that struck my fancy. The master suite had a big bath with a soaking tub, and that sounded perfect after chasing after celebrities and their dogs and then dealing with Betty and the trouble she'd caused.

After a soak, I felt better. I pulled on yoga pants and a well-worn Pacific Marine Mammal Center t-shirt. Settled at my laptop, I tried to think where the online reviews that

Shar told me about might be. I was sure the online sites had policies about creepers like Geoffrey posting multiple negative reviews, but it was irritating to have to take the time to figure all that out.

I thought Yip was one of the sites that specialized in pet-related services. I searched for it and then once I got to the site, had to create a login in order to really see anything. Once through that process, I looked up reviews for PAWS. That's my business name, Professional Animal Wellness Specialist or PAWS for short. Much easier to remember.

Dogbert had moved in close to lie against my leg and the two cats had situated themselves nearby. "Ah, here we go." Dogbert perked up his ears. I shouldn't have used the Go-word. "No, buddy, not that kind of 'go'."

There were at least twenty reviews of PAWS on the site. A few from people who were clients I recognized, and a bunch from obscure email addresses. I clicked through them.

My chicken salad suddenly felt like the chicken was pecking at my stomach as I read through the reviews. They ranged from claims that I was undependable (late, unprepared, etc.) to the more serious: incompetent and unskilled. There wasn't any license in California for doing the type of work I did, so I'd always depended on my reputation. This blast of bad reviews could pose a serious problem.

I'd started an email to the address listed in the help section for lodging a complaint, when my phone rang. I recognized the number.

Can you believe it?

It was none other than the lowlife himself.

A better person would've just let the call go to voicemail.

Not me.

"What the heck, Geoffrey?" I didn't even say hello.

"Are you all right, Carolina?" The voice that used to give me chills now ignited an anger that made me want to reach through the phone and grab him by the throat.

"Don't pretend you don't know what I'm talking about," I bit out.

"You seem a bit tense." I could imagine the smirk on his face. "Could it be that the rumors are true?"

"You no-account bottom-feeder." The calm in my voice should have scared him, but he was so full of himself there was no room for thinking about anyone else.

"Now, now, let's not get nasty."

"You listen to me, you yellow-bellied pond scum. I don't care if you get all cozy with the celebrities or steal my clients. I don't even care that you tell lies about me." I took a deep breath. "But you had better not mess up this event. Because if you do, buddy, I'm coming after you."

I have no idea what his response was because I pulled the phone away from my ear and jammed my finger on the disconnect button.

I was done taking the high road. This was too important to let Mr. Ego cause problems.

I tossed my phone on the coffee table and sank back into the cushions. As soon as I did, it beeped to let me know I had a message. Probably another cancellation at this rate.

Picking up the phone, I checked the number. I'd missed a call from Sam. I tried him back immediately but my call went straight to voicemail.

Shoot. A call from Sam would have been great about now. He always managed to lift my spirits. Handsome, funny, thoughtful. There just wasn't much wrong with the guy. Well, except for that aforementioned periodic pressure for more of a commitment on my part.

As you might imagine, after a disaster like my marriage to Geoffrey, I was a bit gun shy. Who wouldn't be, right?

As I got ready for bed, I found my thoughts going back to Jonathan Trimble and Warriors for the Paws. In my mind's eye, I could see Jonathan struggling for control as he shared his story. And his hands shaking when he talked about being able to do things with his daughter. Barking with the Stars was more than just a fun event for a great cause. It had the potential to make a life-altering difference for veterans like Jonathan.

Before I went to bed, I wrote out a check for Warriors for the Paws and put it in an envelope to mail the next day. I wished I could do more. They deserved more.

One thing was for sure, I would do absolutely everything I could to make sure that my ex-husband's attempts to cause problems for me didn't interfere with the event and that Barking with the Stars was a rousing success.

CHAPTER FOUR

The next morning, the first thing I did was call Purple's suite to apologize for what had happened. There was truly nothing about the incident that was my fault, but still I felt an apology was needed. Also, I really did need to go over the dressing room accommodations for Lavender with Mandy and Purple. There was no answer. I made a note to try later.

Figuring I might as well catch up on paperwork, I decided to spend the morning at the office. I took Dogbert on a walk around the neighborhood and then dressed for the day.

Laguna Beach weather is almost always ridiculously wonderful. The locals were complaining a bit about the heat wave but it wasn't intolerable. Heck, I'd grown up in central Texas where there's no ocean breeze to cool you off. I dressed for the warmth in a new light-blue Maranda shift. A talented

SoCal designer, her classic meshing of fabrics and materials made her one of my favorites. Sandals, bag, sunglasses, and I was out the door.

It was a short drive to the office and I settled in to work on updating records. I share the office space with a real estate agent, a tech firm, and a psychic. We used to have an accountant as well, but he's in prison now. But that's another story. Verdi, our part-time receptionist, wasn't working. Although there were many times I wished Verdi was full time, it mostly worked out. The adorable Goth girl also worked part time at the local coffee shop to make ends meet.

A quiet morning was a nice change after the excitement of yesterday and I made short work of the paperwork. I kept my cell phone handy just in case Mandy or Purple called me back. Truthfully, I was also hoping for a call from Sam. He was probably so tied up in meetings that he wouldn't have an opportunity to call until evening, but just in case he had a break it would be great to talk to a sane person.

I was just wrapping up, when I heard the front door ding and looked up to see Betty Foxx standing in the doorway to my office.

Today the little lady sported deep-gray

velour, the pearls, and a sheepish expression. Unusually subdued for Betty.

"Good morning." I laid aside the list I'd been making. "No bumps or bruises from yesterday?"

"Nope." She stepped closer.

"That's good." I motioned to the comfy conference chair by my desk. Sam called it my "shrink chair." "Would you like to have a seat?"

"I can't stay long." She twisted the strap of her purse. "Raider is waiting for me." Raider was her St. Bernard. "We're going to the dog park."

"Not —"

"Don't worry," she interrupted. "He's not in the car. I'd never do that. He's waiting for me at the groomer's."

"Good." She was right. I had been about to deliver a lecture about leaving animals in vehicles. Leaving an animal in the heat for only a few minutes can be dangerous.

"See, here's the thing. I need your help." Her eyebrows were a dusty rose today, and I tried not to be distracted by them as she talked.

"With Raider?" I had worked with Betty and Raider when she first got the has-no-idea-how-big-he-is canine.

"No . . ." Betty opened her pocketbook,

50

pulled out a baggie, and handed it to me. "See when we got thrown out of that singer's suite, I forgot to put this down, and I must have put it in my pocket, and I sorta left with it."

I held up the baggie which contained several bubble packs of medication. "Good grief, Betty, these are prescription meds that Purple or Mandy may need."

"I know, Carmen," she huffed. "That's why I need your help. I tried to call, but the front desk said they weren't staying there. And I said, yes, they were. And then the lady put me on hold, and when she came back on she said she couldn't connect me. I don't think they want to talk to me."

"Hmmm, wonder why?" I imagined the hotel staff probably had orders to call security if they spotted a little old lady in satin loungewear lurking about.

"I just wanted to see what she looked like under there." Betty didn't sound all that contrite. "Plus, I read on the Internet that no one had a picture of what she looked like and I figured if I could get one, it'd be worth a lot of money."

"Betty! You were going to sell the picture?" I wasn't sure she'd know how to go about selling a photo like that but I'd learned to never underestimate Betty Foxx.

"And I'd be famous and that sexy reporter would be impressed."

"If you mean Callum MacAvoy, I don't know why you'd want to impress him. Besides, Betty, what you did was very wrong."

"So, will you give that baggie back to Her Royal Purpleness and her keeper?"

I didn't think Mandy would appreciate being referred to as Purple's keeper.

"I will." I sighed. "And will you promise not to try anything like that again?"

"Sure." She looked sincere, but she always looked sincere when she was lying.

Betty turned to leave and then stopped in the doorway. "Thanks."

"You're welcome. Give my love to Raider." I'd almost said Melinda too, but my cousin and I had things to sort out and one of the first things we needed to do was to stop communicating through other people.

When Betty left, I took a look at the baggie of medication. Checking to see what the drugs were, I hoped it wasn't something either Mandy or Purple had needed this morning.

The bubble packs were methylphenidate, more commonly known as Ritalin, which I knew was prescribed for Attention Deficit Hyperactivity Disorder or ADHD. As I mentally ran through the symptoms — trouble focusing, impulsivity, and hyperactivity — I wondered if Purple perhaps suffered with the disorder. It looked like the plastic bag contained at least a three-month supply. That amount wouldn't be uncommon for someone like Purple who was on tour for long periods of time. I imagine she had, or rather Mandy had for her, a smaller supply of the meds in a more convenient container, but I still needed to get these to her as soon as possible.

I had time before lunch to stop by the hotel and get the packet of meds to Purple or Mandy. And perhaps I could check the dressing room accommodations for Lavender at the same time.

I pulled up in the circular drive and handed my vintage silver Mercedes convertible off to the valet parking attendant. Because the Ocean Mark P was new to the area, they'd been amenable to staging our Barking with the Stars event which I'd heard was now being referred to in the press with the tag line "Red, White & Purple" because of the star power the pop singer wielded. Hopefully this would be a great kickoff event for the hotel. So far, they'd been an example of a fantastic corporate community partner. I was impressed.

I stopped at the shell-shaped front desk and asked that they connect me to the Starfish Suite. Mandy answered and said she'd be right down.

I parked myself on the other side of the massive fountain where I could watch for her and enjoy the beauty of the lobby. It was only a few minutes before I spotted her striding across the courtyard. No-nonsense khaki shorts, a light-green blouse, and, as usual, eyes straight ahead and focused.

I waved. She walked toward me, her lips a thin line. I couldn't blame her for being upset. What Betty had done was a breach of the confidence Mandy had shown by letting her close to Purple.

"I'm so sorry you had to come down." I handed her the bag. "I could have brought this up."

"No, it's best."

"I'm very sorry about what happened yesterday, and I'm sure Mrs. Foxx is as well." I replayed the whole mess in my head. "I hope you understand, I knew nothing about Mrs. Foxx's camera. I was just as surprised as you."

"I'm sure that's right, Caro." Mandy took a deep breath and pushed her dishwater-blond hair off her forehead. "But here's the thing, Purple has decided to go with a different dog therapist."

"What?" I hadn't anticipated this when I'd agreed to help Betty out. "I had nothing to do with —"

"I know." Mandy held up her hand. "And I know this isn't fair. But when she's made up her mind, there's no discussing anything. She's already hired this other guy and we're just done. I'm sorry."

She walked away before I could get anything else out, and then turned back to me to say, "Send me the bill for what time you've spent so far."

Well, horse feathers.

I was sure my face flamed as red as my hair. I knew which "other guy" Purple had hired, and the names I'd called him the other night were way too good to describe him.

It's a good thing there was nothing nearby to punch because it wouldn't have helped and I'd probably have hurt myself.

I finished my afternoon appointments, went home to take care of pets, and tried to call Sam again. I'd had a message from Diana to remind me we had a late dinner planned with the Barking with the Stars committee members that evening. I had it on my calendar, but I confess it had gone clean out of my mind after dealing with first the sabotage by my ex and then the mess with Betty.

Barking with the Stars was the brainchild of Sunny Simone and she'd had the good sense to snag Diana's expertise right away. Unlike the Laguna Beach Fur Ball, the "cough up some cash" fundraiser Diana and I had been involved with last year, this was a three-pronged approach. A live telethon event with tickets sold to be part of the audience. The celebs would appear on stage with their dogs, talk about Warriors for the Paws, and beg for donations. Some would also do performances, and then the whole kit and caboodle would wrap up with an auction of items that stars had donated.

Brilliant.

I took a quick shower and slipped into a mint-green Armani sheath that always made me feel cool and collected. Flat Kate Spade sandals and unruly red locks tamed into a loose bun and I was out the door.

I'd already filled Diana in on the Betty incident and she'd tried to share my chagrin, but I could tell there was a time or two she'd held back a chuckle. She'd reassured me that I had nothing to worry about. She and Sunny and the rest of the committee had complete confidence in me.

The group had decided to meet for dinner at Posh, the hotel restaurant, to discuss final details. Again, I handed off my car to the parking attendant. I was sure my little vintage Mercedes was lost among the late-model Porsches, Lamborghinis, and Bentleys he'd been parking, but he never batted an eye. I walked through the lobby, taking some time to appreciate the way the architect had made the glittering Pacific part of the design. It was almost as if the lobby framed the beach and the stunning Laguna Beach sunset.

The restaurant décor continued the theme, and the hostess escorted me through a fragrant flower-lined pathway to where the other committee members were already seated.

The event committee was an eclectic bunch. There was Ben McMullin. Or "Big McMoney" as Diana and I referred to him. Only to each other, you understand. Ben had money, big buckets of money, and we were glad that he was interested in animal rescue. He'd been a great benefactor. The man was also just in general a really nice guy. Rumors had it that although he'd bought a house in Laguna Beach, he also maintained his first home in Indiana as a reminder of where he'd come from. As a former veteran from a family steeped in military service, this event was right up his alley.

He had an average build with average looks, and his tan slacks and sports coat did not scream designer togs like most of the crowd in Posh. In fact, they didn't scream anything at all, they just blended in. He politely stood as I was seated and then went back to studying the menu, his forehead wrinkled in concentration.

Beside him, and also in the big-buckets-of-money category, was TV Land script-writer and creative genius extraordinaire, Danny Mahalovich. He'd successfully launched several TV shows known as much for their irreverent humor as their ratings. The best known, *The Search for Signs,* had been so successful, in fact, that big stars were willing to do guest spots, and up-and-coming talent vied for a chance to make appearances. Danny was the terrier of the team. He lent youth and street cred to the Barking with the Stars event, plus his contacts among the insiders covered all the big wigs in the small-screen world that Diana's silver-screen contacts did not. His vivid-blue pants and white polo shirt paired with a navy sports jacket somehow looked hip and not at all out of place in the fancy restaurant.

Then there was Sunny Simone. As the CEO of Warriors for the Paws, she hoped to parlay the committee's support into some great press for her cause as well as have a successful fundraiser. I was glad I'd had the opportunity to hear more about the operation from Jonathan Trimble. Sunny believed in this cause and had been at this for a long while. Her sleeveless bone-white linen dress accentuated her tan, and large gold earrings added to her classy look. She looked more dinner party than dog cause, but I knew from what Diana had shared she was a bulldog where this cause was concerned.

And, of course, the adorable Diana, our link to the stars. Her simple black-and-white Fanny Karst set off her creamy complexion and blond hair to perfection, and her smile was, as always, brighter than all her diamonds. She had, along with her super-agent, brought the star power to the event. It had been Diana who'd initially suggested contacting Purple about the fundraiser in an attempt to engage her huge fan base and all the buzz around the pop star. Sometimes I thought Diana had more savvy than the rest of us combined.

Oh yes, and there was me, who was in theory the onsite keep-the-canines-calm addition to the group. I'd been in charge of working with Diana to identify the pets who'd be coming with the celebs and relaying any special needs in terms of diet or accommodations. I had a list; I had a spreadsheet. Up until the last two days, it had been a pretty simple task. I only hoped Geoff's rumors weren't going to cause more problems. Diana had assured me most of the participants weren't going to be looking me up on rating websites like Yip or GotIt. She doubted they even looked at websites. They had people for that. And their people were already plenty busy making spa appointments and setting up doggie play dates.

When our waiter appeared, we all ordered and then got down to business. We were in the middle of a discussion about the celebrity auction when a stir in the lobby drew every gaze in our section.

Purple, in her signature flowing cape-dress, swept into the lobby area from the outside door with a full entourage of fans and paparazzi. She looked neither right nor left but strode forward, her head up. Again, I was surprised by how agile she was with all that hair covering her eyes.

Nipping at her heels was a pack of adoring fans, or I assumed they were adoring fans, as none took their eyes off her. The group was made up of a variety of ages, sizes, and ethnicities. One petite dark-haired girl was almost glued to Purple's side, her ripped jeans and purple hair in sharp contrast to her timid demeanor. Another woman sported leggings splotched with big purple passion flowers and a t-shirt that proclaimed, "Beware the Haze." I had no idea what that meant. Still another, covered head to toe in purple paint, clutched a "My Heart Bleeds Purple" sign.

Tania, a hotel staff person I'd chatted with as I'd been in and out, had told me that they had guests who had traveled from Australia, Japan, and Brazil to be here for this week and the event weekend. Diana had been right about one thing, the pop star's fans would follow her anywhere.

Lavender, the star's dog, sported a black bow that matched the humongous black velvet bow atop Purple's head. The little pup leaned into the folds of the star's cloak hiding her face. That was worrisome.

I looked away. I was not only disgusted by what Geoffrey had done by underhandedly enticing a client, but I was also sincerely concerned about Purple and her pet. My ex-husband knew nothing about canines and hadn't bothered to learn since he'd followed me to Laguna Beach. He was simply in it for the money. And the attention. I needed to find a way to check on the little pup.

Waiting for the attention of the others to come back to the task at hand, my gaze landed on two ladies at the next table. At first I didn't pay much attention to what they were saying, as I was still preoccupied with trying to rein in my thoughts regarding my ex-husband and his shenanigans.

As I forced myself to tune back in to the present, I noticed their food. Posh certainly hit the high mark for the beauty of its dishes. The two ladies had chosen the sushi, and the rolls looked appetizing but so did the presentation. I wondered what they thought. As I glanced at their faces to see if I could determine whether they were enjoying their choices, I heard one say, "Disgusting."

Golly, I hoped that wasn't a comment on the food.

"They just hang on her," said one.

"She can't even go out without the Posers stalking her," the other agreed.

I looked back at the entourage.

I supposed it would get old for a star to have a crowd everywhere she went. I would also think it would get old going everywhere with a wig that obscured your vision.

Maybe that was part of why Purple protected her identify so much. She could remove the wig, dress in regular clothes, and no one would recognize her. Maybe there was a method to the wig madness.

Purple and her crowd moved through the lobby and across the courtyard. Where was the ever-present Mandy?

"Caro?" I tuned back in to the conversation at my own table in time to realize I'd missed a question that must have been directed my way.

"I'm sorry. What was that?"

"I asked if you were willing to check with your veterinary friend, Dr. Darling, to see who he plans to have onsite?" Sunny asked. "We need to be sure Rufus gets them the proper credentials."

"Of course, no problem." I reached in my bag for my notebook where I kept my daily list and jotted a reminder to myself. I know, I know, you can keep track of all that stuff on your phone, but for me there is something about writing it down that worked. "No problem at all."

We finished up the details and Diana signaled the waiter that we were finished. Our dinner checks were handled and the others hurried off. Diana and I walked out together.

As we approached the valet desk, the doors opened to admit a bald man carrying a purple guitar. He wore a "Purple Live in Central Park" t-shirt tucked into faded, horizontally ripped bell-bottom jeans and white socks with sandals. The socks were an interesting choice given the warmth of our weather. And his jeans?

Dude, the seventies want their jeans back.

"Where have you been, Lew?" asked one of the ladies I'd been eavesdropping on in the restaurant. "Our interview time was eight o'clock."

"I know." He cradled the guitar. "I went to get this out of my car and it took a while. I thought you might like a picture of it for your magazine."

"What about the wig?" she asked.

"I didn't bring it along for this trip." He bounced from one foot to the other. "I can send you a picture."

"Okay, let's go sit down and talk." She pulled a small recorder from her pocket. "You don't mind if I record our interview, do you? It just makes it easier for me when I write the article."

Interview? Article? Who was this guy?

"No. No problem."

They moved on to the mix-and-mingle area and were out of earshot.

Diana and I looked at each other.

"Just when you think things can't get any weirder." She shook her head.

I waited with Diana for her driver and then gave the attendant the ticket for my car. I glanced at my phone for the time; it was only ten o'clock but with the three-hour time difference, it was way too late to try Sam. He was probably sound asleep already.

Tomorrow for sure. I'd fill him in on wigged-out pop stars, Purple Posers, and the Pomegranate Incident.

It's all for a great cause, I reminded myself, as I slid into the driver's seat.

All for a great cause.

CHAPTER FIVE

Early the next morning I pulled into the Ocean Mark valet lane, shifted into park, and handed the tanned young man my keys.

"Nice car," he commented pushing sun-streaked hair off his forehead. In LA and the surrounding area most of the waiters and valets were out-of-work actors waiting for their next big break. In Laguna, they were more likely surfers who only wanted to work between catching the next big wave.

"Thanks." I smiled at the guy. It was always nice when my car got the compliments I felt it deserved.

He slid into the seat and started to pull forward but quickly stopped when a dark SUV shot out of the underground parking. Thank goodness for his quick reflexes. I loved my car so I was glad about that, but ever happier that the guy was okay. Cars the age of mine don't have all the safety features of new cars and that SUV had been flying.

If the valet hadn't been paying attention, that could have been the end of him and my car. The big black SUV looked slightly familiar, but southern California is bumper to bumper with similar cars.

Hopefully the driver slowed it down a bit before merging with regular traffic on PCH. I took a deep breath to calm my heart rate, which was racing after that close call, and then stepped through the doorway.

I'd been such a frequent visitor lately that the hotel staff had become familiar faces.

"Hello, Tania." The young woman looked crisp and, as always, had a ready smile. Her dark hair was pulled back, and her caramel skin, though devoid of makeup, was smooth and fresh looking. She had to be exhausted as I knew she'd been around when the committee had dinner the night before. One afternoon while I was waiting for Diana, Tania had shared that she was completing her degree in Hotel and Hospitality Management. Her time at the Ocean Mark P was part of an internship, and it appeared the hotel was taking full advantage of her time with them.

"Hello, Caro." She stepped forward. "You're here early."

"As are you," I noted. "You were here late last night and now so early today?"

"Oh, I just walked in."

"I stopped by to check on Purple and her dog before the day gets started and we all get busy," I explained.

"Oh, sure," she said. "Do you know where to find her?"

"I do." I shifted my bag to the other shoulder. I felt sort of guilty, as if I were misrepresenting myself, but I didn't want to go into all the details about being fired and getting crossways with the star. "I'll just go on up."

I took the elevator to the sixth floor. I truly did feel compelled to check in on Lavender and Purple. With the way the dog had hidden her face last night when I saw them in the lobby, I was concerned that all the progress we'd made was about to be undone.

Six floors is not very high for most luxury hotels but it was pretty high for Laguna Beach where it's all about the view. Or rather about not blocking the view.

The elevator doors opened to a vista of the deep-blue, early-morning waves of the Pacific. I breathed in the sea air. This. This was why I'd moved here. I promised myself a run on the beach when the day was done. It had been too long. Dogs were permitted on the beach after six so I could take Dogbert. He'd be thrilled.

I got off and made my way to the Starfish Suite. As I moved down the hall I could hear voices. There was a small grouping of people at what appeared to be the entry to the pop star's suite.

A uniformed officer stopped me at the doorway. I could hear Lavender barking.

"What's going on, Officer Hostas?" I know it doesn't speak well of my reputation that I knew the name of the police officer. But I can explain.

"You can't go any farther." His tone said it all. No arguments.

"Has something happened to Purple?" I could see a medical crew over his shoulder. "An accident? Is she okay?"

"Ms. Lamont, we're attempting to sort that out." I guess it didn't speak well of my reputation that he also knew *my* name. "I'll need you to leave." He pointed back the way I'd come.

"But —"

He pointed again.

Concerned, but wanting to let everyone do what they needed to do, I headed back toward the elevators and pushed the down button. When the door slid open and Homicide Detective Judd Malone stepped off, I felt my stomach lurch like a big dog on a short leash.

It was clear whatever the situation was, it definitely was not an accident. You might call the medics to an accident. You might even call the police. But you did not call a homicide detective.

Malone looked up, spotted me, and shook his head in disbelief.

"Caro." He nodded. And, yeah, that I'm on a first-name basis with the homicide detective probably doesn't say much for me either. Or at least that's what my mama would say.

"Detective." I nodded back.

"Come with me." He took my arm and steered me back down the hallway toward Purple's hotel room.

Detective Judd Malone had escorted me away from crime scenes before, but this was the first time the man had ever escorted me *to* one. Tall, dark, and killer handsome (no pun intended), the detective wore his usual dark jeans, dark t-shirt. Today the usual black, bad-boy leather jacket was missing. Perhaps in deference to the early morning or the heat we'd been experiencing. The muscles in his forearm tensed as he stopped me just outside the door.

"Can you please do something about that dog?" He pointed inside at Lavender.

70

Mandy held the dog, but Lavender kept pushing against Mandy and barking incessantly. "I couldn't even hear my officer on the phone with all the barking."

Officer Hostas moved aside to let us enter and Mandy immediately handed Lavender to me.

I glanced around. The room looked much as it had two days ago when Betty and I had been there. Except for the body on the floor. Several people knelt near the body. It was clear from the clothing and the pure-white hair, it was Purple.

Malone carefully stepped around the medic team.

"Is it okay if I take her outside?" The pup had let me take her without resistance, but was shaking.

"I need the dog close by. It'll have to be processed when the crime scene folks get here," he answered over his shoulder as he moved across the room to speak to Officer Hostas.

I guessed that was a no.

Malone returned to where Mandy and I stood.

Lavender continued to bark but not quite so frantically. Her barking had been the reason Purple had initially contacted me. They'd been on the road and in hotels nonstop, and Lavender's barking issue had become a problem.

"Are you the one that found the body?" Detective Malone addressed Mandy.

She nodded. Her eyes were bloodshot, undoubtedly from crying, and her crisp efficient Gal Friday persona was nowhere to be found. This was a Mandy I'd never seen.

"Yes, I came to go over her morning appointments with her and found her on the floor. When I looked closer it was clear she was, she was . . ." She dropped her face in her hands.

"Any idea who might have done this?" Malone was all business.

"Well, when I got here that other pet therapist was leaving." Mandy lifted her face and looked at Malone.

"Another pet shrink?" Malone turned to look at me. His expression said he couldn't believe there were people other than me in the pet therapy line of work. Since the first time we met, I'd had a bit of a problem with the detective taking my profession seriously.

I had a sinking feeling in the pit of my stomach and suddenly I knew why that dark SUV that nearly collided with the parking valet had looked familiar.

"You know him." Mandy pointed at me, her finger shaking. "He took over when she fired you."

"G-Geoffrey?" I stuttered.

"Yes, that's the one. I saw him coming down the hall from this way when I got off the elevator with Purple's pomegranate juice."

"Your ex-husband, Geoffrey?" Malone asked.

I nodded.

He turned to one of the uniformed officers. "Go pick up Geoffrey . . . uhm —"

"Carlisle," I supplied.

"Do you know his address?" Malone waited.

"Sorry. I don't." I'd made it a point to not know where Geoffrey was living. In fact, I continued to hope that he would decide Laguna Beach was not for him and move back to Texas.

Lavender continued to shake and whimper. I turned my back to the group and took a few steps away, shielding the shivering pup from some of the commotion. I took a deep breath and tried to slow my breathing. The dog would tune in to my emotional state and that wouldn't help her.

The truth was I felt a little shaky myself. Just a couple of days ago I'd been in this room, and now Purple was dead and Geoffrey was somehow involved.

"Okay, find Geoffrey Carlisle and take him to the station. We need to question him." I could still hear Malone from where I stood.

"The CSIs should be here shortly." Malone came up behind me. "At least it's not barking."

"She," I corrected. "She's not barking now, but she's still traumatized by the smells and the sounds. It would help if I could take her out of this room."

"Okay, the hallway, but just outside. Stay close." He walked me to the door. Officer Hostas gave me the eye as he stepped aside.

"When we get a couple of more people here, they'll need to go door to door and find out if anyone saw anything," Malone addressed Officer Hostas, and then glanced down the corridor where doors stood open and people poked their heads out.

Tania and a man I assumed to be one of the hotel managers were coming our way. Tall and thin, the man was attired in the hotel's "uniform" of turquoise shirt and tan pants.

"What's going on?" asked the man whose name badge said "Sherman." He didn't have to ask who was in charge. Even without the uniform it was clear that Malone was. Sherman moved as if to enter the room.

"We're sorting that out." Malone blocked their path to Purple's room. "We will need these people" — he indicated the row of rooms — "to stay here for the time being so we can question them."

"Oh, no." Sherman shook his head so hard his gold wire-rimmed glasses nearly flew off. "We can't have that. This is a very exclusive floor, and our guests expect to be treated with luxury and superior service while they're here. We can't have them inconvenienced like this."

Malone slowly turned toward Mr. Hotel. I'd seen that look before. I took Lavender and stepped away a little farther down the hallway. Tania and I made eye contact.

"Perhaps we could offer them a free breakfast from room service for their inconvenience," Tania suggested. "Send up some coffee and muffins?"

Mr. Hotel stared at Tania as if she'd suggested caviar and Dom Perignon, but I could see when he realized it was a really great idea. In fact, such a great idea he could probably take credit for it.

"Yes, why don't you get on that." He waved a hand at Tania. "Notify the kitchen. I'll help sort things out here."

Malone took him aside, I assumed to explain the graveness of the situation. I paced with Lavender, holding the pooch against my chest. She'd stopped shaking and eventually I could feel her relax against me.

The rooms were grouped with clusters of two or three together with open areas in between, so I could see the Pacific on one side and the courtyard on the other as I came to the open spaces. I stopped for a moment by one of the openings and looked down at the patio. Down there everything was normal. People in beach attire were making their way outside; others were sitting at scattered tables with coffee or their morning caffeine of choice. All were simply going about their day. Seeing the people made me that much more aware that Purple would never "go about her day" again.

Back on our floor, Malone had finished filling in Mr. Hotel, who walked back toward the elevator, his face white. Two officers were just getting off the elevator and Malone motioned for them to come forward and follow him, I assumed to begin the questioning of the other guests on the floor. I hoped Tania had ordered plenty of coffee and muffins.

A crime scene tech motioned to me from the doorway of Purple's suite. They must have arrived when I'd been walking the hall.

Mandy was still parked in the chair where Malone had asked her to sit. Though a little more composed than she'd been, the assistant seemed at once bedraggled and tense. I imagined they would need to process her as well. Her dress had spots of blood on it and her hands hung limp.

"Are you okay?" I stopped and leaned down to her. "Is there anything I can get you?"

She raised wide eyes pooled with tears. "I wasn't here. Maybe I could have . . ."

I waited for her to go on. Survivor's guilt can be powerful.

"I'm sure there was nothing you could have done. In fact, you might have also been hurt or killed. Why would Geoffrey have been here so early?" I asked. I'd been mulling that while I was out in the hallway.

"I don't know." She shrugged. "She seemed really taken with him."

"We're ready for you, miss." The taller of the crime scene techs motioned to Mandy. "We'll be ready for the dog after that."

When they were ready for Lavender, the tech asked if I would mind holding the dog while they processed her. I calmed her while they took samples of her fur and brushed the pads of her feet lightly.

"Do you know, was the dog in the room?"

I hoped not, but feared she had been.

"According to the assistant, the pooch was in her own room." The tech answered with a wry half smile. "A whole other level of society that has a separate room for the dog." He shook his head.

"Though maybe in this case, that was a good thing," I noted.

"Yeah, you're probably right about that." He patted her head.

When they were done with Lavender and me, I took her to her room. Replete with a small canopy bed and baskets of toys, I could see the young man's point. I tried to set her down, but she clung to me so I sat with her for a while.

Once Lavender was asleep, and the puppy snores were steady and deep, I carefully put her in her bed and went back out into the main room of the suite. There were still people everywhere.

I was pretty sure I was free to go, but I needed to find out who was going to take over with Lavender. I wasn't sure Mandy was up to it though she seemed to be much more like herself than she had been earlier. They'd removed Purple's body and I was sure that helped, but the shaky grieving assistant of the morning had definitely vanished and she was back to being the Mandy

I knew. She was talking with one of the officers, and I waited for a break in their conversation.

Malone entered the room with Officer Hostas. "We're going to have to get Paul to talk with the media or the hotel is going to have a riot on their hands. Can you check on his ETA?"

"I think we're done here." The CSI I'd been talking with addressed Malone. "From what we've been told, the door was open when she arrived." He nodded toward Mandy. "Apparently was supposed to meet the victim at nine o'clock to go over her schedule for the day. So you'll see her fingerprints on the door and undoubtedly elsewhere. We'll look for others."

I wondered if this was a good time to mention they'd probably also find mine. And Betty's.

"Do we have any idea the last time the victim was seen alive?"

"We saw her about ten o'clock last night," I spoke up.

"Here?" Malone turned to me.

"No, in the lobby," I responded. "She was with a group of fans, and Diana and I were in the restaurant for a meeting with some of the other members of the event committee."

"Event?"

"That's why there are all the Purple fans here. There's a Barking with the Stars fundraiser for Warriors for the Paws. They help train dogs as companions to soldiers with PTSD."

Malone just looked at me for a while. "Sounds like a good cause. I'll need those names."

"Sure." I stepped aside to give the committee members' names to one of the detectives.

I looked around for Mandy and spotted her with the other tech who seemed to be listing the items on the table. I imagined they were trying to figure out if anything was missing. With a celeb like Purple, robbery was a possibility. In fact, it seemed more plausible than Geoffrey as a killer. At least to me.

I crossed to where they stood. "I'm sorry to interrupt. Lavender is asleep in the other room." The room was emptying as the officers and CSIs left. "I wanted you to know before I left."

"Okay." She nodded. "I'll take care of it."

"You'll let me know if you need anything, right?" I touched her arm and felt her stiffen.

Mandy had to be feeling raw. Not only

the loss of Purple, but also having to keep it together and deal with all the details. I couldn't put her to bed like I had with the dog, but I hoped she had someone to call who would provide some comfort. Someone to be with her.

"Anything at all, hon." I started to touch her again but then pulled back. "You have my number."

"Yes, I do. Thank you." She turned back to the tech.

Dismissed, I had no further reason to be there. I stepped out of the suite and walked down the hall toward the elevator.

"Caro?" It was Malone.

"Yes?" I had just pushed the button.

"I just wanted to let you know that we've picked up Mr. Carlisle."

"Thanks," I hesitated, "for letting me know."

"We may need you for a formal statement later." His bright-blue eyes pinned me. "We'll be in touch."

"Got it." I sighed.

I got on the elevator and pushed the button for the main floor.

Downstairs, fans and the press had begun to congregate in the lobby. It was clear the news had somehow leaked, and several of the fans were quietly crying; others seemed stunned. A television crew had just pulled up out front and I saw Callum MacAvoy plowing through the crowd.

I made a quick detour and slipped out a side entrance to make a call to Diana.

She picked up right away. "Caro?" My number must have shown up on her cell phone.

"Yes." I swallowed and took a deep breath. "I'm at the hotel and —"

"So, it's true?" I wasn't sure how she knew but somehow Diana always was in the know when something happened in the community.

"I'm afraid so. I arrived shortly after the police. I'd wanted to check in on her dog. You know, with Geoff working with them I wasn't sure things would go well. And then there was that mess with Betty."

"Is your detective on site?" Diana asked.

"Not *my* detective, but yes, Detective Malone was one of the first arrivals."

"So they must think it wasn't accidental. Do they have any idea what happened? Probably not at this point, right?" I could picture her in her sunny kitchen making coffee and feeding pets.

"No, I think they're at a loss. They've shut down the section of the hotel where she was staying. But, Diana, here's the crazy part. Her assistant, Mandy, identified Geoff as leaving just before she found Purple."

"What?"

"I know. And here's the other thing, as I pulled in to the hotel and gave my car to the valet, I'm pretty sure I saw Geoff's SUV leaving."

"You don't think . . ."

"No, to tell you the truth, I don't. Geoff is a pompous jerk but a killer? No, I really don't think so."

"Be careful, sweetie."

"I will. I'm going to stick around here for the press conference to see what the official statement is."

"I'll call Sunny, McMoney, and Maha-lovich just in case they get calls from the press."

Good thinking on Diana's part. I hadn't considered the impact on the event or that committee members might get questions. I promised to call her later.

I grabbed a hazelnut latte from the hotel coffee shop and situated myself so I could hear what Paul, the Laguna Beach PD spokesperson, had to say. I could see Mac-Avoy across the way talking with fans, and hoped he didn't spot me. I leaned back against the wall. The large potted palm provided some cover. His camera crew was there in full force. No doubt this was big news.

The place was full of tears and chatter as the various groups waited for the spokesperson to arrive. I caught snippets of so many conversations.

What will we do without her?

Poor Drake. The love of his life gone.

I heard the police took pictures of her without the wig. I'll bet those get leaked.

I can't believe we saw her last show. We saw history.

I didn't know who Drake was, but I felt sorry for him because, undoubtedly, he was being inundated with fans and the media as he was hearing about the death of someone he cared about.

The comments about the wig were interesting to me. Although I'd never seen Purple's full face, surely someone had. Definitely Mandy and this Drake at least. And I had to believe her fans had sought out her real identify and found pictures of her before her fame. I mean it was just too easy on the Internet to dig into someone's personal life. Now whether any of it was true or not was another story. Just like all the bad reviews about PAWS that I'd found on Yip. All it took was one bad person on a mission to destroy your business and it became a full-time job quashing rumors.

The two women from last night's dinner excused themselves as they eased past me and situated themselves near the front of the crowd. I stood at an angle to the crowd, so I had a good view of the mob and the press set up. Tania and one of the hotel workers wrestled a podium into place.

Neither of the dinner women were talking, and their body language said they weren't a part of the riff-raff wiping tears and reminiscing about the Purple concert last weekend in San Diego.

The taller one — in my head I was calling her "Curly Sue" because she had great naturally curly brown hair — adjusted her glasses and turned to the smaller Asian woman. I'd dubbed her "Tiny," well, because she was not only short, but petite in every way from her stature to her movements. Tiny head nods. Tiny lips barely moving as she spoke. A tiny but long-fingered hand deliberately tucking short, tiny hair behind her ears. Hopefully I could learn names soon.

Curly turned to Tiny. "Purple doesn't have any relatives. She talked about being raised by her grandfather for most of her life in that interview with *Rock Talk* several years ago."

"That's right," Tiny agreed. "I imagine Mandy will be the one to make all the arrangements."

"We should get in touch with her so that we can pass the information on to our members." Curly Sue pulled out her smartphone and swiped something open. "I have her private number. I could text her."

"I also have it." Tiny was not to be outdone.

The two seemed to know a lot about Purple and her personal life. But I guess that goes along with fame. But members? What did they mean by members? The whole fandom thing had seemed a little creepy to me. Were they members of a Purple Fan Club? I'd not seen these two dressed up in Purple's signature look. Or had I? But then again, how would I know, right? Not when everyone wore face-covering wigs!

Paul, the police spokesperson, took the podium on the platform of the staircase. It was only maybe four or five steps up but it separated him from the mob. I'm guessing maybe a Tania idea. In the background she politely moved people so they weren't blocking exits.

The clamor of sound turned to silence as Paul tapped the microphone, making sure it was on.

"If I could have your attention," he began.

Knowing what he was about to share, I felt the weight of the words I knew were to come. The words that would confirm to fans who had only been speculating, their very worst fears.

CHAPTER SIX

"Sometime after ten o'clock last night someone entered the hotel room of the celebrity known as Purple. There was a struggle, and she was fatally injured." The officer stopped and looked at the crowd.

"There was no forced entry. We believe the victim knew her killer."

A collective gasp shot through the room.

He waited for the room to quiet before continuing. "Anyone with any information about this incident is asked to call the Laguna Beach Police Department at this number." He paused as people scrambled for pen and paper and then gave the number. "Or Orange County Crime Stoppers. You may also submit anonymous tips via our website. Thank you."

As soon as he finished, Callum MacAvoy waved his hand. "We understand that you already have a person of interest in custody. Is that true?"

"We do have a lead, but I'm sure you understand, I'm not at liberty to talk about that."

He had to be referring to Geoffrey. I wondered how that tidbit had leaked so quickly. There had been only a handful of people in the room at the time. And I knew I hadn't told anyone other than Diana who I absolutely knew would not have passed on what I'd told her.

"What was the cause of death?" asked a reporter from another television station.

"The coroner has not yet ruled on cause of death, but we believe the cause to be blunt force trauma."

"Are we in any danger?" asked a girl I recognized from the entourage the night before.

"We don't believe so," he answered, "but if you see anyone acting suspiciously, you should report that to hotel security immediately."

Paul did a great job of stating the facts and then simply repeating them as reporters and fans alike wanted to know more.

By the third time through, I couldn't take any more. I needed some air. Reaction, I told myself. Shock. I'd been busy with Lavender. I'd been worried about Mandy. It had all caught up with me. I felt like I'd been awake for forty-eight hours. Like this morning was days ago.

I moved away from the crowd and slipped outside to the courtyard. People were still going about their business, eating lunch, heading for the beach, but there was a different subdued feel to the atmosphere. I found a table in the shade, sat down, and kicked off my shoes. A hotel staff person offered me a mineral water, and I accepted.

I don't know how long I sat, letting the sounds of people talking, dishes clattering, and children giggling wash over me, but I could tell when the press conference ended because a flood of people swept past me. I watched groups of fans come through the courtyard and either head up to their rooms or go through to the beach.

My phone buzzed and I checked it to see that Diana had sent me a text. The Barking with the Stars committee wanted to meet as soon as possible to discuss the turn of events. She wanted to know if later today or tomorrow morning worked for me. Also, she wanted me to call her when I got home. I responded affirmatively to both.

As I dropped my phone back in my bag, Tania walked by. She spotted me and stopped.

"How are you doing?" she asked.

"I'm okay," I lied. "How about you?"

"The hotel is not at all happy with a murder onsite when they are just barely opened." She shook her head.

"Inconvenient, huh?" I took a sip of the mineral water.

Tania nodded ruefully. "It seems so cold, but the truth is I didn't know her. I feel very sad for her family, though. Those who cared about her."

"I guess she didn't have any family. Only child. Parents deceased. Raised by her grandfather, who is also gone." I held the cool water bottle to my forehead, hoping to stop the ache between my eyes.

"That must be very lonely," Tania observed. "I have one sister, two brothers, and many cousins."

"Me, too. No sisters, but one brother, and tons of cousins." Maybe that was part of my introspection. Purple had no one. I had family. I had a cousin. One who lived right here in Laguna Beach. Our mothers had both done the beauty queen circuit and we'd been expected to do the same. After learning what that life was like, we had each rebelled in our own way, walking away from those expectations. We'd shared so much with each other when we were younger. We had more in common than blood, but we were so divided today, we might as well live on different continents.

"I'm sure the police will solve this very quickly," I mused. "There must be security cameras everywhere." I'd heard the crime scene techs talking about the potential for video. It was a new hotel so that surely meant all kinds of state-of-the-art technology that could help.

"That's a problem." Tania sighed.

"What do you mean?" I took a sip of water from the bottle.

"There are video cameras in the hallway that leads to the Starfish Suite." She lowered her voice. "But they had been disabled."

"What?" The police had seemed to think Purple's murder had been a crime of passion. Someone she'd argued with, things had gotten out of hand. "How were they disabled?"

"I don't know any more than that." The guilty look on her face said she'd realized she probably shouldn't have shared the piece of information.

"Don't worry," I assured her. "I won't be talking to the press."

"Thanks, Caro." Tania straightened her shoulders. "I had better get back to work. We have a large group of financial people checking in, and it will get busy at the front desk."

I could only imagine. A bunch of accountants or bankers here for their conference and then all the Purple fans in their various Purple outfits. What a mixture.

As Tania walked away, I watched the flow of people to and from the courtyard, strolling between wings, and stopping to talk. If I'd been convinced before that Geoffrey wasn't the killer, I was even more convinced after Tania's revelation. Disabling the cameras changed this from an argument gone wrong to premeditated murder. Someone had known where she would be and had planned to kill Purple.

I slipped my shoes back on and gathered my things. I had several things to take care of and sitting here was not going to get them done.

For one, I needed to call my mother before she saw the news and made the connection to Laguna Beach. It was possible Purple's murder had not yet hit the national news. Unlikely, though, right? I dreaded the call, not because I'd have to recall details. Mama Kat was hardly ever interested in the details. Or least only interested in them as they related to her.

And somehow by the end of the conversation, my proximity to a crime would have given her grey hair, caused great embarrassment for her, or made it impossible for me to land a decent husband. Take your pick. There would be something.

I promised myself that I'd take care of it as soon as I got home, but instead I let Dogbert out and then cuddled up with him on my bed and drifted off to sleep fully clothed.

I woke up to the ringing of my cell phone. Oh no. It was Mama Kat's ring. My brief nap had set me back. Maybe she'd already seen the news.

It's a terrible thing to admit, but I always have a little fight-or-flight response when my mama's number shows up on my phone. Because of that I'd set a special ringtone that gave me a little warning.

"Hello, Mama," I croaked, my voice still groggy from sleep. "I've been meaning to call you."

"I would hope so," she responded. "Didn't you get my email?"

I'd been so dead-dog tired with all that had gone on that I'd simply skimmed through emails, and it was likely I'd missed it.

"Probably." I made my way to the kitchen and poured myself a glass of sweet tea hoping it would wake me up. Dogbert followed me to the kitchen and I refilled his water bowl as I listened.

"I need to know as soon as possible if any of those dates work for you and Sam." I could see her on the other end tapping a nail on her desk, or fluffing a pillow while she talked. Mama Kat hardly ever just sat still.

"This is for the barbeque?"

"What else would it be for?" The exasperation was clear in her voice.

The Big Texas Barbeque was her latest mission. She'd never met Sam, but she'd talked with him on the phone. He'd admitted he'd never experienced a genuine Texas barbeque. And she had decided such a serious gap in his life experience must be remedied right away and she was just the woman to do it.

At least she'd stopped setting me up on blind dates with sons and nephews of friends. Ever since Sam Gallanos had come into my life, Mama Kat had decided there might actually be hope for me finding dates on my own. But like everyone else, including Sam, she thought it was time to get serious about what my future plans were with the handsome Greek.

"Mama, Sam is out of town right now." I took a big gulp of my tea and slid open my

95

patio door. I set the glass on the table and dropped into the patio chair. "When he's back, I'll ask him about the dates you emailed to me. Okay?"

She'd not made any connection between Purple's death and me, and I thought it best to get it over with than wait until she did.

"Mama, listen. I don't want you to worry, but you remember the fundraiser for the therapy dogs for veterans that I told you about?"

"Of course, a very good cause, dear." She was probably still tapping or pacing. "I talked to Hub about it, and he said it was a good one."

Hub is my step-father, and the only father I've ever known, and I loved him to pieces. And respected his judgement. However, I was a little irritated that she'd felt the need to check it out with him rather than take my word.

"Well, you'll probably see it on the news but the singer who was to headline the event has been killed."

"What?"

"I said —"

"I know what you said, Carolina Lamont," she interrupted. "I simply cannot believe it. You stay far away from that investigation. Don't even think about getting involved.

The last time you were trying to be helpful, you came very close to —" She stopped. "Well, I can't even say it."

"There's more." I might as well get it all over with at once.

"What more could there be?" I could hear the slide from concern to hysteria in her voice. Maybe I should have called Hub and asked him to break the news to her.

"Take a breath, Mama." I waited and then continued. "Geoffrey is a suspect in the murder."

"That —" She paused, then used a word Grandma Tillie would have taken great exception to, and dropped the phone.

"Mama?" I raised my voice. "Mama? Are you okay?"

Well, I'd definitely underestimated this one. I didn't really believe she was in any physical danger, but was undoubtedly on a rant or prostate with emotion. On our best days we pushed each other's buttons, which was why we functioned best living several states apart.

"Mama?" I waited and tried one more time. "Mama?"

I pushed disconnect and called Hub's cell. It went to voicemail, but he called me right back. I explained the situation, and he said he'd check on her right away. Hub was solid and I adored him and his calm.

He ended our conversation with a caution of his own to be careful. I promised I would.

We hung up and I sat for a few minutes finishing my tea and thinking. The events of the day were still just as shockingly surreal, and yet as I reviewed them in my mind, I still did not believe Geoffrey was capable of murder.

My phone beeped, and I noticed I'd missed another phone call from Sam.

Ah, Sam. What was I to do about Sam? I loved our relationship just as it was. He was smart, funny, and totally got me. Who could ask for more, right? Not me.

Like Purple, Sam had been raised by a grandparent. His American mother and his Greek father had died when he was young. His grandparents had taken on his care and brought him along in the business world. In their case, olive imports. His grandfather had been gone a number of years, and his grandmother, who many believed had always been the business savvy behind the company's success, had continued to run the business after his death. I'd met Yia-Yia, as he called her, and she was still a force to be reckoned with. She reminded me of my Grandma Tillie in so many ways. I grinned to myself. Could be some of the pressure Sam obviously felt to formalize our relationship came from that corner.

I listened to Sam's message and went inside to call him back. Just as my finger hovered over the recall button, the doorbell rang.

Before answering I peered out to see who it was.

Hell's Bells!

I wasn't about to go into hysterics like Mama Kat, but I have to admit I did drop my phone.

It was Geoffrey.

Picking my phone up from the floor, I leaned my head against the door and thought through my options. I could simply not answer. I could tell him to go away. There was no reason I had to talk to him, but the truth was I wanted to hear his version of what had happened. And I didn't think he killed Purple. That would require more backbone than Geoffrey Carlisle had.

I opened the door.

He went straight through to the living room and dropped onto the couch. Dogbert gave him a wary look and moved away. Thelma and Louise raised their heads and then dismissed him as uninteresting and went back to their naps. My pets had better sense than some humans.

"Would you like something to drink? A glass of tea or something else?" My southern hospitality had been bred deep. You offer even your worst enemies food and drink.

"Don't you have something stronger?" He glanced around the room.

"I have wine," I offered.

His expensive blue shirt was rumpled and he looked like he'd missed a shave. "I guess that will have to do." He continued to examine the room while I got out a wine glass and poured him a glass of cabernet.

I handed him the wine glass. "Will this work?"

I knew it would, of course. I knew what wines he liked, the amount of starch he liked in his shirts, his favorite brand of socks. At one point in my life, I'd made a point of knowing everything about him. All of his preferences.

I'd be willing to bet he would be unable to name a single one of mine.

"This is quite a change from what you grew up with." He waved a hand at the room in general. "You've come down in the world, Carolina."

Of course, he would see my house that way. What I'd created was a home instead of a showplace. Comfortable sturdy furniture you could sit on, books I enjoyed, a

100

place accessorized with things that meant something to me.

I refused to take the bait. I'd come a long way.

He continued to look around. "I thought the pet shrink business was booming?"

"Is that why you're trying to take it away from me?" Okay, I hadn't come as far as I'd thought.

"Whoa there." He set his glass on the coffee table. "Who says I'm taking anything away from you? You don't have your clients under contract and if they want to work with someone else, I assume they're free to do so."

"Stop it, Geoffrey," I bit out.

His head whipped around and he stared at me.

"Just stop it." I wasn't going to let him off the hook with the fake innocence. "I know what you're doing. And you know what, go right ahead. My good clients know me and will stick with me. I don't even care about that. What I am concerned about is that you have no experience, no love for animals, and obviously, no scruples. But then this isn't your first rodeo as a cheat."

His bloodshot blue eyes hardened. "Come on, Carolina, you aren't going to dredge up ancient history, are you?"

"No, as a matter of fact, I'm not." I went back to the cupboard and took down another glass and splashed some cabernet for myself.

It's five o'clock somewhere, right?

"So, what are you doing here, Geoffrey?"

"You seem to have some pull with the homicide detective." He leaned back in the cushions. "I thought you could put in a good word for me."

The absolute embodiment of an ego so huge that he truly believed the woman he had cheated on, destroyed professionally, and now was attempting to put out of business would "put in a good word."

"What planet are you from?" I could not believe he'd just said that.

He looked confused.

"So what happened, Geoffrey?" I took my glass and sat in the chair opposite him. "As crazy as it seems, I actually don't think you killed Purple. But I'm pretty sure the police don't have any other suspects."

"She was dead when I got there." He shrugged. "I was supposed to meet her, and the door was unlocked when I got to her suite. I went in and there she was."

"You're sure she was dead?" I leaned in to look him in the eye. Though I didn't have the best track record with Geoffrey Carlisle lie-detecting. "You checked?"

"No, I panicked and left." He looked away. Now that sounded much more like the Geoffrey I knew.

"Did you see anyone?"

"No one." He shook his head. "I mean there were people in the courtyard and around the hotel but I didn't really notice."

"How far into the room did you go?"

"Far enough I could see her and the blood on the rug."

"You didn't even call for medical help?" I downed my wine. "What if she were still alive and could have been saved?"

"Trust me, she wasn't alive." He exaggerated a shiver. "Still, you have to know running out like that makes you look guilty."

"Like I said, I panicked. I wasn't thinking about whether or not it made me look guilty."

"Well, it does." I resisted the urge to add additional commentary on how incredibly heartless it was to not give aid. To not call someone. "What did Detective Malone say?"

"He said they were going to check security cameras, but I needed to stay close. Not to leave town. That sort of thing." He cleared his throat. "I think I need to get an attorney. Do you have any recommendations?"

I couldn't tell Geoffrey that the cameras were not going to be any help. Frankly, I thought the tampering confirmed that he wasn't involved. Unless he had an accomplice, and why would he, dealing with electronics was beyond his area of expertise.

"I can get you some names." I regretted the offer as soon as it was out of my mouth. I'd wanted to hear his side of the story, but I sure didn't need to be Hannah Helpful with all that he'd done to make my life miserable.

"I should go." He drained the last of his wine and handed me the glass.

I didn't disagree. I'd been civil about as long as I could, and my patience was wearing thin.

He stood. "Here's my cell number." He handed me a card.

I didn't even look at it. Placing it on the coffee table, I walked him to the door.

He stopped in the open doorway. "And you'll put in a good word with your pal, Detective Malone?"

"I've already told him I didn't think you did it."

"Thanks, Carolina." He leaned in as if to kiss my cheek.

I backed up. "You're welcome. Don't make me regret it."

I closed the door quickly and leaned on it.

Walking back to the couch, I picked up the wine glasses and rinsed them in the sink.

I picked up my phone to check the time. I had missed a call from Diana, probably with a time and place for the committee meeting.

I called her back right away and grabbed Dogbert's leash from its hook by the door. He heard the sound and came galloping down the hallway from the living room.

Diana picked up immediately. "How are you, sweetie?" she asked.

"I'm okay." I clipped the leash to Dogbert's collar and we stepped out into the warm evening. "I'm so sorry I missed your call. I'm afraid I just crashed after I got home and then when I woke up my mother called."

"Oh." Her pause said she knew what that meant. "How did that go?"

"As you might imagine."

The sun was just beginning to set, and the slight breeze off the ocean reminded me of all the things I loved about Laguna. I breathed in the fragrance of my neighbor's evening primrose mixed with salt air. The perfect SoCal evening.

"The committee would like to meet for brunch tomorrow at ten at the hotel to discuss our next steps." Diana brought me back to the conversation at hand. "I hope you can make that work."

"I'll be there." Dogbert picked up the pace a bit and I let him. We both needed to stretch our legs and a brisk walk would do us both good.

"Great, I'll see you then."

Dogbert and I finished our walk in no time. Once we were back home, I suddenly realized I had not only skipped lunch but I'd also missed supper.

I tried Sam as I was throwing together a sandwich but got his voicemail again. These meetings must be keeping him hopping. I checked the time and left a message. Tomorrow I'd keep trying until we connected.

The next morning, I lay in bed a few minutes after I woke up, hoping it was all a bad dream. Life can take the most tragic turns at the drop of a hat. I thought about Purple and the plans that she'd had. A new house, a career taking off, and it sounded like a significant someone in her life.

I shifted cats from against my legs, Thelma on one side and Louise on the other, and made myself get up. The two looked at me in offense and meowed in protest before stretching and settling back into the soft covers. Dogbert, on the other hand, was a morning person and was immediately ready for whatever was to come next.

Starting coffee, I turned on the local news. The heat wave continued. Thunderstorms were predicted for the evening, which was unusual for SoCal. High surf warnings were a possibility as the storms moved in. Of course, the murder was the biggest news story but the coverage simply recounted what the police spokesman had said the day before.

I dressed for the day knowing I'd be going to my pet appointments directly from the meeting with the committee. Dark Lucky jeans and a lightweight, pink silk shell were simple and casual. I threw on my embroidered Valentino varsity jacket over the shell in deference to the brunch crowd.

I checked Diana's message. We were to meet in the Sea Horse Room for brunch and talk about what would happen now that the event had no headliner.

I arrived and again handed the valet my keys. I checked with the desk to make sure I knew where the Sea Horse Room was. It was the other side of the courtyard and didn't have a view of the lobby. The quiet breakfast and brunch bistro had been situated to take full advantage of the ocean view.

Diana was already seated but rose to kiss my cheek and give me a badly needed hug. Her bright-blue Michael Kors wrap dress matched the bright blue of her eyes and cheered me immensely.

Diana's presence had drawn the attention of a few people in the restaurant. She was genuinely loved by all ages. Her fans were, certainly, people who've seen her movies or even re-runs of her movies. And she continued to do special projects. But she'd moved from movie star to animal advocate in recent years and was in the news as much, if not more, than she had been in her heyday.

A young woman approached just as I arrived at the table.

"I'm very sorry to bother you." She held out a notebook to Diana. "But could I have your autograph? It would mean so much to me."

"Of course, you may." Diana was always gracious with fans. She signed the notebook with a flourish and smiled at the girl.

"Who is that with Diana Knight?" I heard a whisper from the table behind me.

"Oh, she's nobody," the whisperer's companion responded.

That's right. That's me. I'm nobody, and I am thoroughly thrilled about that fact. I'd had enough fame and notoriety to last me a lifetime. When Geoffrey's affair with a client back in Texas where we'd shared a joint counseling practice had resulted in both of us losing our licenses, there had been a media feeding frenzy. As well as an almost daily feature in the *Dallas Morning News* about all the details, the lawsuits, and the divorce. I was beyond happy to be "nobody."

"How are you?" Diana patted the chair next to her.

I cringed a little, remembering. "I've been better. You?"

"I'll be better when we can figure out what we're going to do for a star for our event." She tapped the table with one polished nail. "I don't mean to be unfeeling, but we'd booked Purple months ago and we were lucky she was willing to fit us in. Now with only a week to go, it's going to be difficult to find someone who is both willing and available."

"That's true." I sat down and placed my tote on the floor. "Do we even go on at this point?"

"I hadn't considered that possibility but I suppose we have to think about it." Diana leaned back.

"It would be a shame. Warriors for the Paws is doing such important work and so many people are not even aware of what's happening with our veterans. I had no idea the scope of the problems before you told me about them."

Diana raised a brow. "You know you're preaching to the choir, hon."

"Ah, there you are." Sunny had arrived, looking sharp as always but with a furrow in her brow that hadn't been there the last time we'd met. We chatted only a few minutes more, and Ben and Danny were seated. A quick look at the menu and we all ordered.

"Let's get down to business, shall we, while we're waiting for our food?" Sunny was a straight-shooter, but I could tell she was shaken by both the murder and what this might mean for the fundraising efforts. "Do we go on? Is there time to find someone else?" She looked at the group.

"Diana and Sunny, you're better at this than the rest of us," Ben commented. "You've probably done tons of fundraisers. What do you think?"

"Our biggest issue, I believe, is finding a big name to take Purple's place." Danny reached for the energy drink he'd brought with him. He was right, of course. Without Purple we had stars, but no one as big as she was. No one with her following.

"When I spoke with a few of the stars today, they were shaken but no one was talking about bailing on us," Diana spoke up.

"What would you think of Nora Worthington?" Danny asked.

"She'd be great. And I know she's an avid animal lover." Diana beamed at the thought, but then her face fell. "But I can't imagine she'd be available at this late date. And if by some miracle she was, would she be willing?"

"Her agent has been putting out feelers about Nora being on *Search for Signs,*" he said. "I could have my office call the agent and see if we couldn't arrange some sort of in-kind agreement."

"I love her stuff." I'd recently been listening to her latest. She was a gutsy R & B singer who'd had several hits and had also dipped her toes into acting with cameos on several popular television shows.

"Of course, you all would have to be sworn to secrecy. If it gets out that I'm open to barter, it will be the end." Danny finished the rest of his energy drink in one gulp.

We laughed.

"You all laugh, but I'm serious. I don't want my office staff to find themselves in the middle of *Let's Make a Deal.*"

"I think she'd be a great choice." Ben signaled the waiter for more coffee. "If you can make that happen, I'd say go ahead."

"We might think about a sort of tribute to Purple as a part of the show," I added. I thought about the people in the lobby yesterday and their reactions to the news. "I'm sure her fans would appreciate that."

"Any word on services?" Sunny asked.

"Not that I've heard." I could ask Mandy. Or one of the super-fans, they seemed to know everything.

"I met with Drake Owen this morning on another matter." Danny drummed his fingers on the table. "He's been in town working with us on a new project. His expectation was that there would be a private service at a later date."

"Drake Owen?" I knew who the country mega-star was but I hadn't made the connection when I'd heard the Purple fans mention Drake.

"Yes, her fiancé, he's pretty broken up over this." Danny moved to tapping his phone on the table. Maybe he needed to lay off the energy drinks.

"I think a tribute of some sort would be a great idea," Sunny leaned forward to say. "Look around you at all the Purple fans in the hotel."

We agreed to hold for one more day before making any sort of decision. Danny would contact Nora Worthington's agent and see if she would consider helping us out and if her schedule would permit. He would let us know. We really had a very short time to decide what to do. If we could find another headliner with star power to step in, there would still be a lot of work to do to see if we could salvage the remains of this event.

Food had arrived and Danny asked to have his food boxed so he could take off. The rest of us moved on to small talk as we ate. I don't know if Diana had briefed them or if they were all just extremely well mannered, but no one mentioned the questioning of my ex-husband in conjunction with the murder investigation.

As soon as we were done, I left the hotel and turned back toward downtown. I had one appointment to attend to and then, I'd decided, I would pay Mandy a visit. I'd phoned her, but she hadn't returned my call. Tania had confirmed for me that Purple's suite was still being treated as a crime scene and that Mandy was back at Purple's Laguna Beach house. I decided to take a chance on stopping by. It would give me a chance to clear up some things with Mandy.

Besides I really wanted to check in on Lavender.

CHAPTER SEVEN

Purple's house was in Diamond Cove, a super-gated community that was into privacy and security in a big way. As I drove up to the guard shack, I wondered if I was still on the list. I had been because of working with Lavender, but who knew if the very efficient Mandy had had me removed when Geoffrey replaced me. I probably should have called ahead.

"Good morning, Ms. Lamont." The guard was the regular one for this time of day, and after asking me to sign in on his tablet computer, he waved me through. Diamond Cove was so high tech, I was surprised they didn't just use your fingerprint or one of those retina scan things like they have in the movies. If eye scans aren't already in play, they are probably coming soon to a paranoid SoCal subdivision near you.

I drove through the winding streets and pulled into the half-circle driveway. The beautiful modern house was so new I couldn't imagine what needed to be remodeled. But apparently, the project continued as there was a Pacific Coast Construction truck already in the drive. I parked beside it.

The doorbell was answered quickly by a redheaded apron-wearing woman I'd not met in previous visits. I wondered where Pat, the usual lady, was. Maybe they had particular days and I'd come during one of her off days. I would have definitely remembered this one. My hair is red — as in my-ancestry-must-definitely-have-some-Scots/Irish — but apron lady's red was more of a Crayola primary red color. I explained to her that I was Lavender's pet therapist and was just here to check on her.

"Yes, yes." The lady motioned me to come in. "The doggie is out on the terrace with Sheron, the hair lady."

I was confused by that. I thought Purple was very much the hair lady herself. Not sure what to expect, I followed her as she wound her way through the living room and out to the stunning pool and patio.

An ash-blond woman in white capris and a gauzy taupe top played fetch with the little dog. Lhasa Apsos, like most dogs, need enough exercise to keep them fit, but most of all they need attention. They're such a loyal breed that they crave as much attention as a pet parent is willing to give. Part of the reason I'd been concerned about Lavender's state, given her dog mom's death.

"Very good, girl." The lady picked up the little dog and cuddled her to her chest. The dog leaned in and tucked her head.

Aww. I felt my throat tighten. I was so glad that Lavender had someone to comfort her. So many people are dismissive of the effect of grief on animals, but believe me, they know. They often provide comfort to us when we're dealing with a loss, but sometimes they also need comfort themselves.

"Sheron," the apron lady called out, "it's the doggie therapist."

Sheron turned and set Lavender down on the terrace. She stepped forward and held out her hand. "Hello, I don't believe we've met. I'm Sheron, the resident hair stylist."

I clasped her hand. Strong fingers and unpainted nails. Not like the stylists I'd been used to on the beauty pageant circuit.

"You do . . . uh . . . did, Purple's hair?" I wasn't sure how much doing that entailed but I guessed it was all about the look.

"That's right." Sheron stepped back and patted Lavender who'd not left her side since she'd set her down. "All the wigs and such. And then when a person is wearing wigs all the time you've got to worry about the health of their real hair."

I hadn't considered the perils of wig-wearing but it made sense.

"I also do Lavender's hair." She patted the dog's head. "I'm not a groomer, but once the groomer has the trim completed I take care of the purple hair coloring."

"Oh, I see." I reached down and let Lavender sniff my fingers. "I guess you're one of the few people who actually saw her, Purple that is, without her face almost totally covered by hair."

"I guess. Though that was mostly about being out in public. Around home she was like anyone else."

I couldn't imagine.

"Though she did have to be careful any time she went outside. The paparazzi were always trying to get a photograph. I think that's why she liked the idea of this." She swept her hand around. "A gated community with very strictly controlled access."

"You live here at the house?" I was beginning to see a pattern. I'd asked about other people at the house and on the road with whom Lavender came in contact, and Purple had insisted it was just her and Mandy.

"I was planning to." She brushed the dirt

off her knees. "I've been with Purple for a little over ten years. Most days it's just MB, Lavie here, and me around the house."

"MB?" I hadn't heard anyone by that name mentioned either. But then I hadn't heard of Sheron until today.

"Oh, sorry." She laughed. "Mandy Barton, Purple's assistant. You know her, right? She's the one that keeps everything running around here. What am I saying? Not just around here, but in all facets of Purple's life."

"Oh, yes. Mandy."

"I'm sure the girl could run a country if asked. And some days between the concerts, and the recordings, and the appearances, and all, it is almost like running a country."

"Can you think who would have wanted to kill, Purple?" I had to ask. Here was someone with intimate knowledge of the singer, and I couldn't pass up the chance.

Her eyes teared up. "She was a challenge at times, but I will miss her. She was a tough business woman, and I can't imagine you make it in the entertainment business without making some people upset. But upset enough to kill her? No, I don't think so."

"I'm sorry for your loss."

"Now what can I help you with?" She

blotted her eyes with the sleeve of her top. "You're the pet therapist?"

She seemed like a really nice lady and I hated to mislead her. I really was there under false pretenses.

"Well, it's a long story but she actually fired me a couple of days ago. But I wasn't sure if the new person would be following up with Lavender given the circumstances, and I wanted to check in and make sure she was doing okay."

"She's a good dog." Sheron's voice got a reaction from the dog who came running and barreled into her. "Oops, I used my treat voice." Sheron smiled.

"Seems like you two have a good relationship." Truth was the little dog seemed more attached to Sheron than I'd seen her with Purple. Which might explain Purple's failure to mention the hair lady. I'd worried that Lavender was more accessory than companion to the star, but Purple had insisted they were inseparable. Even so, I'd sensed something lacking.

"We both do a lot of waiting and so I guess we sort of bonded."

"Well, I'm glad to see everything is okay." I glanced back at the house. "Is Mandy around?"

"I believe so." With Lavender following

her closely, she ushered me back through the house to the living room where the red-haired lady was cleaning windows. "Do you know where Mandy is?"

"She's out front," she answered without missing a swipe.

"Thanks, Sheron. It was nice to meet you." I handed her one of my business cards. "Please feel free to call me if Lavender runs in to any problems."

"Thank you. We appreciate your concern." She reached down and picked up the dog. "Don't we, poochie?"

After thanking Sheron again, I stepped outside. Mandy was out front near the street talking with a guy with spiky hair who looked vaguely familiar. They stood near a late-model white Subaru. A nice enough car but one that looked out of place in the posh Diamond Cove community. He reached for Mandy's arms and held them at her side.

As I descended the wide front steps, I couldn't quite make out what they were saying, but it was clear there was a problem.

Mandy's face was pink and she looked upset. Never afraid to wade in, I started toward them. He suddenly let her go and stepped back.

The guy got in his car but leaned out and said loud enough for me to hear this time,

"We had an agreement. I don't know what I was thinking trying to deal with someone who holds grudges."

He put the car in gear and sped off just as I reached Mandy's side.

"Are you okay?" I asked.

Mandy pulled herself together quickly but a tear slipped down her cheek. "I'm fine."

That's what they always said.

I waited. Sometimes silence will bring forth honesty. It didn't, so I asked, "Your boyfriend?"

"What? No." She shook her head. "That's Trevor. He had some dealings with Purple and they were not settled when she . . ." Mandy gulped. "Anyway, we'll get them sorted out."

"Still, to take it out on you."

"It's no big deal." She wiped her face. "Now what can I do for you?"

Back to business. Mandy was the epitome of control. Well, you know what. People deal with grief in all sorts of ways. I worried that by holding it in too long, there would come time when all that emotion came out in a rush.

"I stopped by to check on Lavender."

"But, you aren't —" she began.

"I know I'm no longer Lavender's pet therapist and that Geoffrey will probably be checking in, but I wasn't sure what your arrangement was with him and was just concerned about her."

"Oh, she's with —" Mandy turned toward the house.

"I already spoke with the hair stylist. Lavender seems attached to her. Purple had never mentioned Sheron."

Had Purple's pride kept her from mentioning Sheron? Had she not wanted to admit the pooch's attachment to someone other than her? It seemed really callous to be upset with a dead woman, but I couldn't help the irritation I felt. Seriously, people. I can't help your pets if you won't be honest with me.

"Yes, I'm pretty sure she left the care of the dog to Sheron in her will," Mandy noted. Again, the one dealing with all the details. "At least I hope so."

"Is there extended family? I mean anyone other than the grandpa she talked about."

"Just him and he died last year," Mandy affirmed.

"That must have been hard for her."

"It was." Mandy swept her hair off her face. "She canceled a performance in London and went home for the funeral."

"Have you worked for her for a long time?" This had to be more difficult for

Mandy than she was letting on.

"We met in college. She had a band and I fancied myself a singer," she answered, her voice flat. "Turned out I was a much better manager of things than a singer."

"What will you do now?" It suddenly occurred to me she'd lost both a friend and an employer. "Or have you even had time to think about it?"

"I've got so many loose ends to clear up that I can't even think about it right now." Mandy looked off into the distance. "What will the Barking with the Stars group do?" she asked. "Will the show go on?"

"That's still up in the air." I couldn't share Danny Mahalovich's idea to snag Nora Worthington. "If the event continues, we'd definitely want to do some sort of tribute to Purple."

"Still the big star even after she's gone. Well, I'd better get back to work." Mandy turned and walked back toward the house.

I climbed into my car and started it. As I drove away I suddenly realized where I'd seen the guy, Trevor, who had been arguing with Mandy. He'd been the one in the dressing room area the day we'd been checking accommodations, chasing Purple down the hallway, after her curse-filled pomegranate rant.

CHAPTER EIGHT

Mulling the implications of the guy's presence both backstage and now at Purple's house, I wondered what Mandy had meant by "dealings" with Purple. She'd dismissed my concern for her, and I was sure if there had been any reason to think he might have been the killer, she would have told the police about him. Nevertheless, when I arrived back home, I made a note to be sure to mention him to Malone.

The opportunity to do so presented itself sooner than I'd thought it would. Once I'd greeted pets, taken care of needs, and brewed myself a cup of tea, I checked my phone for messages and saw I had a phone call from Malone wanting to meet with me. I called him back and we agreed to meet at the Koffee Klatch the next morning. A local spot right on PCH, it seemed the easiest location as it was on my way, close for him, and I liked it because it was neutral ground.

Promising Dogbert and the cats I'd be back soon, I headed out for my afternoon appointments. I had a packed schedule and though I enjoyed all my clients by the time I'd headed back home, I was mentally and physically ready to be done with the day. I stopped by to pick up a few groceries and added the ingredients I needed for a new pupcake recipe I'd wanted to try. I liked experimenting with different dog and cat treat recipes and I found cooking relaxing. It was probably all those weekends making cookies with Grandma Tillie in her big country kitchen at the Montgomery ranch. Mama Kat didn't allow cookies at our house. She was perpetually on a diet and endlessly worrying about both her own figure and mine.

Once home, I went through what had become a nightly routine: feed the cats, walk the dog, feed myself, and call it a day. Yes, I lead a very exciting life.

I debated about a run on the beach or staying in and looking up some information on Purple. It was still daylight and the storm had not materialized. I truly needed a relaxing, head-clearing run, but curiosity won out. I settled in in front of my computer and did a little research on the pop star and her career.

In the past, Detective Malone has not always had the greatest respect for my insights. Maybe if I could figure out what exactly was the connection between this Trevor and Purple, he'd take my information on the exchange I'd observed between Mandy and the guy more seriously. And then, of course, I was curious about the missing pieces in what I'd known about Purple and her life. She was engaged but had never mentioned her fiancé to me. And the mysterious Sheron who claimed to have been with Purple for ten years and yet had never been present during my appointments with Purple and Lavender. Hopping from site to site can suck you in and before I knew it hours had passed.

The gossip sites confirmed Mandy's mention that she'd taken a break when her grandfather passed away. There were several sites with really bizarre reasons for why she wore the wigs. She was severely disfigured, she'd been in a fire, she was a twin and they took turns making appearances, she was a man, she was an alien.

She'd been in multiple relationships. Currently engaged. I already knew that.

I didn't learn a lot that I hadn't already known, but there was one news site that mentioned she'd had a stalker a year or so ago. Again, like the dealings with Trevor, I would like to think Malone and his people had access to way better information than online sites and had followed up on the stalker angle already. But I made a note to myself to ask Mandy about the incident.

Dogbert, who'd been sitting at my feet, stood and gave me the I-need-to-go-out woof, so I shut down my computer and took him out for a quick break. When we returned, my cell phone, which I'd left on the counter, buzzed letting me know I'd missed a couple of phone calls. One was from my mother and the other was from Sam.

I sighed. I wasn't wild about returning either call at the moment, but for very different reasons. What a chicken I'd turned into lately. I straightened up my attitude and made the calls, but had to admit I was a bit relieved when I got voicemail with both Mama Kat and Sam.

When I arrived at the Koffee Klatch the next morning, Verdi, my favorite barista who also worked as a part-time receptionist at my office, was on duty. She spotted me and automatically called out my hazelnut latte to the guy in the prep area. Then she nodded toward the back of the coffee shop.

I glanced in that direction. Malone was already at a table.

I waited for my drink and then carried it to the secluded corner where he sipped a black coffee. No fancy coffee for this guy.

I dropped my bag on the floor and slid into a chair. "Good morning, Detective."

He grunted hello and took another sip of his coffee, his expression unreadable. Obviously, he had not yet had enough caffeine. I felt his pain.

"How's the investigation going?"

"About as you'd expect." He leaned back and crossed his long jean-clad legs at the ankle.

"I'm guessing from your phone call you didn't want to just chat."

"I just have a few questions." He tipped his head back and gave me a look I was sure he'd perfected questioning bad guys.

This was the place in the movies and television shows where the detective always pulls out his little notebook and references his notes or writes things down. Not Detective Malone, he kept it all in his head.

"We think there may have been multiple people in Purple's room at the hotel." He waited for me to respond.

"Hard to tell with the security cameras out of commission, though, right?" I felt a little twinge of satisfaction at his flinch of surprise.

See, Detective, I'm not just some dumb former therapist who now practices therapy on foo-foo pets. I'm a smart former therapist who now practices therapy mostly on the parents of foo-foo pets.

"That's true." He sighed. "There's no usable recording on the security feed after seven in the evening."

"We are concentrating on the time between ten and when she was found by her assistant. You and your group saw her in the lobby around ten o'clock."

"That's right." I nodded. "Maybe a little bit before. Her assistant said she was staying at the hotel because the noise of the remodeling at her house was so bad." I was sure he knew that already.

"But the workers don't work at night." He sipped his coffee thoughtfully.

"True. Any theories on who disabled the security cameras?" Of course, they had theories but whether Malone would share them with me was something else.

"No, the footage prior to that is just the usual coming and going of guests and staff. And then starting about seven the recordings have nothing."

"Nothing on the tape?" I wondered how

that was possible.

"No one uses tape recordings anymore. It's all cloud-based so our culprit had to have enough computer knowledge to access the recordings or the controls."

"When I was at Purple's house yesterday . . ." I began.

Malone gave me a look.

"I was checking on the dog."

"Has it finally stopped barking?" The pained expression on his face said he wasn't a Lavender fan.

"Yes, she has." I paused, remembering the dog's reaction to Sheron. "I think she's going to be okay."

He waited for me to continue.

"Anyway, when I was at the house, there was a guy there. Mandy called him Trevor. Young, spiky hair." I thought back to the conversation. "He and Mandy were arguing and it sounded like there was something he had wanted from Purple. Something she had promised but he didn't receive."

"Here's the thing." Malone took a deep breath. Apparently, we weren't going to talk about Trevor. "I need some clarification about when you saw Purple."

"Oh, no." A flash of bright color had caught my eye.

"What?"

"Don't look up. Betty Foxx at your two o'clock."

"Oh, man." Malone dropped his chin and slid down in his chair as if he'd like to disappear.

I'd come to love the feisty senior rascal, but I swear I would never get used to her penchant for lipstick eyebrows and PJs as day wear. Today's ensemble was a nod to the warm days we were having. A tropical print cotton, the bright pinks, oranges, and yellows were an assault on the eyes of the unwary. And, as always, the finishing touch. Her ever present pearls.

She picked up her carrier of coffee cups and had started out the door when she spotted us. An order for the Bow Wow Boutique, I'd bet. I could almost smell Mel's chai tea latte. Betty made a hairpin turn and stopped at our table.

She parked the drink carrier right in front of me. Now I really could smell the spices of the chai tea. Up close, the pink slashes that were Betty's eyebrows were startling. It was a good thing I'd had my coffee.

"Hey there, Detective." She sidled a little closer to Malone and wiggled her rosy eyebrows. "I've been a bad girl. Want to frisk me?"

Malone had to try hard not to spit his coffee across the table.

"Are you okay, Carmen?" She leaned in to look at me.

"I'm fine, Bertha." As I said, I was never sure if she really couldn't remember my name or if she was messing with me. Some days I let it go, some days I messed with her.

"Cookie's worried about you."

"Why?" Cookie was her pet name for Melinda. Surely Mel knew I wasn't in any danger. It wasn't like this was my first encounter with a murder investigation. Nor hers.

"She's worried about you and the Greek."

"The Greek? Oh, Sam."

"Yeah, Sam." Betty shook her head. "Keep up, will ya."

"Why is she worried?" I was trying to keep up.

"This." Betty snapped open the white patent-leather pocketbook she carried and pulled out a newspaper clipping and handed it to me.

It was a color shot of a New York society event, and sure enough there was Sam, his arm around a buxom blond who was identified in the caption as the daughter of French billionaire, William Bellerose.

I handed it back. "I'm fine."

"You sure?" She peered at me, her lipstick eyebrows scrunched together.

"Yes, I'm sure."

"Okay, Carly." She slipped the paper back in her purse, clipped it shut, and picked up her carrier. "If you need us to deal with the blond, you just let us know."

And with that, Betty race-walked out the door.

I laid my head down on the table.

"Carly?" Malone smirked. "What was that about?"

"Nothing." I lifted my head. "Just my wildly dysfunctional relationship with my cousin and her senior citizen assistant."

"At least it's not about that ugly brooch." Malone leaned back and stretched out his legs. He didn't have a lot of patience with our feud over the family brooch. Maybe because it had gotten in the way of police business a couple of times.

"Anyway, you were saying?" I changed the subject. Yeah, I didn't want to talk about Mel and our problems and I didn't want to talk about Grandma Tillie's brooch. And I sure didn't want to talk about that newspaper clipping.

"I'd like you to think about when you saw Purple and the other people who were with her the evening before she was killed."

"Okay." I didn't know any of the people so I wasn't sure I could give any additional insight but I would try.

"Here's the thing." He paused. "I now have more information on the time of death, and the woman would have already been dead at that time."

"What?" How was that possible? I pictured Purple and the group in my mind. As a trained therapist, I knew the dangers of false memory. You remember something in a certain way and you think about it and that cements your version in your mind. But I hadn't imagined that I saw Purple and the crazy group of fans.

"We believe —" he began.

"Don't talk." I held up my hand. I closed my eyes and thought about the group.

Purple in her flowing cape and the group of fans following her. Posers, I'd heard the others call them. A small girl with purple hair, another with the "Beware the Haze" t-shirt, and the one with the "My Heart Bleeds Purple" sign. Surprising that such a big celebrity didn't have security, many did. Where were the body guards? For that matter, where was Lavender? I pictured Purple again with the white dog in her arms, the dog cuddling close.

Wait a minute! Lavender had done that

with Sheron, the hair stylist, but I'd never seen the dog do that with Purple. The reason there wasn't any security was that she wasn't Purple. Instead, *she* — or he I guess — could have been someone dressed like Purple.

"It wasn't her." I opened my eyes and looked into Malone's amused blue gaze. "With the wig and all, it's impossible to say for sure, but her body language was off."

"So, you're not sure it was her?" Malone asked.

"I'm not even sure it was Lavender, come to think of it." I hesitated before continuing. "I didn't actually see the dog's face, but the way the person was holding the dog isn't in keeping with how Purple and her dog normally interacted."

"So the person you saw could have been someone dressed to look like her?"

"Yes, it could have been." I hoped I hadn't confused things with my eyewitness account. Perhaps given the killer time to get away.

I sat quietly for a few minutes thinking about seeing the group and not really taking time to question what I saw.

Malone waited.

"I'm sorry. Does that change your investigation?"

"It's always about putting all the pieces together, Caro. Figuring out where everyone was. Who had a motive. What anything looks like at first is almost never where we end up. But then sometimes it is."

"Have you figured out where everyone was?"

"Mostly." He rubbed his chin. "Geoffrey Carlisle, for instance, could not account for where he was before, but may be able to for this new time."

"Does that mean Geoffrey is no longer your primary suspect?"

"It absolutely does not. I said, it *may* mean that he's able to account for his whereabouts." Malone's face was suddenly serious. "Listen, Caro, he's still a person of interest."

"But —"

"I know you don't believe he's capable of murder, but sometimes we find the people closest to a killer don't see it. They don't want to believe it."

"It's not his style," I insisted. "He's a low-life, untrustworthy, bottom-feeder, but —"

"I can see you're a big fan." Malone fought a smile. "What do you really think of the guy?"

"Listen." I laid my hand on Malone's arm. "I know him. He'd weasel his way out of any responsibility. He'd lie. He'd cheat. But he doesn't have it in him to kill." I couldn't believe I was defending the jerk, but I believed it to be true.

"I know you believe that, but be careful, Caro." Malone's bright-blue eyes pinned me. "Not everyone can be saved."

A realization suddenly occurred to me — Malone knew Geoffrey had come to my house last night. Of course, they were having him followed. They'd released him because they didn't have any evidence, but they were still keeping tabs on him.

"I promise you, I'll be careful." I took a sip of my latte. "Tomorrow we're planning to try to meet with some of the fans to discuss doing some sort of memorial for Purple. I can keep my eyes and ears open."

Malone's cell phone rang and he glanced at the display. "I've got to take this." He stood. "You have my number. Call." And with that he walked away.

I gathered up my bag and coffee. The rush had slowed a bit so I chatted with Verdi for a few minutes. For her, being at the coffee shop meant she heard all the gossip, and like Malone and Diana, Verdi was not convinced of Geoffrey's innocence. While walking thoughtfully to my car I remembered I'd forgotten to ask Malone about the stalker.

Once again at the office, I settled in at my computer to organize my notes and update my files. Due to the Geoffrey-induced cancellations, I didn't have another client appointment until afternoon.

I needed to make some notes about the client because this was a new one. A Sheltie named Bosco who belonged to Les Bratten. Les owned a shop on the main drag not far from Mel's Bow Wow Boutique. The shop sold leather goods, and Bosco had become a problem with customers. Les, understandably, didn't want to keep him kenneled for long periods, but was going to have to think about doggie daycare as an alternative if we couldn't get Bosco's behavior under control.

Shelties need exercise and Les had insisted he was walking the dog as well as taking him to the dog park and letting him run on a regular basis. If that was true, then the problem might be more a need for mental exercise.

I jotted down a few questions to ask Les.

The breed is actually a Shetland Sheepdog, but most people call them Shelties and they're herding dogs, so that fact made it a bit more likely Bosco simply needed a job.

I'd know more after I'd observed him during my meeting at the shop.

I made a few more notes.

Then my thoughts turned to my conversation with Malone. If Purple had been killed earlier and Geoffrey had someone who could vouch for him at that time, the police would need to expand their investigation. The problem didn't seem to be opportunity; the question was who would want to kill Purple.

I flipped over the page of my notebook and wrote down the names of the people I'd met within the pop star's circle. Mandy, Trevor, Sheron, the fans, mostly I didn't know their names, but the two I'd overheard at dinner had seemed to have more access to Purple than the rest. I wrote down Curly Sue and Tiny. And the guy with the purple guitar. What was his name? I thought I'd heard them call him Lew.

I hadn't met Drake, her fiancé, but I put him on the list anyway. Wasn't there something about the killer often being the person closest to the victim?

Next, I started another column for motive. I didn't think this was how Malone and his crew sorted out suspects, but sometimes I had to see things in black and white to wrap my brain around them. It sounds cliché but most times people kill other people for a very limited number of reasons. Money is right there at the top. Secrets also. They are hiding something or wanting to keep something hidden. In this case, with the security cameras being disabled, it seemed the murder had been planned, which would mean the killer needed the expertise to deactivate the cameras. I had no idea how you'd go about that but I'd bet Graham Cash, my techie officemate from next door, would know.

I stepped outside my office to see if Graham was in and ran smack dab into reporter Callum MacAvoy.

"Sorry." He grabbed my arms to steady me. Television anchor, handsome with flashy green eyes and a camera-ready smile, MacAvoy was not one of my favorite people. He and I had clashed more than once.

Mostly because I thought he should mind his own business, and he seemed to think everything was his business. Probably went with the journalism career. And undoubtedly, I had some built-in mistrust because of how I'd been hounded by the press when my crash-and-burn divorce had been big news back in Dallas.

"What are you doing here?" I stepped back.

"Can't a guy simply stop by to say hello?" He smiled his on-camera smile.

"No," I snapped, then realized how impolite that had sounded. "I'm sorry, that was rude."

"If you're not busy . . ." He glanced behind me. "I did want to ask you a couple of questions." He brushed past me and entered.

"Make yourself at home." I followed him to the easy chairs that I'd placed in the office to make conversations more comfortable. I had not, however, envisioned conversations with people like MacAvoy.

"Will the Barking with the Stars group be making an announcement soon?" He didn't waste any time getting right to the point.

"What do you mean?"

"Well, I understand the event has been canceled." His eyes were alert like Dogbert when he was waiting for a ball to be thrown or expecting a treat. The man was baiting me, hoping for a reaction.

"Oh, are you the Lifestyle and Entertainment reporter now?" I leaned forward in my chair. "I wasn't aware you'd been reassigned."

He sat for a moment eyeing me.

"Point to you," he finally said. "What do you know about the investigation?"

142

"See?" I smiled. "How hard was that? Honesty is always the best policy, Mr. MacAvoy."

He rolled his eyes. "Whatever you say. What do you know?"

"I'm not sure I'd share with you if I did know something, but the truth is that I know very little."

"Still I heard you were at the Koffee Klatch with Detective Malone earlier today. You must know something."

Wow, he had some pretty up-to-the-minute intel. "You'd have to talk with Detective Malone about that."

"Tried."

"MacAvoy, you know they can't give you information about an active investigation."

"What about your ex-husband?" He perked up. "They haven't charged him. Is he still a suspect?"

"How would I know? He's my ex — emphasis on ex — husband."

"Fine." He stood. "I'm just trying to keep the public informed."

That'd be great if it really were Mac-Avoy's motive, but I suspected it was more about ratings and pressure from the station to find out the latest on the investigation. I'd seen the news vans from the national networks parked in front of the police station, and I imagined, as the local affiliate, there was some pressure to get the jump on the others.

"Sorry, I can't help you out." I wasn't really sorry.

"I talked to a couple of the fan club presidents this morning." He ambled toward the door. "The one national president and the one from Japan. They had tons of info about Purple. Apparently, these groups of fans follow her from venue to venue. I got some quotes from them."

He didn't sound too enthusiast about his quotes.

"Describe the two you talked to."

He frowned slightly at my question. "One kind of tall, glasses, curly hair. The other very petite, Asian, dark hair."

That sounded like Curly Sue and Tiny. I'd been trying to figure out how I could get in touch with them since I didn't know their names. But short of hanging out in the lobby of the Ocean Mark P, I hadn't come up with anything.

"Did you get their names?" I hated to owe MacAvoy anything but if he had these names, I would be beholden to him for the information.

"Wait. Yes, I think so." He reached into his jacket pocket and pulled out two business cards.

I snatched them from his hand before he could decide to bargain for them. "If you don't mind, I'll make a copy. Be right back."

I hurried to the lobby area where the office copier was located and laid the cards on the glass. Done, I returned to my office to find MacAvoy holding my notebook.

"Doing a little investigating on your own, Ms. Lamont?"

I plucked it from his fingers and handed the cards back to him. "Thank you for the information. I'm sorry I can't chat longer but I've got an appointment and I'm sure you have tons of other people to harass. Oh, I mean, interview."

Linking my arm with his, I steered him in the direction of the front door.

Back in my office I looked at the copy I'd made. Cindy Bradford, Purple Fan Club USA, and Yuki Kimoto, Murasaki — Purple Fans of Japan. Both cards listed PO Boxes and phone numbers. Now that I had names, I'd try the hotel since I knew they were staying there. If I couldn't reach them that way I could always try the numbers on the cards. I folded the paper and put it in my bag.

I checked to see if Graham was in his office so I could ask about the security cameras, but I found his office door closed. That wasn't unusual; the kind of work he did wasn't really in-the-office type work. Maybe I'd give him a call this evening and see what he could tell me.

I packed up my things and locked up. I'd decided to run home for lunch. The stop could be dual purpose. I would be able to let Dogbert out for a break and grab a bite to eat before my one o'clock with Les Bratten.

After Dogbert and I enjoyed our short walk around the neighborhood, I slapped together a healthy avocado, cucumber, and tomato salad and ate it while checking my phone for message and emails. Thank God, no more cancellations. I imagined Geoffrey'd been busy being almost arrested the past few days, but now that the heat was off, I was sure he'd be back at it. I couldn't undo what Geoffrey had done, but I certainly could do damage control. I made a note on my to-do list to follow up with clients who could be potential targets for Geoffrey.

Blowing kisses to the felines and giving a head pat to Dogbert, I packed up for the afternoon. I threw in some new organic dog treats I'd been trying, tossed my phone in my bag, and I was off.

My office is so close to downtown, I

parked in the lot there and walked to Les's shop. Parking in Laguna this time of year is a challenge and gets worse before it gets better. During the height of tourist season, it was better to walk wherever you needed to go than waste time trying to find a parking place.

I'd worn a lightweight Rag & Bone pop-over dress in off-white in hopes of staying cool, but by the time I reached the shop I was still overheated.

Les was behind the counter when I entered, and Bosco immediately came out to greet me.

"Hi there, boy." I gave him a scratch behind the ears and he responded with a friendly bark.

"Good afternoon, Caro." Les had also come out to greet me. His handshake was strong, his forearms muscled and weathered by the sun. The combination of his Sawdust Festival t-shirt which was a few seasons old, his faded jeans, and his man bun, created a look that would not have clued the casual observer to his reputation as a leather artisan or the high demand for his work. His handcrafted leather goods were all the rage with the celebrities and uber-rich in nearby Newport Beach, Bel Air, and Beverly Hills. I had one of his weekenders myself and I loved it. I'd planned a clutch for Mama Kat for her birthday but hadn't decided on a color yet.

"Tell me a little about the issues that have come up recently with Bosco," I invited as I walked to the counter and set my bag on the floor. Still a bit warm from my walk, I picked up a brochure and fanned myself.

"He's always been interested in the customers when they come in." He patted Bosco's head and the dog leaned in to him. "Just like he did with you."

"He's always been friendly." I placed the brochure back on the counter. "Never a problem before, right?"

"No, but he's gotten a little aggressive lately and it worries me."

"Changes in routine, diet, or his health?" I asked.

"Nothing I can think of," Les answered.

"You've had Dr. Darling check him out?"

"I took him in a week ago, and the doc found nothing at all."

"He's getting enough exercise?"

"Oh, yeah." Les grinned. "We've been getting regular walks in. After six at Main Beach, dog park every weekend. When it's open anyway. They closed it a couple of weekends ago because it was so muddy."

The Laguna Beach dog park sat in a valley off Laurel Canyon Road and a big rain created a flow of water off the hills that could sometimes turn it into a swamp. Luckily that didn't happen often.

"Walk me through an example of a problem with a customer." I knew Les had said nothing was different, but something had changed in Bosco's world.

"Well, the worst case wasn't a customer, it was Mason Reed, the guy who owns the high-end handbag shop across the street. He and his wife, Quinn, have only been there a few months. Used to be that import place. You know?" He looked at me to make sure I was following.

"Right," I affirmed. "What did Bosco do?"

"At first, he barked." Les moved back behind the counter and sat down on a high stool. "Then as Reed came closer, Bosco started kind of this deep growl and kind of nipped at the guy."

"That's interesting." I watched Bosco as he kept his eyes trained on Les. "The same with others?"

"Not so much the nipping but definitely checking them out."

"Let me go back outside and come in." I went out and as I came through the door, the bell rang and Bosco tensed but didn't bark or growl. I tested Bosco's reaction to my approaching Les. No reaction at all.

It could be there was something about this particular guy. His size, his attitude, for that matter even his smell. Dog's often assess via their noses. It could have been his aftershave or even deodorant. Maybe something he'd stepped in or walked through.

"What did you do when it happened?"

"I gave Bosco an order to get back, which he did. But he continued growling, sort of deep in his throat, until the guy left."

"How long before someone else came into the shop?"

"Probably fifteen or twenty minutes, and then Bosco went on alert with them, too."

We covered some different tactics that Les could try. I explained about Shelties being herders and how sometimes when they become a problem, it's simply a matter of giving them a job to do. I suggested some puzzle toys or having him help pick up. If Les scattered a few items around the shop and made it Bosco's job to find them and put them away, that activity would go a long way toward keeping Bosco engaged in something useful. Heck, we all like to be useful, don't we?

"I don't want to kennel him here at the shop. He's good company while I'm working." Les patted the dog's head.

"I think we can figure this out." I smiled at Les and Bosco. "Let's try some of the tasks. I'm not sure it's the full solution on the alert behavior but it will keep him busy and result in a calmer canine."

After saying my good-byes to Les and Bosco and leaving a couple of pup treats for Bosco, I headed down the street in the direction of my office.

I'd not gone more than a few steps when I was accosted by Mr. Swanson. Great. I'd been wondering when he was going to pop up.

"Caro Lamont." A straw hat protected his balding head from the sun.

"Mr. Swanson."

My unhappiness at finding Swanson in my path is part of a long story involving Betty Foxx, but the Cliff Notes version is that through a series of events, Mr. Swanson had ended up with my Grandma Tillie's antique brooch.

"What a coincidence." He positioned himself directly in front of me so I had to stop or run in to people walking the other way on the sidewalk.

"Probably not." I was sure he'd been watching from somewhere and had spotted me.

"Been thinking about getting your bid in?"

His beady eyes searched my face.

"No, but I've been thinking about talking with my friend at the police department about you." I couldn't believe he had the gall to think Melinda and I would pay him for something that was rightfully ours.

"Better hurry," he cackled. "Your cousin won't dither like you. She'll snap it up."

I certainly was not dithering, but I was not going to reward such high-handed behavior by paying the man. It wasn't the money. It was the principle.

"If you're ready to do the right thing and hand over the brooch, we'll call it good." Over his shoulder, I saw the guy that Mandy had been arguing with get out of his Subaru and go into a guitar shop. Trevor, she'd called him. I had some questions for Trevor.

"No proof the piece of jewelry is yours. No labels." He peered up at me. "But if you're interested, well, we should talk. If not, I'll simply let your cousin pay what she's offered."

Dang it, Mel. I hoped he was bluffing. I hoped she hadn't made an offer, but the girl was impatient. I wasn't sure.

"Maybe no label, but I have insurance papers with a description and picture of the brooch." That wasn't strictly true. I think Grandma Tillie had had the thing appraised at some point so there probably was some documentation back in Texas. The only pictures I could produce were photos of Mel or me wearing the brooch at various functions. Not because of its beauty. Far from it. It had been worn strictly to torment the other. But Mr. Pay-to-Play didn't need to know that.

He squirmed a little and wiped a couple of drops of sweat from his forehead before resituating his hat.

"Why don't I stop by your house and we can discuss it?" I wanted to know where he lived. I didn't see Malone being willing to put a scare into Mr. Swanson, but if I knew his address I could have my attorney send him a letter that might shake him up. And hopefully get him to voluntarily return the piece of jewelry. At this point, I didn't even know the guy's first name.

I kept my eyes on the guitar shop door, watching for Trevor.

"No, I don't think so." He gave a smarmy smile. "I don't want you breaking into my house and stealing the brooch."

"Steal?" He seemed to miss that part where the brooch was not his property. "Steal something that rightfully belongs to me?"

Out of the corner of my eye, I saw Trevor

come out of the guitar shop and head back to his car.

"Mr. Swanson." I clutched his arm. I needed to get him to tell me where he lived but I really needed to catch Trevor. This might be my only opportunity. I had no idea how to reach him and I needed to know what his dealings with Purple had been.

"What?" He looked confused.

"Stay right there." I stepped around him and took off down the street. "I'll be right back," I said over my shoulder as I tried to get to Trevor before he got in his car.

"Trevor," I called. "Trevor, wait up."

"Trevor." I finally got close enough that he could hear me. He had his car door open and he paused.

There was a moment of confusion and then I think he must have recognized me from yesterday at Purple's house because his expression changed. He tossed the bag he had in his hand into the car, slid in, and pulled out into traffic.

I was close enough I could see the license plate. A California plate. I pulled my note-book from my bag and wrote down the numbers. Hopefully, Malone would follow up on the information I'd given him earlier and probably he could get Trevor's contact information from Mandy. But if she didn't have it, now we (and by *we,* I meant Detective Malone) had another way to track him down.

I turned back the way I'd come, hoping to finish my business with Mr. Swanson, but he had disappeared. The little troll seemed to pop up out of nowhere and then disappear. There had to be a way to find him. Right now, I only hoped to convince him to turn over the brooch, but I wasn't above a little pressure. His attempt at deal-making with Grandma Tillie's brooch was just plain wrong.

With Mr. Swanson gone, I decided to see if the guitar shop could give me any intel on Trevor. The place wasn't busy and I only waited a few minutes to talk to the guy at the counter, but Trevor had apparently just purchased guitar picks and had paid cash. Nothing at all that would help in tracking him down.

Back at the office, it was quiet. None of my officemates were in. The real estate lady was often out, and after a couple of years of sharing the office, I still wasn't sure what Suzanne the psychic's hours were. Maybe she "knew" when someone was going to need her services and just showed up then.

I typed up my notes on Les and Bosco and was just closing down my computer when my cell phone rang. I recognized Diana's number.

"Hello, sugar," I answered while packing up to leave.

"Oh, Caro, I'm so glad I caught you." She seemed slightly breathless.

"Why?" I stopped what I was doing. "Is something wrong?"

"Well, you know that famous Tom Hanks movie quote?"

" 'There is no crying in baseball?' " I offered.

"No. 'Houston we have a problem.' "

"Oh, no." I couldn't imagine what else could go awry. "What now?"

"The fans aren't able to get into Diamond Cove where Purple's house is and so they've taken to leaving tributes at the hotel."

"Tributes?"

"You know, flowers and such," she explained.

"Understandable. I don't see how that would be a problem."

"It's not just the flowers. They're leaving signs. And balloons and all kinds of purple items which are blocking the hotel entrance."

"Oh." Well, that *could* be an issue.

"The hotel is very unhappy with the situation and they've told Rufus they're looking at their legal options."

"What do they mean by that?"

"It means, they're looking for ways out of working with us," Diana explained. "I'm sure it's not the image they're after with their fancy suites and high-end clients."

"But we have a contract, right?"

Diana said nothing for a moment. "We do and it's unlikely they have an out, but in the meantime, they are making it very difficult for Rufus."

"I'm sure." I picked up my notebook, noting my earlier list of suspects, and flipped it closed. "But what can we do? We're not in control of the fans."

"Sunny seems to think if I went and talked to the hotel that maybe I could smooth some ruffled feathers. And I've been calling Danny to see if he's made any progress on Nora Worthington as our headliner. I thought if they knew she would be filling in, that might influence them."

"It's unfortunate that the flowers and things are creating a problem for the hotel, but it's not unusual." I dropped the notebook in my bag. "People express grief in a lot of different ways."

"I have an appointment with the hotel general manager at four o'clock. Would you be willing to come along?" she asked.

"I'm happy to come along as moral support, sugar." I was sure Diana's influence would be our best chance to charm them, but I was happy to provide backup.

"Great, thanks. I knew I could count on you."

"Do you want me to pick you up or meet you there?"

"It would be wonderful for you to pick me up if you'd don't mind."

"No worries, hon. I'll get you about twenty minutes before four."

"Thanks."

We ended our call and I finished packing up my things, and headed home to let Dogbert out and freshen up.

I parked in my drive not bothering to pull into the garage since I was leaving so soon. As usual the two felines glanced up as if to say, "Oh, it's just you." And Dogbert greeted me like I'd been gone for months.

"I know you're glad to see me, even though you pretend you're not." I called to Thelma and Louise as I grabbed Dogbert's leash and led him back outside. We did a quick once around the neighborhood again and we were back home.

I promised Dogbert a beach run or a dog park visit sometime this weekend. Not only was my pooch not getting enough exercise but neither was I. Since walking away from the beauty pageant scene several years ago, I've never stressed about my weight. But I feel so much better when I'm able to burn off some worries with a run, and my favorite was an early morning or evening run on the beach.

I freshened up my makeup, slipped on a new Lela Rose checked knit that looked a bit more business-like than the popover dress I'd been wearing. I pulled my hair back in a beaded clip I'd picked up at a little shop in downtown Laguna and even slipped on some heels. My mama would have been proud.

As I stepped outside I blew kisses to my fur babies. "I'll be back in no time," I called. Dogbert cocked his head to one side as if he understood. Again, the cats barely opened their eyes. "It's a good thing I know you love me."

I started to get into my car when I noticed a paper stuck under the windshield wiper. A flyer maybe?

I unfolded it and froze.

SHE'S DEAD & SO IS UR BIG EVENT — CANCEL B4 SOME1 ELSE DIES.

CHAPTER NINE

I swung around but didn't spot anyone. I'd only been in the house a few minutes after returning with Dogbert. No strange cars. No figures lurking in the bushes.

Carefully carrying the note by a corner, I hurried back into the house and grabbed a plastic sandwich bag to put it in and called Malone. My call went straight to voicemail. Not wanting to be late for our appointment at the hotel, I stowed the plastic bag in my purse, dashed back to my car, and put it in gear.

The drive to Diana's was only a few minutes. Her castle-like home was located in Ruby Point, another of Laguna's exclusive gated communities.

Diana must have been watching for me because when I pulled into her drive she came out immediately. Her Carolina Herrera shirtdress was a bright-blue leaf print and accented her peaches-and-cream complexion and bright-blue eyes. We should all look so good at eighty. Diana had outlived four husbands and was currently dating a handsome Italian restaurateur. Dino owned a popular Laguna Beach restaurant and adored Diana. Diana wasn't quite ready for marriage number five.

"Thanks for picking me up, kid." She slid in and buckled her seat belt. "Don't you look great." She touched the fabric of the dress. "New?"

"It is." I had figured she would notice. "I thought I'd look a little more professional in a dress than my usual dog drool-covered jeans."

"Caro, you look good in everything, but my favorite is dog drool." Diana chuckled. "All right. Let's see if we can talk down an anxious hotel manager."

"There's something else." I fished in my purse and handed her the bag with the note. "It was on my car. In my driveway."

"Have you called Detective Malone?"

"I left him a message."

"It sounds like someone doesn't want our fundraiser to be a success."

"I guess not. But why? Could it be that Purple's death had something to do with the event itself?"

"I can't imagine who would be against

such an important cause. It doesn't make sense." Diana shook her head.

"No, it doesn't," I agreed. "Let's go take care of the hotel and then I'll drop this off to Malone."

"It's an important cause, Caro. But nothing is more important than your safety. If Malone thinks we should cancel, we cancel. We'll figure out another way to help Warriors for the Paws."

"We're not cancelling." I would not give in to someone who thought a note could scare me.

When we arrived at the hotel, two of the valets rushed out to open our car doors. I handed over my keys. The valets were all beginning to look familiar to me. Lately it seemed like my car had spent more time in the hotel garage than my garage at home.

A wilting carnation smell hit us as we neared the hotel entrance. Diana and I picked our way around a large mound of flowers, homemade signs, stuffed animals, and other sorts of tributes. At least twenty purple balloons bobbed in the breeze. A group of maintenance workers worked to clear a path on the sidewalk.

We checked in with the concierge who phoned Mr. Sherman's office. A young woman showed up to escort us to the offices. The lobby was a mixture of business people and Purple fans. It was a strange combination but in all everyone seemed to be minding their own business.

The executive offices were as nicely appointed as the rest of the hotel but had a behind-the-scenes vibe. While the lobby, restaurants, and suites were all about the resort experience, this area was all about function. Not unlike the behind-the-scenes at pageants, there was a steady hum of people working hard to make every detail perfect on the "show" side. We were ushered into a board room to wait.

The hotel manager Sherman arrived with a couple of other people in tow. Tania, I recognized, and the other person he introduced was Jamie, their head of maintenance.

"Thank you for seeing us." Diana didn't wait for the others to introduce the topic. She commanded the stage immediately. "We know the Purple tributes have become a problem for your staff."

Tania nodded in agreement. "The crew gets them cleaned up and more appear. Guests can hardly get to the entrance at times."

"I completely understand the problem that creates." Diana smiled at Jamie and though he was probably half her age, he was taken in by the Diana Knight charm.

Mr. Sherman, not so much.

"We just can't have it. We have other guests. Other events." He shook his head. "It's not in keeping with our corporate image." He looked to Tania for backup.

"It's the way some people deal with their grief," I explained. "You see the phenomena frequently with a celebrity death. Princess Diana or Prince, for example. There were huge fan tributes."

"But you understand the hotel is simply not equipped to handle something like this." He pushed up his glasses with such force I was afraid he'd hurt himself.

"We do understand." Diana was so calm it helped to keep the tone of the conversation civil. "However, I don't believe that if we were to cancel or move the event that the tributes would stop."

"I believe you're right, Diana," I agreed. "The truth of the matter is this is where Purple died. And that's the connection, not Barking with the Stars. Regardless of what we decide to do, the fans will keep coming."

"True." Jamie, the facilities guy rubbed his chin.

"I agree." Tania stood and went to look out the window. "The fans will keep bringing more and more flowers and signs and purple balloons."

"What if we gave them a better place to leave those things? Perhaps away from the front of the hotel," I offered.

"I like that idea." Jamie perked up.

"And what if we gave them a different focus for their tributes?"

"Like what?" Sherman asked.

"I don't know, but we have presidents of two of the biggest Purple fans clubs right here." I was thinking of those two names on the note in my bag. "Diana and I could talk with them and see if they might have some ideas and if they'd be willing to help get the word out."

"That could help tremendously." Tania sat back down at the table.

"I could also call Callum MacAvoy from TV 5 and ask for his help in spreading the word once we came up with a plan," I said.

Wait a minute. What was I thinking? Somehow MacAvoy would figure I owed him if he helped out. Maybe this would act as repayment for those fan club presidents' names.

"I can look around to see what we could come up with for a better spot for the flowers and stuff." It seemed Jamie was on board.

We all looked at Sherman. He seemed a little put out that there wasn't going to be a fuss, but his face said he couldn't come up with any arguments against the plan.

"We'll see what we can do then and get back to you." Diana stood. "Who should we coordinate with?"

"I can be the point of contact," Jamie offered. He handed Diana a business card. "Just call me directly once you've talked with these fan club presidents. I'll keep Sherman in the loop."

I followed Diana out of the board room. The lady in the outer office asked if we needed help getting back to the lobby and I said I thought we could find our way.

We waited for the elevator in silence, but once we'd boarded and the doors closed, we both let out a big sigh.

"Are we a dynamic duo, or what?" Diana grinned.

"We are," I agreed, smiling back.

"They don't even know what hit them." Diana punched the lobby button. "Brilliant idea, by the way, to move the tribute area."

"I believe that it's true. That the fans will keep coming no matter whether the event is going forward or not."

"Do you want to see if we can get in touch with the fan club people before we leave?"

"That's a great idea." I liked how Diana thought.

We stopped in the lobby and called Cindy Bradford first. She answered right away but sounded a bit groggy for four thirty in the afternoon. When I explained that Diana Knight and I would like to see her, she perked right up. Cindy agreed to meet us in the coffee shop in ten to fifteen minutes. Next, we placed a call to Yuki Kimoto. She answered immediately and also agreed to meet us.

We found a quiet corner in the coffee shop and I ordered lattes for Diana and me.

The ocean theme throughout the hotel didn't translate well to a coffee shop and so the interior designer had gone for beachside café in the décor. We settled into bamboo beach chairs to wait.

Once Cindy and Yuki arrived and introductions had been made, we got right down to business. We filled them in on our meeting with the hotel.

"We've put reminders out to our online groups already asking that they channel their love for Purple into supporting causes that were near and dear to her heart," Cindy explained. "My group specifically has a list of charities that Purple supported. We're happy to add your group to the list."

Wow, very organized and a bit more corporate than I had expected.

"My online group is the same." Yuri folded her hands in her lap. "We are all so sad. But we can honor her life by helping those she tried to help."

"That's great." Diana leaned forward. "What we were hoping is that you could also encourage fans to stop dropping flowers and things off in front of the hotel."

"Those probably aren't coming from our base." Cindy pulled out her phone. "I have over thirty thousand subscribers, but most of them are not within driving distance." She swiped and opened a website. "Eighty percent United States, another ten percent UK, and the rest scattered." She held the phone so we could see the site.

Again, I'd thought this fan club thing was a fun little hobby and clearly it was a business venture as well.

"Thirty thousand!" Diana exclaimed. "Good grief, child. Where were you when I needed a fan club manager?"

Cindy's face lit up at the praise. "And growing."

"I do not have as many people who signed up as Cindy's Purple People, but we have a respectable fifteen thousand or so," Yuki commented.

"The hotel has agreed to see if they can find a place for the tributes that wouldn't obstruct people checking in the hotel." I was impressed with their numbers and their organization. "Maybe getting the word out to your members would help."

"We're hoping to move forward with the Barking with the Stars event as a tribute to Purple." Diana tapped a polished nail on the table. "But we have a lot of details to take care of if that's going to be possible."

Yuki's expression was serious. "I would be happy to get the word out if you think that would help."

"It would help," Diana answered. "And we appreciate it."

"We'd also appreciate any ideas you have." I reached into my bag and pulled out a couple of my cards. "Let me give you my phone number."

"Maybe," Diana continued thoughtfully, "if we manage to keep this event alive, you would each like to say a few words during the tribute."

They both stopped and looked at Diana.

After a pause, Cindy said quietly, "That would be cool."

Yuki nodded. "Yes."

I handed each of them one of my business cards. "We'll keep you posted on what the hotel comes up with for a tribute area."

Cindy handed her card to me and one to Diana, and Yuki followed suit.

"We should know something by tomorrow." Diana accepted the cards and tucked them into her bright-blue Kate Spade satchel.

"Any scuttlebutt among the fans staying at the hotel around the investigation?" I had to ask.

"You mean other than the missing items?" Cindy asked.

"Missing items?" Diana had been about to stand but sat back down.

"Auction items that were in Purple's suite," Yuki explained. "Many fans came specifically to bid on these things."

From the look on Diana's face it was clear that no one had told her there were auction items unaccounted for. I hadn't known but then I wasn't really involved with that part of the event.

This was another blow to a fundraiser that was already in trouble. "Are there many things missing?" I asked.

"Pretty much everything that had been in her room is my understanding." Cindy shrugged. "I'm not sure of the specifics."

I thought of all the items Mandy had been unpacking in Purple's suite the day we'd been there. An award, a doll, a poster. I tried to remember what the other items had been.

"They were worth a lot of money." Cindy propped her chin in her hand, her elbow on the table. "They're worth even more now."

"Is it possible the police took them as evidence?" Diana asked hopefully.

"No, it doesn't sound like it." Cindy seemed to be in the know. I wasn't sure how, but she seemed certain the police hadn't taken them.

We wrapped up and with a promise to call them as soon as we knew anything, Diana and I stopped at the valet station and I handed off the ticket. Most of the flowers had been cleared from the walkway, but cars with fans continued to pull up as we waited for my car.

I dropped Diana off and then drove back toward Laguna proper. She would call Sunny and see if she knew anything about the auction items and I would ask Malone about them when I dropped off the note that had been left on my car.

Traffic was still heavy but it didn't take long to get back to the downtown area. I started toward my place and then decided I would just swing by the Laguna Beach police station and see if Malone was in.

I figured he would want the note anyway,

171

so it would be easier to simply talk to him in person.

The police station was in a low brick building right next door to City Hall and like the rest of Laguna, parking was at a premium. I had to park several blocks away so I was regretting the high heels by the time I got in the door.

I walked in and looked around for Sally and Lorraine who were usually there. Yes, I know. Being on a first-name basis with the police station staff, also on the list of things that don't speak well of me. Not seeing either Sally or Lorraine, I approached the desk. That's when I noticed Betty Foxx sitting on the bench in the entryway, her white patent-leather purse perched on her knobby knees.

Attired in white "loungewear" with crimson lip imprints scattered across the fabric, Betty's lips and eyebrows matched the bright-red accents. And one eyebrow was halfway up her forehead. A disconcerting Picasso-like effect.

"Betty." I stopped. "What are you doing here?"

"I had to come down and get finger-printed." She held up her hands, fingernails also painted red. "You know, on account of all that stuff I touched when we were in that dead singer's hotel room."

I guess that made sense. They needed to rule out all the random fingerprints. In a hotel that could probably be a bit more difficult.

"I had my hair done in case they needed a mug shot too." She shared a big grin, seemingly thrilled about this fortunate turn of events. "What do you think?" She turned her head back and forth so I could see.

What did I think?

As usual where Betty was concerned, I didn't know what to think.

Chapter Ten

We didn't have long to wait before Malone appeared. He glanced at Betty and then spotted me and did a doubletake.

"I know what you're doing here," he addressed Betty, "but *you*?" He turned to look at me. "Did we have an appointment?"

"I left you a message. Something has come up I need to share with you." I'd intended to simply hand over the note, but I wasn't going to do that in front of Betty.

"Sounds pretty cozy." Betty snickered. "It's okay, you two can talk in front of me. I can keep a secret."

The truth of the matter was the silver-haired imp could not keep a secret. Not for five minutes.

"All right." Malone motioned to the young officer working the desk. "Would you take Mrs. Foxx back to the lab for fingerprinting? They're expecting her."

Betty stood and followed the officer down

the hallway. "Are you single?" I could hear her ask as they walked away.

They called older women who went after younger men cougars. I didn't think Betty fell into the cougar category. She was more of a harmless kitten trying to act like a predator.

"My office," Malone said. It was more of an order than an invitation.

I followed Malone down the same hallway that the officer had taken Betty, but then we took a turn into another corridor where the offices were located.

Malone's work area was no-nonsense, like the man himself. There was a desk, a chair, and a filing cabinet. He pulled a tan folding chair from behind the door and offered me a seat and then sat himself.

I sat down, pulled the plastic bag with the note in it out of my bag, and handed it to Malone. "I found this on the windshield of my car."

He read the note carefully and then looked up at me. "When?"

"Earlier this afternoon." I knew better than to try to explain.

"Where was your car when you found the note?"

"In my driveway."

"Okay." He blew out a breath and tipped

back in his chair. "Walk me through finding it. What had you been doing before that?"

I started with arriving at home, taking Dogbert for a walk, going inside to change, and ended with coming out to find the note.

"How long would you say that was?"

"Fifteen, twenty minutes, tops."

"Caro." Malone's jaw hardened. "Whoever left this on your car must have followed you home or already knew where you lived." He crossed his arms and leaned forward. "Who would want the event canceled?"

"Other than the hotel?" I asked.

"Why would they want the event canceled?"

"I don't think they truly do. They just wish it didn't involve a murder investigation and a steady stream of mourning fans leaving flowers that block their entrance." I told him about the problem with the tributes on the property and the meeting Diana and I had had with the hotel management.

"Sounds like a good solution." He picked up the note and looked at it again. "Can you think of anyone who would benefit if your big event didn't happen?"

"Diana and I met with the presidents of two of the biggest Purple fan clubs while we were at the hotel. It seems like they're hoping the event will go on." I thought hard.

"I simply can't come up with anyone who I think would want Barking with the Stars to be canceled."

"All right. We'll process this and if you come up with any ideas let me know. If you happen to get another threat" — Malone looked at me pointedly — "don't wait for me. Call dispatch."

"Got it." I didn't move right away.

Malone raised a brow. "Is there something else?"

"You know about the stalker Purple had, right?" I asked.

He nodded.

"And the missing items from the hotel suite?" I didn't want to be accused of keeping anything from the police.

"Yes, the assistant gave us a list of things that had gone missing from the hotel room."

"And?"

"And, it's all part of our investigation." He stood.

I gathered our time was up. As usual with Detective Malone, the sharing all went in one direction.

I took my leave and peeked at the front desk as I left to see if the young officer had survived his time with Betty. He had his head down working on some paperwork and didn't look up as I passed by, but I thought

I detected a smudge of red lipstick on his cheek. I wasn't sure whether that was a lip print or an eyebrow smudge though.

Once home, I confess I felt a little unsettled by the events of the day. I hadn't really been frightened by the note on my car, but Malone's reaction now made me feel uneasy about the whole deal.

I changed out of my dress and heels and into yoga pants and an oversized Laguna Beach Dog Park tee. Taking Dogbert out and then feeding him and the cats was comforting. A part of my regular routine.

I flipped on the television to see what was going on in the world and caught sight of Callum MacAvoy on the Channel 5 News.

"Here we are in front of the Ocean Mark P, an elegant hotel by any standards." He looked directly at the camera. "But also, the scene of the tragic death of the star known as Purple."

"As you can see for the past day and a half, since Purple's death, people have been coming here. Leaving mementos of all sorts, flowers, CDs, cards in her honor." The camera panned the piles of flowers, candles, pictures, and balloons in front of the hotel.

Hell's Bells.

I smacked my forehead. If it hadn't already

occurred to fans to bring things to the hotel, they'd be doing it now. And, the hotel was probably going to think I had something to do with telling him about the growing mound of flowers and notes. Why had I even mentioned MacAvoy's name?

My cell phone rang. Hoping it was Sam returning my call, I was disappointed to see that it was a number I didn't recognize.

"Hello?" I answered, my eyes still on the television.

"Caro Lamont?" A male on the other end of the line asked.

"Yes."

"This is Jamie, from the Ocean Mark P."

"Hello, Jamie." I hoped he hadn't called about the news story.

"I believe I've identified an area that might work to redirect fans who want to drop off flowers and things."

"That's great." I was impressed. He'd done fast work to come up with a place so quickly.

"So, you can let people know about it?" he asked.

"Would you mind if I came and took a look at it?" I asked.

"Absolutely. That would be fine."

"Great. I'll be right there." I could check it out and then let MacAvoy and the fan club presidents know the details.

I had no sooner hung up from talking to Jamie than my phone rang again. This time I recognized the number; it was Diana.

Diana had just gotten off a call with Danny Mahalovich. Danny had heard back from Nora Worthington's agent, and the singer was thrilled to help out by stepping in as the new headliner for the event.

"That's wonderful." I felt a weight lifted. The show could go on. "Thanks for letting me know. I also just got some good news."

"Did you hear from Sam?" Diana asked.

"No, we're still playing phone tag. We keep missing each other." I flipped off the television. "My good news is that I heard from Jamie at the hotel, and they've identified a space for the flowers and other items. I was just about to go take a look."

"Well, that is good news!" she exclaimed. "Still, I want to get back to the Sam issue."

There was a beep.

"Hold on." The beep was from Diana's end. "I'm sorry, sweetie, I've got to take this. It's Sunny and I've been trying to reach her. She'll be thrilled with the news about Nora, and I'll fill her in on the hotel."

"No problem, hon." I was already moving down the hall. "You take care of that. I'm running back to the hotel to see what we can do to get these tributes taken care of."

I changed my clothes yet again and grabbed my car keys.

The trip to the hotel was short but long enough for my mind to wander off in a million different ways. The event was back on track but the police was no closer to solving Purple's murder. If things had been taken from the suite, had that happened before or after the murder? Or was it possible Purple had interrupted the thief and her murder was the result of the break-in?

And, on the personal front, though I really didn't want to go there, when had Sam and I become an issue Diana felt we needed to talk about?

I pulled into the valet lane and got out. Handing my keys to the young man, I crossed the other lanes and met Jamie who was talking with Tania. From the body language, there was more than a business interest on Jamie's part, but not so much on Tania's. She was a girl on the mission to make it in the hotel business so I wasn't sure he was going to get anywhere with her.

"Hello, Caro," Tania said, as I walked up. "Jamie was telling me about the new solution. That will be good. It allows the fans to grieve and still our regular guests can check in without a problem."

Just as Tania spoke, another car pulled up and let out a group of teens carrying bouquets of purple flowers. Two of the people, hard to say if they were male or female, were dressed in full Purple garb with flowing black cape and a white wig with a streak of purple. At least they weren't carrying around dogs like the Purple imitator we had seen the night Purple was killed.

"Ms. Lamont, if you'll come with me." Jamie pointed to a golf cart parked near the hotel entrance. "I'll talk to you later, Tania."

"I'd better get back inside. We have had an extremely busy day and some staff absences." She turned to go back in. "Caro, if you have a moment would you stop by before you leave?"

"Certainly." I climbed into the golf cart with Jamie.

What he proposed was a great alternative. It was a waiting area beyond the hotel entrance with patio brick and stone benches and a fountain at the center. Planned as a pick-up-and-drop-off area for ferrying guests to excursions such as whale watching or para-sailing, it was not yet being used. There wasn't really parking, but there was a small turnaround lane for vans and buses.

"We'll eventually fill pots with tropical plants and bring in some other vegetation, but we weren't quite ready. The fountain hasn't been turned on, but I believe I could get it working by tomorrow."

"This is perfect. Close enough to the hotel but it gets the congestion away from the entrance." I walked around the area. "I know your staff will probably have to clean up on a regular basis, at least until after the event, but this will keep the traffic out of the hotel entrance." I peered into the basin of the currently non-working fountain. "Any chance you could replace some of those bulbs with purple lights?"

"Bet I can find some." Jamie made a note. "And we can put up some signage to direct people to this area."

"Great." We climbed back into the golf cart. "I'll touch base with Tania before I leave, and we'll see if we can get a news story on this tomorrow. I'll check in with you before we talk with any news people and make sure you're ready."

Back at the hotel, I thanked Jamie and headed inside to talk with Tania. I found her behind the long front counter talking with one of the desk clerks. She spotted me right away.

"You wanted to talk to me?" We walked toward the lobby conversation area. It was early but the hotel restaurants and bars were already packed with people, and there were several groups waiting to be seated.

"I was asked to give you this." She handed me a plain white envelope.

I opened it and inside was a handwritten note that said simply, "Call me tomorrow at noon." And there was a phone number. The number wasn't a local one.

"Who gave you this?" I turned the note over in my hand.

Tania shrugged. "It was a lady. I'm not sure how old, but she was not tall." She held her hand to indicate shorter than I was.

"One of the ladies that Diana and I met with earlier today?"

"No, this was a different lady." She frowned. "I'm sorry, I didn't pay that much attention to what she looked like. There was a problem with the cleaning crew, and I just took the note and told her I'd see that you got it."

"Don't worry about it, Tania." I smiled at her. The girl had plenty going on. "I'll call her tomorrow."

"Okay, I'd better get back." She hurried back to the front desk and I dug in my bag for my valet ticket. Though, at this point, it seemed I was in and out so much the parking attendant knew me and my car.

Finally home and getting ready for bed, I felt like the day had been three days rolled into one. The meeting at the Koffee Klatch with Detective Malone that morning seemed weeks ago. I was flat out exhausted.

Grandma Tillie used to say, "My get up and go, got up and went." And boy that was how I felt tonight. I changed into PJs, brewed a chamomile tea, and cuddled up with my fur babies.

I missed Grandma Tillie so much. She'd been the steadiness in my life when there hadn't been much solid. Always there, always the same. She took people at face value and would have been baffled by a star who hid her face, by a gaggle of people who mourned someone they hadn't really known, and, if I were honest, by my own resistance to simply sorting things out with Sam and with Melinda.

Grandma Tillie always called it like she saw it.

Things were always simpler when we were at Grandma Tillie's.

Which was probably what had started the whole fight between my cousin and me over Grandma Tillie's brooch. I suppose in a way we both were trying to hang on to her.

My thoughts turned to Mr. Swanson. I needed to do something to deal with him and his offer to surrender the brooch to the highest bidder. I didn't think it was right to pay, but I also couldn't walk away. I had to admit there was a part of me that wanted to be the one to take possession of it. I wanted to be the one to give it to Mel and say, "Let's stop this."

How crazy was that? We'd fought over the dang thing, stolen it from each other, flaunted our possession of it, and now when it came down to it there was still the competition wanting to be the one to do the right thing — first.

I sank back into the couch cushions and reached for my tea and a book I'd been in the middle of reading. Escape time.

I was almost asleep when my cell phone rang. It was Sam.

I scrambled out of the cushions and reached for my cell. "Hello, there," I answered.

"I'm sorry. It sounds like I woke you." I didn't detect any background noise this time.

"I'm afraid I was half-asleep, sitting here pretending to read."

"Well, I won't keep you long." He hesitated. "I wanted to check in. I heard on the news that the artist, Purple, had been killed. Wasn't that the main star for the event you and Diana have been working on?"

"Yes, that's her. A sad situation and clearly a lot of changes with the event. I'll fill you in when you get back." I didn't go into detail. I simply wasn't up to it. "Are your meetings going well?"

"So far so good," he answered without elaborating.

I twirled the fringe on the throw I'd put on my lap for the cats. The strain of what we weren't saying hung between us.

I asked about his Border Collie, Mac, who was staying with Sam's grandmother while he was gone. I offered to stop by and take Mac to the dog park if that would help. In reality, the offer was no sacrifice on my part. I'm partial to the breed; I'd had one as a kid and would have one now if I had the space for the kind of physical activity needed.

And, Mac was special. Not just because he was the reason Sam and I had met, but also because he was smart and loyal and clever. What a great dog.

When we said good-bye, Sam had still not mentioned the beautiful blond on his arm in the picture Betty had shown me. I still hadn't mentioned that my ex-husband was the prime suspect in a murder investigation. And neither of us had acknowledged there was any sort of a problem between us.

I normally wasn't one to kick a problem down the road to deal with later, but in this case, I needed some time to think about where I stood.

I was the one who'd insisted on no commitments. I'd argued let's just enjoy the present and not look too far into the future.

Be careful what you wish for.

CHAPTER ELEVEN

Morning and coffee made for a better attitude on my part. And, anyhow, I wasn't one to wallow. At least not for very long.

There were things between Sam and me that needed to be sorted out, but that was best done in person. And I needed to sort some thoughts out myself before then.

As I got ready to head out to my first appointment of the day, I was more optimistic than I'd been in a while. The hotel had identified a place for the tribute, Danny had used his influence to get us a great headliner, the fundraiser would go on. It would benefit some very deserving heroes.

I pulled out my phone, called Jamie, and made sure he was ready. Then I called Callum MacAvoy's number, left a brief message about the tributes, and gave him Jamie's number to call for information about the location.

I had hoped to arrange a time with Mandy

to stop by and talk to her. I wanted to know more about Trevor. I'd given the information to Malone but I thought, if Trevor had threatened her, she might be more apt to talk to me. Also, I wondered if she'd received any mail for Purple that might give a clue as to someone who wanted the event shut down. And I also wanted to ask her about Purple's stalker. The information I'd found online didn't mention that they'd ever identified who he/she was.

Mandy didn't answer her cell. Instead, the call went straight to voicemail so I left a message. I'd try again after my first appointment.

And maybe the mystery woman who wanted me to call at noon would shed some light on what was going on.

When I pulled up in front of John and Marilyn Halston's house, I noticed the black SUV and felt my blood pressure kick up a notch.

Geoffrey, you continue to amaze me with boorish behavior.

I hadn't called to confirm our appointment, but I'd had a standing appointment with the Halstons at this time for several months.

I rang the doorbell and Marilyn seemed surprised to see me. "Oh my goodness, hello

Caro. We weren't expecting you."

We? I'm not often speechless, but I was this time.

The utter gall of the man. And how had he known about this appointment? He must have somehow gotten access to my appointment calendar to have both the time and the address.

I could hear Hamilton, the Halstons' pug, barking like crazy in the other room. It was just a matter of time until the poor guy got himself so agitated he couldn't breathe. Marilyn held open the door and I stepped in and followed her down the hall.

"Your colleague said you were taking a little time off to re-group, and so I was filling him in on what we'd been doing with Hamilton based on your advice," she explained over her shoulder as I followed her to the family room where Geoff was seated on the couch. The pug raced around the room and hurried to greet me with snuffles and barks of excitement. A behavior we'd been working on eliminating for at least three months.

What an ever-loving mess.

And I knew Geoff's tactics. He was counting on me to not make a scene.

I turned to Marilyn. "I am so sorry this has happened. Geoffrey Carlisle is not my colleague. He is not working with me. He is here under false pretenses."

She looked at Geoff. I was pleased to see the shocked look on his face.

I turned back to Marilyn. "I can't throw him out of your house, but I sure as Sam Hill would if I could."

She looked at Geoff. Looked at me. And back at Geoff.

"I think you should go." Marilyn's voice was firm.

Geoffrey stopped on his way out and whispered in my ear. "That lady may think you're stable, but we both know you're not."

I blame my slow reflexes that he was able to exit walking normally.

Once I heard the front door shut, I said to Marilyn, "I'm very sorry about that."

"Not your fault." She held back a grin. "Shall we get started?"

After a good thirty minutes with Hamilton and Marilyn, seeing how they were doing with the exercise I'd recommended, we went outside and tried some new things.

At the end of the hour, I apologized again for the problem with Geoff and promised to check back in a couple of weeks to see what progress Hamilton had made.

This time I didn't waste any time dealing with the Geoffrey problem. I went straight to the office, pulled up my client list, and composed an email that I hoped was both frank and professional. The people who had trusted me enough to work with them and their furry family members deserved to know a slime ball like Geoffrey was out there, not only spreading rumors about me, but also attempting to take advantage of them.

I took a deep breath and hit send.

I looked at my phone and read a text from Diana confirming our mid-afternoon meeting at the hotel with Purple's fiancé, Drake Owen.

Then, I looked at the time. It was almost noon. Pulling the notecard out of my bag, I dialed the number on the paper. It rang and rang. No answer. Not even a recording so I could leave a message. How strange was that? To ask me to call and then not answer.

I'd try later. But the note had specifically said to call at noon.

I grabbed lunch at Zinc on the way to my next appointment. I'd called these clients to confirm just to make sure. I hoped for real progress for recently married Dan and Jennifer Moore's Basset Hound. Gustav was young and adorable, and Basset Hounds are relatively easy to work with. But when Gustav got tired of walking, he would simply lie down on the sidewalk. They would be forced to either drag him or carry him home. Walking the pup for ten blocks, and then carrying him the ten blocks back home was getting old fast.

The couple had never had a dog before, and so they also needed to adjust expectations about the amount of work involved.

I'd given them some options to try with him such as incentives to keep him moving. The breed, like most hounds, are driven by their nose so the incentive didn't always have to be a treat, it could be something like tracking an item by scent. They reported making good progress with the suggestions so far. I left them with a few more ideas. Bassets are notoriously stubborn so working with them is mostly about being just as stubborn. Slow and consistent are the watchwords. I also left Gustav with a few samples of some apple pupcakes, that new recipe I'd tried, but cautioned the couple against overdoing the treats because obesity can be a problem for Basset Hounds.

Leaving the Moores' top-of-the-world home high in the Laguna hills, I made a quick stop at home to change out of my jeans and give Dogbert a break. And then I was off to the hotel for our meeting with Purple's fiancé.

The line of people who filed toward the area set up for fans to leave mementos confirmed that the new location was working. The hotel had put up some tasteful signage directing people to the area.

I'd just stepped out of my car, handed my keys to the valet, and started toward the entrance when Callum MacAvoy pulled up in the News 5 van.

He got out and motioned for the driver to pull forward where the fans were lined up. "Thanks for the tip, Caro." He held out his hand to shake mine.

"Consider it a public service." I shook his hand reluctantly, still leery of him and reporters in general. Carry-over baggage, I know, but there it was.

"What are you doing here?" MacAvoy looked around. "What's the news on the event?"

"There will be an official announcement later today." It wasn't up to me to share the news.

"A new headliner?" He sidled closer.

Somehow, he knew just what to zero in on. How did he do that?

"Perhaps." I moved back.

"Aw, come on, Caro, I deserve the scoop."

"I would if I could, MacAvoy." Not only had he given me the fan club presidents' names, but I really did appreciate him getting the word out about the new area for flowers and memorials.

"I can't promise anything" — I turned to go inside — "but I'll see what I can do."

"Great!!" His TV smile became a genuine one. "Thanks."

I checked in at the front desk for a location for the meeting and then followed the directions I'd been given to the second-floor terrace and to the Coral Reef room.

The Coral Reef room was a private meeting space the hotel had provided to us. While the committee could meet in the restaurant or at the coffee bar, meeting with a country star this big would have caused a media storm. We'd dealt with one problem. We didn't want to create another.

I'm not sure how I ended up being the first committee member to arrive for the meeting with Drake Owen, but I confess I found myself a little star-struck when I entered the room. He'd been standing at the window looking outside and he crossed the room to meet me. Very few guys tower over me, but this cowboy sure did.

Tall, lanky, and aw-shucks handsome, he was a favorite of country music fans and the current hot ticket on the concert circuit.

And heck, I was from Texas, I could appreciate a nice-looking cowboy hat tipped back on a tanned forehead. Though I was pretty dang sure this one cost a good piece more than the ones worn to round up cattle on the Montgomery family ranch. Drake's shaggy haircut probably cost as much as my high-end salon cut, but it gave him a "just walked in from the great outdoors" look.

"Hello, Drake. I'm Caro Lamont." I held out my hand. "I'm part of the committee that's been working on this event."

"Nice to meet you." He removed his hat, ushered me to the table that had been set up with a pitcher of iced tea, a pitcher of lemonade, a bucket of ice, and glasses. He pulled out a chair and invited me to sit.

Grandma Tillie would have been impressed.

For that matter, I was impressed.

"My condolences." I sat, tucking my dark-blue Dolce & Gabbana lace skirt around my knees. "I'm sure this is very difficult for you." I swallowed. "I'm sorry we need to bother you at a time like this."

"It's okay." He sat down and tossed his hat on the chair next to him. Some emotion passed over his face. I wasn't sure if it was pain or something else, but I try not to judge. Everyone handles grief in different ways.

"The rest of the group should be here soon." I hoped.

"You knew Pan?" He tipped his head sideways and looked at me, perhaps trying to figure out my role in all of this.

"Pan?" I was confused.

"Yeah, sorry." He gave a small chuckle. "Pandora. Pandora was her real name." There was something wistful in his smile. "Never understood why she didn't just use it. It's a fine name. Marketable even. But then what do I know. I'm a country boy. I was actually born with this dumb name."

"I guess I must have realized she had another name, but everyone around here called her Purple." I hadn't heard anyone, even Mandy, call her anything but Purple.

"Part of the mystique she'd built. Her brand, she called it." He went silent.

I let the silence settle. Sometimes, especially around a loss, people don't get a chance to process. They're so busy taking care of things that need taking care of, they don't have the opportunity to stop and reflect.

"How did you two meet?" It was probably out there in the press or on the Internet, but I hadn't followed the tabloid-worthy romance.

"You'd think a music thing, right?" He grinned.

"That would seem natural." I nodded.

"No, it was one of those big Hollywood after-party deals." He looked across the room as if remembering. "I won't out the movie star because a guy like me is lucky to be invited to an A-list shindig. But Pan was as bored with the party as I was."

"Kindred spirits." I had seen photos of them online, of course, when I'd searched for info about Purple.

"I used a stupid line and said, 'Do you want to blow this popsicle stand?' " He looked off in the distance as if remembering. "She said, yes. And, as they say, the rest is history."

"You're going to miss her."

"You know, I am." Again, that hesitation. "You have a significant other?" His green eyes pinned me.

I was caught off guard. Did I?

"Sort of," I answered.

"There's no 'sort of' in relationships." He leaned forward, elbows on his knees. "At least that's what I think. You're either all in or you're nowhere."

Was that where Sam and I were? Nowhere?
And was Drake referring to his own en-

gagement with Purple (or Pan as he called her)? Had there been problems between them? Two big stars. It had to be hard to have any time together at all with both of them on the road. The fan club ladies, my source of all things Purple, hadn't mentioned anything, but we hadn't really talked about the engagement.

The door to the suite opened and Diana and Sunny stepped inside. Diana elegant, as always, in a vivid-blue summer knit and Sunny in an all-white linen ensemble completed with a bright-pink scarf.

"Thanks, sis." Drake reached over and patted my knee as he rose to greet them. "You're a real good listener."

I was happy to provide an ear to anyone dealing with such a terrible loss. Drake was right; I was a good listener, and I was pretty sure I detected something other than grief. There was something else. Something he wasn't being quite forthcoming about in his relationship with Purple.

Now, I'm not saying I have liar radar. If I had that superpower, I sure as heck would have never gotten involved with Geoffrey Carlisle. And I also wouldn't have been so shocked when I found out he'd been having affairs right under my oblivious nose.

Introductions were made and Drake was

again the epitome of old-fashioned southern charm as he shook hands with both Diana and Sunny. He then ushered them to the conference table as he had me. Diana and Sunny expressed condolences to Drake and again I noted the bit of distance as he spoke about Purple.

"I don't know if Caro has filled you in but one of our committee members, Danny Mahalovich, has arranged with Nora Worthington to participate in the Barking with the Stars event this weekend," Sunny explained.

"Wow." He paused, reached for the pitcher of tea on the table, and poured a glass, offering it to Diana. "But, wow, that's quite a coup. She's bound to be a draw."

"We're grateful she's agreed to help out." Diana accepted the glass of tea. "However, we wanted to talk with you about an idea we had, and we wanted to be sure you were okay with it."

Drake nodded, encouraging her to go ahead. He offered drinks to Sunny and me before pouring himself a glass of lemonade.

"Purple had become so much a part of the event and so supportive of the cause that, in fact, the press began referring to it as the 'Red, White, and Purple' fundraiser," Sunny said. "So, we'd like to plan a segment that is a tribute to Purple."

"We don't want it to be construed that we're taking advantage of these tragic circumstances in any way," Diana continued.

"In talking with her fans that have remained at the hotel, it seems that it might give them a bit of an outlet for their grief," I added.

"I think that's a great idea. And, in fact, I'm sure Pan would love the idea. She was doing a thing at the end with her dog, right?"

"A song honoring her grandfather." I had been touched by her idea.

"Ya'll have done a bang-up job under awful circumstances." Drake wiped some of the condensation off his glass. "I can't imagine why anyone would have a problem with what you've got planned."

"Have arrangements been made for services?" Diana asked.

"Well, I don't know if you know this or not, but she didn't have any family left. It had been just her and her Gramps for quite a while. So, I guess I'm kind of it. I'm not planning anything public. We'll do a little memorial back in Oakwood, her hometown, and inter her ashes in the little country cemetery where her grandfather is buried. Though Purple was very public in her professional life and played it to the hilt, she was very private in her personal life. I'd like to keep it that way."

"I'm so sorry, I didn't mean to intrude." Diana touched his hand.

"No offense taken, ma'am."

"Would you like to attend the event and maybe say a few words?" Sunny suggested.

"I'd sure like that but I'm not positive I can commit at this point." He put his glass down. "I interrupted recording sessions in Nashville to come here and deal with the details, so I'm not sure if I'll even be in town on the weekend."

"Of course." Sunny gathered her things. "Please let us know if there's anything we can do."

Diana and I stood as well and shook hands with Drake. We promised to keep in touch and let him know how the plans shaped up for the tribute at the event. And he promised to let Sunny know whether he'd be in town for the weekend event.

Interesting. He'd either deliberately lied about interrupting his recording sessions in Nashville to come or Danny had his information wrong. He'd said Drake had been in the area. There was no reason to doubt Danny, but if Drake had lied to Danny, that begged an additional question. Was Drake hiding something?

Was the distance I'd noticed simply how Drake was handling dealing with his loss? Or was the good-old-country-boy persona an act and there was something more going on?

Diana, Sunny, and I went our separate ways. The lobby was busy with people checking out and checking in. I spotted Tania helping with something behind the desk and waved at her. The valet brought my car around and I slipped behind the wheel.

Leaving the hotel and heading back to the office, I mused about Drake's view of relationships. All in or nowhere.

Sam had lately pressed for more of a commitment on my part, and I'd resisted. Had he decided to move on? I'd been the one unwilling to make any promises, and so I had no right at all to get my knickers in a knot if he'd decided to see someone else.

My greatest fear when I'd first started seeing Sam was that he had all the earmarks of a player. Fancy car, entry into the exclusive clubs, invites to the best parties, surrounded by luxury. Then as I got to know the substance of the man, I changed my thinking. When I met the grandmother who raised him, I'd understood the essence of who Sam

Gallanos really was. Or thought I had.

Apparently, the fear still lived on. The mistakes I'd made. You didn't have to be a psychologist to figure out that my reluctance to be "all in," as Drake described it, was directly related to my poor judgment in falling all in with Geoffrey.

Sam was different. I could trust Sam, couldn't I?

Could I?

I didn't trust myself to know.

CHAPTER TWELVE

Back in the office, I updated my files and checked my email. I had a couple of really nice responses to my earlier email about Geoffrey. He'd underestimated the value of the relationships I'd built working with people and their pets over the years.

I wished I'd approached the problem head on to begin with, but I'd been trained to bite my lip and put a good face on it rather than air my dirty laundry. No matter how hard you fight it, that southern training runs deep.

When I'd moved to Laguna Beach after the divorce, I hadn't known for sure what I would do. Initially, it had simply seemed like a good place to lick my wounds. But it was really a close-knit community and my business had flourished on word of mouth. I still sometimes longed for Texas, but I loved Laguna. And though some of that was the amazing weather and the beach, mostly it was the people. I'd hated it when Geoffrey had shown up and begun causing problems in the spot I'd chosen to start over, but I had every confidence that he'd move on when it became clear that the pet therapist gig wasn't the easy money he'd thought it was.

Even more reason to get him cleared and find the real killer so he could move on and leave town.

I didn't have any more appointments, so I decided to pack up and call it a day. The Barking with the Stars event had monopolized my time and attention lately, and I was okay with that, but I had to admit I was counting the days. I'd be glad when it was over and things could get back to some semblance of normal.

I'd closed down my computer and gathered my tote bag when I heard the bell on the front door of the office ding. With Verdi only part-time, we were used to not always having a receptionist to greet people. More often than not, it was a delivery.

"Hello," I called. "Be right there."

I stepped out into the reception area to see Cindy and Yuki, the two fan club presidents. Cindy towered over the smaller woman. She wore a sun dress with big multi-colored pansies and Yuki sported a tunic with scattered lilacs. They seemed an odd combination in some ways and yet complemented each other in so many others.

"We hope it's okay that we came here." Cindy looked around.

"Of course, it is." I motioned toward the door of my office. "Come on in."

"We didn't know if we needed an appointment." Yuki's voice was soft. "We wanted to talk to you and didn't want to talk at the hotel."

"It's not a problem." I moved the bag I'd been packing off my desk and pointed toward the easy chairs. "Have a seat. Would you like some water or something else to drink?"

"No, thank you," Cindy answered for them both.

"You wanted to talk to me?" I sat down with them. "What can I do for you?"

"We just wanted you to know that Marsha Reilley has been asking around about you." Cindy said the words in a rush.

"Marsha Reilley?" I didn't recognize the name. "Should I know who that is?"

"She's a crazy Poser." Yuki bit her lip. "You know, not a real fan."

"One of the ones that dress up like Purple," Cindy explained. "She has the whole wig, outfits, and even a dog."

"Oh." Now I got the "Poser" reference. "Why would she want information about me?"

"She claims she needs to talk to you about her dog." Cindy twisted the handle of her purse. "But I think she's just looking for information about the investigation."

"Why would she think I'd have that kind of information?" I asked. "For that matter, why would she want that kind of info?"

"Just to be a big shot." Yuki sat up straighter. "There are many of us who admired Purple. We loved her music. We loved the real her."

Cindy nodded, her eyes suddenly misty. "Then there are those who weren't respectful of her privacy and wanted the attention on themselves."

A part of me was listening to what they were saying and was empathetic to the upset pair. Another part of me was fascinated with the whole fandom phenomena. These two had bonded because they agreed on what being a fan meant. Trading on Purple's image and fame they felt was disrespectful. I was sure the "Posers" would have a different opinion.

"Well, I really appreciate you letting me know." I smiled at the two.

"Neither of us provided her with your contact information." Cindy stood. "But she can no doubt find your office location just like we did."

I had an office number on my business cards but the number was either forwarded to voicemail or to my cell phone. Most people were referred to me by one of my current clients, so very few just dropped by. Giving out the info on my business card would not have been a problem, but I appreciated that they were concerned about my privacy and wanted to protect me from the Posers.

"Say." I had a thought. "I received a note with a phone number." I got up and pulled the note card out of my bag. "Do you happen to know this number?"

I handed the card to Cindy. She looked at it for a few seconds.

"I don't recognize the number." She handed the card to Yuki.

Yuki looked at it and then shook her head. "I don't know it."

"I got the card from a hotel staff person and I called it at the time that was on there, but no one answered." I took the note back. "And there was no opportunity to leave a message."

"It sounds like the kind of drama a Poser

would resort to." Cindy rolled her eyes.

"There were a couple of other things I wanted to ask you about." Malone would say I should leave the asking to him, but I couldn't resist when I had the Purple experts right in front of me. "If you have time."

"Sure," Cindy said.

Yuki nodded agreement.

"I understand that about a year ago, Purple had a problem with a stalker." I was sure they must know about the stalker, but neither had mentioned anything.

"She did," Cindy confirmed. "An online troll."

"The troll person posted bad things online and sent Purple emails," Yuki explained. "According to Mandy, they also came to her shows and sent notes backstage."

"What kind of notes?" I asked. "Did Mandy ever say?"

"We never actually saw one of the notes, but Mandy said they were threatening." Cindy's brow furrowed. "She said they'd taken measures to protect Purple. Do you think . . ." She stopped, and swallowed, eyes wide. "Do you think Purple's killer might be the stalker?"

"I'm sure the police are following up on every lead." I hadn't meant to alarm the two very sweet fans. "I just read about it and wondered if they'd ever caught the person."

"They did not." Yuki sighed. "We did talk about it in our newsletters, but just to keep Purple's fans informed."

"Mandy gave us permission." Cindy traced one of the flowers on her sundress thoughtfully. "We wouldn't have covered it otherwise. You don't want to give people ideas."

"That makes sense." I loved their concern with the consequences of what they were putting out there. Mr. TV, Callum Mac-Avoy, could use a lesson in that kind of thinking. "The other question I had for you was about the fan with the purple guitar I saw you talking to a couple of nights ago."

"That's Lew Simpson." Cindy folded her hands. "He's more of a collector than a fan."

Ah. So, another category. There were true fans, there were Posers, and there were collectors.

"He has many very cool Purple collectibles." Yuki brushed her long straight hair off her face. "Items no one else has."

"If I remember correctly, you were interviewing him?"

"Yes," Cindy confirmed. "He talked about some items he brought to be signed, like the guitar. And other memorabilia he has at home. I once saw a picture of his house in another fanzine and it is stuffed to overflowing with collectibles from, not just Purple, but other popular stars."

"I imagine that's a pretty competitive market." It seemed to me given the hundreds, if not thousands, of fans who been coming to the hotel to leave tributes since Purple's death, that there must be people willing to pay a high price for the types of items this guy traded in. Were there also people willing to kill to get their hands on it?

"That's true," Cindy agreed. "I allow advertising in the newsletter, but only reputable dealers or fans who may need to sell items from their collection."

"Thank you so much for your information." I was glad the two had stopped by. "I have to confess this is all new to me, so I appreciate the education."

"We won't bother you any further." Yuki stood, her delicate flowered tunic and her slight stature made her look younger than I knew she probably was. "We did have a request of you." She looked at Cindy.

"We don't want you to think that we're taking advantage of you in any way." Cindy hesitated. "But our fan base would love to know about this event and your role in working with Purple."

"Your remembrance of her," Yuki added.

"We're hoping you'd consider doing an interview for us. We'd write it together and then it would appear in both the *Purple Fan Club, USA* newsletter and the *Murasaki* in Japan."

They seemed so sincere. And truly the two were completely oblivious to the idea that though the "Posers" took advantage of Purple's fame, they were doing much the same.

"I'm sure Mandy would love to do something like that," I suggested. "Or maybe Sunny Simone, the head of the Warriors for the Paws?"

"Mandy hasn't been talking to us since Purple's death." Cindy frowned. "She's always been good about getting us interviews and answering questions."

"She's probably grieving herself," I said gently.

"Oh, I'm sure you're right." Cindy had the grace to look a bit guilty. "That's undoubtedly the case. It's just so out of the ordinary for her."

"If you would think about an interview, we'd be very grateful." Yuki made one last pitch.

After the two left, I packed up, made a quick stop at the grocery store, and headed home.

I had a text from Diana that Rufus would be sending me an email with the new lineup for this weekend's event. I answered, threw together a quick dinner, and then changed into comfy clothes.

Wow. I really needed that run on the beach. I considered Malone's caution about being aware of my surroundings, but there would be plenty of people on Main Beach on a beautiful evening like this. It really wouldn't be risky.

I sighed. Ultimately, Malone's caution and all the things I needed to do won out and I decided to postpone it yet again.

I sat down with a cup of tea and the list that Rufus had emailed. There weren't a lot of changes to the event lineup, other than, of course, the main star who would open the show and do the finale.

We'd planned to have a few of the veterans and their therapy dogs for both, and I'd talked with Purple and the others about the potential for issues with pet dogs and therapy dogs. It probably wouldn't hurt to remind the stars, who were appearing with their dogs, that they shouldn't pet or give treats to the therapy dogs. It seems clear to those of us who work with dogs that therapy dogs are working, but I know from experience that well-meaning people simply forget. The important thing, if we were to pull this off, was to keep a stable environment for the canines. A high-maintenance temperament would be stressed by the tension of a big event. What things could we do that would keep the atmosphere calm?

I smiled to myself as I realized the direction of my thoughts. I wasn't sure if I was worried about the dogs or the stars. Probably a bit of both.

Nora Worthington would come in just before the event. Probably just the night before, I thought. Because I hadn't had a chance to talk with her like I had with Purple, I should probably email her some of my ideas for keeping everything on an even keel. I picked up my phone and texted Rufus to see if he could get me her email address or forward an email to her.

Just as I hit send and leaned back on the couch, my doorbell rang.

Setting aside my cup of tea and the two cats, I went to see who it was.

Peeking through the curtains, I spotted Detective Malone's silver Camaro, and unlocked the door.

"Detective." I waved him in. "Can I get

you something to drink?"

"I wanted to stop by and let you know that we didn't find any fingerprints on the note that was left on your car." He followed me into the kitchen. "Other than yours."

"I'm not surprised." I held up a glass. "I have soda, tea, wine, or something stronger if you like."

"Water's fine." He leaned on the counter. "Unless you have coffee."

"Kinda late for coffee, isn't it?"

"I've still got a bunch of paperwork to finish." He walked back to the living room and sat on the arm of the sofa. The two cats eyed him. "It's back to the office after this."

"I'll make some coffee." I reached for the freshly ground beans. "It won't take a minute. Dare I ask how the investigation is going?"

"Unfortunately, it's not going anywhere." He rose from the arm of the couch not even noticing the cats who switched their tails and frowned at him. "There's not much to report."

Malone paced my small living room and then walked to the patio door and stared outside. I wondered if he even saw my color- ful terrace or the ocean view. Eventually he went back to the arm of the sofa.

"Anything turn up on Trevor from the

license plate?" I asked casually, afraid to show too much interest.

"Not much." He got up and began pacing again. Thelma and Louise tipped their heads and followed his movements back and forth. "His name is Trevor Lang, and he's known the victim for a very long time. They were in a band together when she was just starting out."

"They were?" I wished I'd known that little tidbit. I could have asked my new friends, Cindy and Yuki. I'd bet they had some background info on Mr. Trevor Lang.

The coffee was done and the bold aroma made me crave a cup of my own. But unlike Malone, I was not going back to the office, and sure didn't need caffeine to keep me awake. Unfortunately, my worries about Barking with the Stars, and my theories about Purple's murder were more than enough to do that.

"I'll make a call tomorrow and ask Mandy about their disagreement and what she knows about his relationship with Purple." I could tell he was making a note in his head.

I handed him a mug of coffee, and he stopped pacing long enough to take a sip.

"The guy seemed really wound up when he was at Purple's house. Got kind of physical with Mandy." I refilled my tea infuser and dropped it into a cup. "And when I tried to talk to him, he took off. Seemed like someone with something to hide."

"Caro, I'll check it out, but I'm afraid our best suspect is still your ex-husband." Malone had always been nothing if not straight with me.

"I know." I sighed. "And you know what I think about that."

"I do." Malone almost smiled. "He had the opportunity and leaving the scene without offering aid or calling for help doesn't help his case." He paused and took another sip of coffee. "But I tend to agree with you that he doesn't have much of a motive. But the truth is we haven't uncovered anyone with much of a motive."

"You've talked to Drake Owen, her fiancé?"

"He came to collect her effects today and to find out about when the autopsy would be done."

"I guess he was here to help with the arrangements. She didn't have any family left." I hesitated to mention the discrepancy in Drake's story. Danny could have easily been mistaken, or I could have misunderstood.

"That's what Mandy, the assistant, told us," Malone said.

"What about the will?" I'd wondered about the inheritance with no relatives in the picture. "Does anyone stand to profit?"

"Not really." He finished off the coffee. "She left some to Mandy Barton, the assistant. She left her dog to the lady that helped her with it and a considerable amount of money to take care of the dog. She left a chunk to a veteran's group in her grandfather's name. Nothing remarkable to any one person."

"Any word on the security cameras?" As long as he was chatty, I would continue to ask questions. "Or the missing auction items?"

"Appears the cameras were hacked." He took his empty cup to the kitchen and set it in the sink. "We have a list of the items, but there's no rhyme or reason to why some things were taken and others weren't."

There had to be a reason. We just weren't seeing it. "Was there something that was extremely valuable that was taken?"

He shook his head. "A doll, a wig, lunch box, bobblehead, that kind of thing. Crazy stuff."

Believe me, I knew. I'd watched as Mandy had unpacked most of it.

"I understand the price depends on both the rarity and the fans' interest." I hadn't realized what a market there was for memorabilia, but after talking to Cindy and Yuki, it seemed there was the potential to make a killing, no pun intended, in the collectible market. "I assume you're looking at robbery."

"We're looking at everything." Malone headed for the door just as my phone rang.

I picked it up and glanced at the number. It was Sam.

Shoot. I had one more thing I needed to mention to Malone before he got away.

"Do you need to get that?" he asked.

"Not right now." I hesitated and then pushed the button to let the call go directly to voicemail. "I assume you've done some follow-up on Purple's stalker?"

"We have." He crossed his arms. "Do you have additional info on the stalker?"

"No, it just came up when I was talking to the fan club presidents."

"Talking or questioning?" Malone interrupted.

"Talking." I shrugged. "They came to me. Stopped by my office."

Now I had his attention.

"They say anything else pertinent to my murder investigation?"

"Not really." I ran my hand through my hair, reviewing the day in my head. I thought

I'd covered everything.

He watched me for a couple of beats and then started toward the door again.

"Oh, I almost forgot." I grabbed the bag I'd dropped right by the entry when I'd gotten home. "What do you make of this?" I pulled out the cryptic note with the phone number Tania had given me. Like the other note, I'd put this one in a plastic bag. I was becoming a regular CSI.

Malone looked at it, flipped it over, and then looked at me. "Nothing more?"

I shook my head.

"Where'd you get it?" he asked.

"One of the staff people at the hotel said she was asked to give it to me."

Malone handed it back to me.

"I don't think it has anything to do with Purple's death or with the investigation." In fact, I wondered if it might be Mr. Swanson trying another tactic on the brooch. Tania had described a female but she didn't have much of a description, and for all I knew Swanson was married and his wife was in on the scam. However, given the situation I felt like I needed to at least show it to Malone.

"What makes you think it doesn't?" Malone waited.

"It didn't seem threatening, just kind of

222

cloak and dagger-ish." I shrugged.

"You called the number?" Malone asked and then slapped his forehead. "What am I saying? Of course, you called it."

"I did. But no one answered and there wasn't an option to leave a message." I frowned. "It seems like a lot of trouble to go to and then not answer."

"I'll take it and have the lab run it for prints." Malone held out his hand.

"I'd like to try the call again." Though I didn't think it had a connection to Purple's murder, I didn't know that for sure. There'd been the other note and now this.

"Try it right now," he suggested.

I glanced at my phone. The voicemail icon on the screen blinked indicating a waiting message. I punched in the number on the notecard and pushed the button for speaker. The call rang and rang. No answer.

Malone held out his hand again, and I reluctantly gave up the note. "We may find some prints or we may be able to tell something from the paper."

"It doesn't look like the other note. It may have nothing to do with the investigation." If it was Swanson, I'd love to have some intel on him, but I wasn't ready to bring up the brooch hostage situation to Malone.

"It may not." Malone opened the door.

"Or it may."

"Fine."

"I'll let you know if they find anything." He didn't say "lock this door behind me," but he gave me the look.

When Malone was gone, I locked up.

It wasn't that late. I could call Sam back. But he would be home in a couple of days and we could talk in person. He'd said he definitely planned to be in town for the big event.

I set the phone aside. What a chicken I was. I couldn't handle another awkward conversation where Sam and I danced around anything of substance with polite talk. Heck, we were on a verge of talking about the weather.

Then I picked the phone back up and played the message.

"I can't wait," his message said. "I miss you so much."

The truth was, I missed him, too. Though I wasn't clear about where we were going, or even where I wanted our relationship to go. That's why not calling him was so much safer than calling him. Schrodinger's cat and all that.

CHAPTER THIRTEEN

After a night of tossing and turning, I was glad I'd pre-loaded the coffee pot before going to bed. I unloaded the dishwasher as I waited for the coffee to brew, thinking again about the information Malone had shared.

I flipped open the notebook with my to-do list for the day. On one of the pages was the list of suspects I'd started the day after the murder. Callum MacAvoy had shown up at the office, and I'd never gone back to it.

MacAvoy. I added a note to my to-do list to check with Sunny and see what the timing was on the Nora Worthington news. Was I okay to share that with MacAvoy now? He truly had helped with getting the news out about the new place for fans to leave memorials.

After jotting down the reminder, I went back to my suspect list. I'd listed all the people I'd met that had anything to do with

Purple. Mandy, Sheron, Geoffrey. I had Drake on the list, though at the time I'd not yet met him. I'd listed "the fans." I hadn't known names at that point, but I added Cindy and Yuki, though clearly it was extremely unlikely as neither had any motive. However, as Malone had said, so far no one had motive. I added Trevor Lang to the list. And the Purple Poser, Marsha Reilley, who Cindy and Yuki had said was trying to get in touch with me. I also added Lew Simpson, the collector, they had told me about.

Ah, thank goodness, my coffee was done. I took my cup and sat down with my laptop. I looked up "security cameras." Whoo boy, had times changed. I was still imagining the security systems you saw in the movies where blurry movements and shady motions were recorded. And where disabling a security system required fancy moves such as repelling down an elevator shaft like George Clooney and Matt Damon in *Ocean's Eleven.*

According to the companies offering security, you could retrieve recordings, reposition cameras, and download videos from a computer or even a phone. I'd seen the ads where you could monitor your home while lying on the beach, but I'd wanted a better understanding of how the corporate versions worked.

I knew Malone and crew had undoubtedly already talked to hotel security and the security camera company and knew all this. They had that part covered. What Malone and crew didn't have was the access to the fan club folks and the Purple Posers like I did. The fans had intimate knowledge about the memorabilia and the auction items and, the way I looked at it, they'd be much more likely to give up intel to me than to the police.

I didn't have anything planned for the day, except the meeting with Rufus later to go over logistics on the PTSD dogs. Mandy had not returned my call, but she had told me to send a bill for my services to date the day Purple had fired me. Maybe I'd just get that ready and drop it off in person. I wanted to better understand what it was Trevor had been after. He topped my list at the moment.

I assumed Geoffrey was still working with Lavender. Hopefully I wouldn't run in to him. I was afraid I was completely out of patience where he was concerned.

He had KK's dog, Scamp, and a couple of others that he'd convinced to drop me, so I would have to see him during the event.

I hoped Warriors for the Paws would raise a ton of money. I hoped Nora Worthington would bring a boatload of attention to Barking with the Stars. I hoped we would help a ton of veterans. But I also couldn't wait for this weekend to be over.

The unseasonably warm weather was predicted to continue, but the morning temp was decent. The bright blue of the sky promised a perfect southern California day. I showered and dressed for the day in a bright Johnny Was handkerchief-hem dress. It was light and fun and I hoped it would transition from snooping to working. I slipped on low canvas Via Spiga sneakers. They were a bright cobalt blue and would be easy on my feet.

The morning rush was over so the drive from my house to the exclusive Diamond Cove gated community didn't take long. Apparently I was still on the visitor list because the security guard had me sign in like before on his tablet and then waved me through.

I parked my car in Purple's drive. There wasn't a construction truck on site today. I wondered if the remodeling was complete or if the crew had moved on. Would the renovations continue with the homeowner dead? Mandy had her hands full with sorting everything out.

I wondered about her relationship with Drake and who would be making those kinds of decisions. Sometimes situations like this brought out either the best or the worst in people. Hopefully Mandy and Drake were in agreement on things. I supposed there was an executor. Malone hadn't said anything about who that was and I hadn't thought to ask.

I rang the doorbell and the crimson-haired lady answered again.

"I'm sorry, I didn't get your name last time," I apologized. "I'm the pet therapist."

"Greta," she said. "Sheron is eating. Doggie too." Greta didn't smile but her expression wasn't unpleasant. I couldn't figure out her role. Was she a sort of housekeeper?

"Is Mandy in?" I hoped for the best.

"No, she is gone." Greta was a woman of few words.

Shoot, I had hoped to catch her.

"Do you think she'll be back soon?" I knew Mandy was probably dealing with all kinds of details and press questions, but she'd been scarce the last couple of days.

"No idea." She opened the door wider. "Come."

Off she went and I had no option but to follow. I didn't want to intrude if Sheron, the "hair lady," was eating breakfast.

"There." Greta pointed to a small breakfast nook where Sheron was seated. She had juice, toast, and what appeared to be orange marmalade on a pretty, flowered china plate. A matching teapot sat on the table, and Lavender slept at her feet. It looked like a picture from a glossy *Elegant Living* magazine.

"I'm so sorry. I didn't intend to interrupt your breakfast." I hesitated in the doorway. "I stopped by to give this to Mandy." I held up the envelope.

"I can see that she gets it." She took the envelope from me and placed it off to the side. "She left early this morning. No time for breakfast that one."

"I'm sure she has a lot of things to deal with."

"Yes, always busy. I don't know what on earth Handy Mandy will do without someone's life to run." Sheron smiled, taking away the sting of her comment. "I'm not being unkind. Mandy is good at her job, but that type of job doesn't leave much room for a life of your own."

"It will be an adjustment," I agreed.

"Would you like coffee or tea? It's a nice English breakfast tea," Sheron offered, and indicated the chair across from her.

"I'd love one."

She poured steaming liquid into another of the pretty flowered cups. I could see they were purple irises now that I was closer.

"There's honey and sugar on the tray." She pointed to some containers.

"It must be hard for you." I tasted the tea. It was full-bodied but brisk, and I didn't see the need for any sweetener. "And for Lavender." I reached down and scratched the top of the dog's head. "Have you noticed any problems?"

"You mean like separation anxiety?" The hair lady was pretty savvy about dogs. She took a sip of tea. "And did you mean me or the dog?"

"I meant Lavender." I met her gaze. "But how *are* you doing?"

"I'm doing okay." She set the cup down carefully. "It's crazy, the house is so quiet. Don't get me wrong, Pandora could be demanding. She had an ego. I guess you have to think you're all that in order to get up on a stage in front of thousands. I don't miss the drama, but I do miss her."

I waited for her to go on.

"Lavender is used to the sporadic schedules and the coming and going that life on the road presented. She's a pretty adaptable girl, aren't you?"

231

The dog looked up at her like she understood and then rested her chin on Sheron's foot with a satisfied doggie sigh.

"Has the new therapist been to check in on her?" I continued sipping the tea enjoying the flavor.

"Oh, yes." Sheron looked up from petting Lavender. "And then I fired him."

I almost choked on my tea. "You did?"

"I most certainly did." Her blue eyes narrowed. "I like to think I'm a pretty good judge of people and that guy was a waste of time. If he's a pet therapist then I'm a brain surgeon. I don't think he even likes animals."

Something must have shown on my face.

"I'm sorry if he's a friend of yours, but I was not impressed."

"No, I wouldn't say Geoffrey is a friend of mine."

"But you know him?" She looked me in the eye.

"Ex-husband," I explained.

"Oh." She paused. "I'm sorry."

"Not as sorry as I am," I answered before I could stop myself. "Don't worry about it. You're right, he really doesn't have that much interest in the animals."

"Besides I understand he's a suspect." She poured me another cup of tea without asking. "Until the police figure out who killed Pandora and why, we need to be careful about who we allow around here."

Though Sheron was matter-of-fact in her delivery, I had the sense the opinion might be one she'd already delivered perhaps to Greta or even Mandy.

"Are you sure you wouldn't like something to eat?" She held out a plate.

"No, thank you." Maybe it was fortunate that Mandy had been out. I might learn just as much if not more from Sheron. "I met Drake Owen yesterday."

"He stopped by here to talk with Mandy." She refilled her own cup.

"He seems nice." I kept my tone neutral.

"I've been around this business for probably longer than you've been alive." Sheron pushed back her platinum-blond hair, tucking a strand behind her ear.

"I'm sure that's not true." I truly didn't think so, but if that were the case I'd have to get the name of her plastic surgeon or whatever fountain-of-youth elixir the woman was using.

"Well, a long time anyway." She sipped her tea. "It's incredibly hard if not impossible for two stars to fit their egos inside a marriage."

"I can see that would be a challenge." I

nodded.

"That's no comment or criticism on either of them, you understand. It's simply that it takes one heck of a lot of grounding to walk on stage to thousands of screaming fans and not begin to think that you were somewhere above the rest of us mortals."

I hadn't considered the dynamics of that kind of fame.

"Most begin to believe that they're some kind of special."

"So, I guess there were problems?" I asked.

"I'm just the hair lady, but I see and hear a lot. I'm not sure that engagement was ever going to turn into a marriage." She set her cup carefully on the saucer. "Not that they didn't love each other. Who am I to say. But . . . well, love isn't easy."

No, it sure isn't. Whether you're a big star or a pet therapist.

We sat without speaking for a few minutes. Sheron was a great observer and a great listener. If she hadn't been a stylist, she would have made a great therapist. I wondered what else she'd observed.

"There was a guy here the last time I stopped by. He seemed to be having a disagreement with Mandy." Again, I strove for a neutral tone though I was pretty sure she was on to me and my questions. "His name is Trevor, and I was told he used to be in a band with Purple."

I sensed a change in her posture immediately. If she were a dog, I'd say the mention of Trevor got her hackles up.

She waited a couple of beats before answering. "There were some things Trevor needed to straighten out with Pan. Unfortunately, that didn't happen before she died."

"Things?" I asked.

"Business things. An artistic disagreement of sorts." She waved her hand and shifted in her seat. Lavender looked up at Sheron as if wondering why her convenient headrest had moved. "I don't really know the details but no doubt Mandy and Drake will make sure it's sorted out in a fair way."

"I saw Trevor downtown and tried to talk to him, but he didn't seem to want to talk to me."

"Like I said." Sheron picked up her teacup and then put it back down. "Mandy will figure it out."

"But you don't think she's in danger from him?"

"Mandy?" she scoffed. "No, I think Mandy can hold her own."

Sheron was clearly done discussing Trevor so I didn't press further. I asked a few questions about Lavender and what plans Sheron had made about going forward. She seemed to have a good strategy for getting things settled with Lavender and then making arrangements to travel with the dog to her own home in northern California.

I asked Sheron to let Mandy know I had stopped by. She confirmed that she'd make sure Mandy got the envelope I'd left.

As I navigated the traffic on PCH and drove back toward the downtown area, I glanced at the time. It was coming up on noon. I wondered about the note that had asked me to call at noon yesterday. I pulled onto Ocean Avenue and parked along the street across from the little bungalow that housed the Laguna Beach Historical Society.

Pulling out my phone, I checked the outgoing call history. There it was. Though Malone had the note, the phone number was in my recent calls from where I'd tried it yesterday. I pushed the call-back button.

One ring, two rings. Suddenly the caller picked up.

"Hello?" The voice was a whisper.

"I'm sorry. This is Caro Lamont and you left me a note to call you at noon yesterday. There was no answer then or last night when I tried, so I tried again today." I blame it on my upbringing that I found myself apologizing to someone I didn't even know.

"Check the missing Purple memorabilia that's showing up for sale."

"What —" I began.

There was dead silence on the other end.

The caller had hung up. I tried to think about the voice. Had I heard it before? Was there anything familiar about it? The problem was the whisper had been so soft I wasn't even sure whether it was a male or female. I considered the timbre. Definitely higher. Either a female or a guy with a higher voice.

I picked up my cell again and dialed Detective Malone. I didn't exactly have him on speed dial but I did have his number programmed into my phone. I know. My mama would be appalled.

"Malone." He answered on the first ring.

"Hey." I took a deep breath. "I called that number again and this time a person answered."

I spotted Mr. Swanson walking along the sidewalk. He carried a Whole Foods bag and was headed in the opposite direction my car was facing.

"You what?" Malone asked.

"Hold on." I got out of the car so I could see where Swanson went.

Oh, for crying in a bucket. I seemed to be cursed with always encountering Swanson when I was trying to deal with something else.

"Caro?" Malone raised his voice slightly in the same way I do when I want to get Dogbert's attention.

"Just a minute." The short man wasn't moving that fast. I should be able to catch up with him. He got in an older dark-blue Range Rover, started it, and immediately pulled away. I stopped on the sidewalk to note the license number.

"SWNM4019," I said.

"What?" Malone was losing patience.

"Nothing." I needed to focus. "I called that number and a person answered this time."

"Of course, you did." I could only imagine the expression on his face. "What did this person say?"

"They said the missing items are showing up for sale." I hurried back to my car so I could write down the license plate number before I forgot it.

"Did the person say where?" Malone had his you're-trying-my-patience voice engaged.

"No." I pulled out my notebook and jotted down the plate number. "The call lasted twenty seconds at the most and the voice was just a whisper."

"Okay, we'll check it out." He paused. "Where are you?"

"I'm parked by Whole Foods," I answered. Not a fib, really. I was near the store. I knew he was actually trying to discover why I had been so distracted, but I was not going to bring Malone into the problem with the brooch unless I had exhausted all other options. The trouble was I didn't know what those options were.

"All right, thanks for the info." Malone signed off before I could ask if he'd let me know what he found out.

I tucked the notebook back in my bag, not sure what I would do with the license number. Would it be unethical for me to ask Sally or Lorraine at the police station to look it up? They knew all about Melinda and me and the family brooch. Heck, it had once been police evidence for a short time. They would probably do it as a favor, but I didn't want to ask them to do something that might be over the line as far as using police resources. I decided not to go that route.

I had a little bit of time before my meeting at the hotel with Rufus. I'd decided to see what I could find out from Lew Simpson. Maybe he and I could have a chat. I called the hotel and asked to be connected with his room.

He'd been reluctant to meet with me until I'd name-dropped that I knew Danny Mahalovich. Seemed Lew was quite *The Search for Signs* fan. Or *TSFS* as I'd recently found out true aficionados called it. I hadn't made any promises about asking Danny for any favors, but had hinted that as a committee member he might be around over the next couple of days.

I couldn't use the information about our new headliner yet. No official announcement had been made. Besides that, the news wasn't mine to share. But I'm betting that might have put Lew over the top.

We arranged a time and planned to meet in the hotel bar. I had the sense that most of the fans in attendance didn't venture far from the venue. That was good for the hotel because they spent their food and drink dollars on site, but from Tania's reports it seemed that the hotel was more than a little fed up with the idiosyncrasies of the Purple Posers and the other fans.

Lew was already there when I arrived. I asked the bartender for an iced tea. It was a little early in the day for a cocktail for me.

"Hello, Lew. I'm Caro Lamont." I started

to hold out my hand in introduction, but then hesitated. I could tell from the way he had his hands tucked away that there might be an issue with contact. Maybe haphephobia, which is a fear of being touched, or maybe just an intense germaphobe. Or the syndrome is actually called mysophobia. I spotted a hand sanitizer in a pocket on his backpack. Hmmm, could be either. Or both.

He waved in my direction and re-tucked his hands. "I've seen you around. I didn't know you were part of the committee though."

"So you're a Purple fan, huh?"

"Yeah, but not crazy like those Purple Poser folks." He relaxed a little. "They're over the top."

"I understand you're kind of a big collector."

"I am." He nodded. "I'm not like the extreme collector like you see on TV. I mean my house isn't packed with stuff."

That's not what Cindy and Yuki had said.

"You collect not just Purple memorabilia, but other stars?"

"Sort of." He perked up a bit. "Why? Is there something you're interested in?"

"I was just curious." I noticed his leg bouncing had increased. "I guess the Purple memorabilia has gone up in price."

"That always happens when a star dies," he explained. "You can't believe the prices on Prince items. Marilyn Monroe, even after all these years, off the charts."

"I guess our missing auction items have a pretty high market value now, huh?"

"Oh, yeah." He ran a hand over his bald head. "Except I'm sure the cops have alerted most of the re-sale places. No legit seller would want to be caught handling stolen stuff."

"You're probably right. I'm sure the police have covered those bases." I couldn't imagine they hadn't, but I would check with Malone to be sure. "Just out of curiosity, what's your most valuable Purple item?"

"I have a guitar that she used on her first solo album." He reached in his back pocket and pulled out a wallet. "Here, I've got a picture of it."

He flipped through the pictures and pulled a photo out of the sleeve. Where most people carried pictures of their kids or family members, Lew carried photos of his collectibles.

I took the picture from him. It was the purple guitar I'd seen him with. I couldn't tell for sure, but it looked like it might be signed. "Autographed?" I asked.

"It is." His leg bouncing increased with

his excitement. "She signed it for me at her Planet Hollywood concert in Las Vegas. I got backstage passes and I have a picture of me with her when she signed it."

"That makes it even more special." I smiled at his enthusiasm.

"It does. The provenance on this kind of stuff is really important."

Okay, so the excitement wasn't about meeting Purple and having her sign a keepsake. It was about the increased value of the item. I was beginning to understand the distinction that Cindy and Yuki had made in explaining to me the difference between collectors and fans. And, of course, what they considered *true* fans.

"Provenance, huh? That seems like such fancy word for talking about something like a guitar." I paused. "Or a bobblehead, or statue, or CD." I tried to think of other things I'd seen in Purple's suite, hoping a long leash and his ardent interest would yield some clues as to why certain items had been taken and others left behind.

"Yeah." He laughed. "It is kinda a fancy word, I guess. But also a word we use in programming. You know, like the execution history of a computer process."

I didn't know, but the reference raised a question. Was the collecting of star memorabilia Lew's only support or was it a sideline?

"I assume you're still planning to stick around for the Warriors for the Paws event." I wondered if the auction had been his sole interest. "Or do you have a job you have to get back to?"

"I'm sticking around mostly because of the investigation." He picked an imaginary piece of lint off his jeans. "I had given Mandy Barton, Purple's assistant, an album for Purple to sign. It's an actual vinyl record. They only made a few. The vinyl is actually purple and very rare." He finally took a breath.

"Did she sign it?"

"I don't know." He was really agitated now. "I gave it to Mandy. I assumed she gave it to Purple, but I don't know whether she signed it before . . . you know. And now, it was probably either stolen with the other missing things or tied up as evidence."

"Wow, that must be frustrating."

"No kidding." He'd gotten louder and his face was pink with emotion. "I left my information with the police, but I haven't heard anything. I'm here for the next few days but then I've got to go back to work."

"Where do you work?"

"I work for FinZone. They're a financial services company."

"Oh." I hadn't heard of them. "What do you do?"

"I'm an application developer. I do the internal apps."

I still wasn't absolutely sure what that meant, but it had answered my unasked question. Did Lew have the skills to hack the security cameras?

My vote was yes.

"I appreciate you educating me about the world of collectibles, Lew." I stood to leave. Again, I noticed he tucked his hands under his legs so I didn't offer a handshake. I laid one of my cards on the table. "If you think of anything else or run across any info on our missing auction items, please call me. After you call the police, of course."

"Okay." He looked at the card but didn't pick it up. "PAWS? Animal wellness, like a pet therapist?"

I nodded.

"Like a shrink for dogs?" He snickered.

"That's right." I was used to the reaction, but found it a little ironic that a guy who collected things like purple vinyl and bobbleheads found it amusing that my job was helping people with their pets.

"If I hear anything from the police about your missing record, I'll let you know." I turned to go.

"That'd be great." He was still staring at my business card. "For sure, that'd be great."

It was almost time for my meeting with Rufus, so I stopped by the ladies' room. I'd just opened the door of a stall and started to step out when a gaggle of Purple fans entered. All in white wigs, they were in the way of my opening the door so I waited for them to pass.

"Marsha, you aren't the only one that's grieving," one girl said.

"That's right," another piped up. "I haven't been able to eat for days. I don't know what we're going to do without her."

Marsha? As in the Marsha Reilley who the fan club presidents had said was looking for me?

I paused, struck as I had been before with how they talked as if they really knew Purple. And, I was torn between thinking they should be living "real" lives of their own and fascination with the phenomena.

They felt sad. In some alternate reality, they each believed they'd had some sort of relationship with the singer. They grieved as if they truly knew her. In psychology circles, we sometimes call that alief. Someone acts as if something they know isn't really true, is true. They know they aren't friends with

Purple, may have not even met her in person, probably only saw her on stage. But still believed their lives would be altered because she was gone.

Was it harmful? Who knows. Maybe it was just innocent fantasy, like cosplay where people dress up like a character from a book or movie. But, if it produced a problem in real life, or a real murder investigation, maybe not so innocent.

I opened the door and stepped out. "Hello." I squeezed between them to get to the sink. "Purple fans, I see."

Five blond wigs with purple streaks nodded, suddenly quiet.

I washed my hands and then reached through the crowd to get a paper towel. "Y'all look very nice."

"Are you the pet therapist?" I couldn't see who had asked.

"Yes, I am." I dried my hands and tossed the paper into the trash.

"I need to talk to you." The tallest of the group stepped forward.

"Are you Marsha?" I asked. "I'd been told you were looking for me."

"Yes." She didn't elaborate.

"I'm afraid I'm on my way to a meeting, but I could meet you afterward." I glanced at my watch. "Say in an hour."

"Oh, thank you." The tall one threw back her shoulders and swept the long magenta scarf she wore around her neck. "I'll meet you in the lobby by the front desk."

When I left the ladies' room, the chatter started back up. I didn't stick around to hear what they had to say, but I was certainly curious about why the Purple Poser, who I assumed was Marsha Reilley, wanted to talk to me.

Rufus McGrill waited by the staircase where just days ago Paul, the police spokesperson, had held the press conference announcing Purple's death. So little progress in the investigation since then had to be frustrating for Malone and his crew. The negative publicity and onslaught of fans had to be annoying for the hotel management and their staff. But all of that together must also have been a whole other level of craziness for Rufus. He had his ever-present tablet computer in hand and looked up as I approached.

"Hi, Caro." He glanced back down. "Let me just finish this email."

"No problem." I waited until he was done. "Pretty crazy, huh?"

"Unbelievable," he agreed. "Are you ready?"

I nodded.

He took me through a staff entrance and into the back hallways to the auditorium where the event would take place. We stood looking at the stage which was big and empty.

"Just a few more days." I patted his arm. "You've put forth a heroic effort keeping this all from imploding."

"I've tried." He tucked the tablet under his arm. "The veterans are the real heroes and I just kept reminding myself that's why we're all doing this."

"That's right." I'd had that same talk with myself the past few days.

"Okay, the celebrities will be in their dressing rooms." He walked down the aisle and to the backstage area. "And enter the stage here." He pointed to some stairs.

"They all have their assigned rooms?" Even as I said it, I knew Rufus wouldn't have missed a detail like room assignments.

"They do." He didn't seem offended by my question. "They'll have their dogs with them. You should check with each of them once they're here." He stopped for a moment. "Except for KK and Scamp, Heidi and . . ."

"Carson," I finished for him. Those were the other two clients who, in addition to Purple, had fired me and signed on with

Geoffrey. Geoff was such a smooth operator they probably thought I'd recommended him.

"I've got a list of all of the celebs, their dogs, what time they go on stage, and if I could just get room assignments from you, I'll add that and I should be set."

"Perfect." Rufus made a note. "I'll get that to you later today."

"Thanks." I loved that like me he had a list. His was electronic and mine was a notebook, but still we were kindred spirits on the list-maker front.

"The veterans and their therapy dogs will arrive just before they go on." He walked across the back where all the cords and pulleys were for the backdrops and curtains. "We thought the less waiting they have, the better. And the venue doesn't have a lot of waiting space."

"Probably a good idea." I stepped over a rope as thick as my wrist. "Have they been here?"

"We did a couple of run-throughs with them yesterday," he replied. "Why? Are you worried they won't know what to do?"

"Not the veterans," I clarified. "The dogs. Although they've been here before, it will look and smell differently with all the people and their pets in here."

"Dress rehearsal should take care of that though, right?"

"I think so." I walked around the area. "Let's just have a Plan B."

"Like what?"

"Like if one of the dogs gets unruly or hard to handle, the dog's human knows what to do. Maybe he or she should simply take the dog out of the environment."

"Okay, great." Rufus added another note to himself. "I'll make sure that instruction is given during dress rehearsal."

"I'm sure you and Sunny have thought of this," I added, "but probably the same goes for the veterans. If the chaos or the noise or anything about the situation becomes too much for them, they should also just take a break. Go outside. There should be no pressure to handle more than they are able to."

"You give us too much credit." Rufus pushed aside some electrical cords so he could walk through. "Neither Sunny nor I had thought about the strain their appearance might be on the veterans. Jonathan Trimble, who you met, is organizing that part of the schedule. I'll make sure he knows to communicate your Plan B to the veterans who are participating."

"Super." I felt good about the prep. There was no reason to think things wouldn't go very smoothly. "Seven o'clock tomorrow night for rehearsal?"

"The celebs were told seven," Rufus confirmed. "If you wouldn't mind getting here around six thirty or so, that would help."

"No problem." I followed him down the stairs and out to the staff hallway. "I can do that."

Rufus talked through a few more details, promised to get me the room assignment list, and then was off to take care of other last-minute details.

"It's almost over," I told myself, then added Rufus's reminder. "It's for a very good cause."

Back in the lobby I glanced around but didn't see Marsha, so I grabbed a latte, and parked myself in one of the chairs where I could see people coming and going. I pulled out my phone and checked email. Rufus had already sent me the list with room assignments for the celebrities appearing at Barking with the Stars. The man was amazing.

I also had an email from Sam with his itinerary. He was arriving tomorrow and would be on hand as promised. Unfortunately, I'd be tied up with the final things I needed to do to get ready for the big event.

I emailed a reply, letting him know if he called and I didn't answer it was probably that I was in the middle of calming a diva or a dog.

I had a lot to fill him in on, and we had a lot to talk about. Could it wait until after this weekend's affair? Probably not.

I also had a text from Diana. She'd discovered some phone app where she could switch her face with her dog's face. Diana's face on Mr. Wiggles's body was funny, but Mr. Wiggles's face on Diana Knight's body was hilarious.

I snorted coffee and nearly dropped my phone.

"Ms. Lamont?" An attractive dark-haired girl slipped into the chair beside me. Her lush brown curls framed a heart-shaped face. Dark eyes that reminded me of Sam, were beautiful but her expression was bleak.

"Yes?" I fought for composure after that text from Diana.

"I'm Marsha Reilley." She held out her hand in introduction.

It took me a second or two to respond. I'd been expecting the Purple Poser I'd spoken with earlier.

Recovering from the surprise, I shook her hand, noting the dark-magenta polish. "Pardon me for being taken aback." I tried not to stare. "But, girl, you look nothing like the person I just saw in the ladies' room."

That garnered an almost smile. "I suppose not."

I tucked my phone away and gave her my attention. "What did you want to talk to me about?"

"I had wanted to get in touch with you because my dog, Peri, has been having some problems lately, and I know you worked with Purple and Lavender." The words came out in a rush.

"Peri, short for Periwinkle?" I asked.

She nodded. "That's right."

"What seems to be the problem?" I asked.

"I don't have a lot after this trip," she interrupted, "but I can pay for your services. Do you want to see Peri?"

"Probably, yes." I couldn't stop staring. The girl was beautiful for one thing, but the biggest difference was her demeanor. In the ladies' room and when I'd seen her in the hotel as a part of the group of Posers, she was tall and bold and walked with confidence. This girl hunched into herself and spoke with hesitation. Probably if she'd asked Cindy and Yuki for my contact information as herself, they would have provided it.

"Can you tell me what has you worried about Peri?" I asked. "He's a Lhasa Apso like Lavender?"

"That's right. He's doing things he's never done before. He's a good dog." Her dark eyes pleaded with me to understand. "But he chewed up the bath mat. I'm going to pay to replace it," she was quick to assure me.

"Anything else?" Chewing wasn't unusual behavior for a dog away from home, but it sounded like she'd traveled with him before and not had any issues.

"Well, there's also the accidents." She dropped her head down. "And some aggressive behavior toward housekeeping staff."

"He's not done these things before?"

She shook her head.

"And you've traveled with him before, I assume." I wanted to be sure.

Her head bobbed in agreement. "Lots of times."

"Is there any pattern to the behavior?"

"I'm not sure what you mean." She tipped her head like Dogbert does when he's not sure of what I'm trying to communicate.

"When do these things mostly happen?" I clarified my questions. "Is it a particular time of day? Is it when he's around certain people? Or smells? In other words, can you think of any triggers?"

"Not really." She twisted the hem of her blouse. "What's odd is that it never happens when I'm there with him. He's just a sweetie, perfect as anything."

Ah-ha. Sometimes the clue isn't what's there but what's not there.

"Marsha, I'm happy to meet with you and Peri, together if you'd like," I offered, "but let me just share what I'm initially thinking."

"I can pay you," she broke in. "Maybe I could do installments or something."

"Let's not worry about that right now." I touched her hand which still clutched the fabric of her blouse. "My initial consultation with you and Peri would be free."

"Oh, that would be great." The girl dropped the hem she'd almost twisted beyond any hope of it being able to return to its original state and looked up at me.

"The thing is that you're grieving for Purple." I held her gaze. "Peri senses your feelings, and that can create some instability. He wants to be with you. To comfort you, and when he's left alone, he gets anxious and acts out."

"Hmmm . . ."

I could see the wheels turning. Hopefully it was making sense to her.

"Is there a way you can have him with you more? Or spend more time with him?"

"We haven't been cuddling at night like we always have," she mused. "I kind of thought he was just going through a phase."

"Is brushing time a good experience for him?" I asked. Lhasa Apso dogs need a lot of brushing. A *lot* of brushing.

"Yes, he loves it. We make a big production of it, and it's sort of bonding time."

"Maybe some extra brushing time would help," I suggested. "Some extra cuddle time."

"You really think that's what is causing him to do these things?" Her brow furrowed.

Her questioning of what I'd said was typical. People can never believe it's that easy.

"I do." I reached in my bag and handed her one of my cards. "Why don't you try it and let me know? I'll be around tomorrow and I can always meet with you and Peri then."

"Thank you so much for talking with me." She tucked the card in the pocket of her jeans.

"It will be busy tomorrow, so I may not answer right away, but I'll call you back if you leave a message." Hopefully my ideas were on target and would work, but if not, I had some other ideas. "Tomorrow will be crazy."

"The next two days will be bonkers," she muttered under her breath.

That was a fact I knew to be true.

"Before you go, I have a quick question for you."

"Okay."

"How many of you are there that dress up like Purple?"

"You mean here at the hotel?"

"Yes, I guess that's what I'm asking."

"There are twelve still here. Two had to leave. They said that they had to get back to work but I think they were kind of spooked by the whole murder thing."

"Who wouldn't be, right?" I waited for her reaction.

She nodded.

"So there are twelve of you now?"

"That's right. I think so anyway." She thought for a moment. "It's always kind of a fluctuating number as more could arrive at any time, and we're pretty protective of our real identities so I'm not sure anyone really knows."

"But you had to give your real names to the police, didn't you?" I couldn't imagine Malone and company going for anything less.

"We did."

"The night before Purple was killed I saw an entourage walk through the lobby." I wished I'd paid better attention at the time. "I thought it was Purple, but now I'm thinking it might have been you."

"It could have been." Her eyes slid away from mine. "A bunch of us went out."

"You play the role very well," I complimented her. It was true, when she was in costume she nailed the role.

"Thank you." She smiled for the first time.

"What will you do now? Will you continue to . . . uhm . . . play the role now that the real Purple is gone?" I'd almost said, "continue to be a Poser" but caught myself in time.

"I'm not sure." She slumped. "There was one thing I didn't mention to the police officer I talked to. He seemed sort of condescending about the role play and so I don't think he would have been interested. Part of the fun of dressing up like Purple was that sometimes, especially when there were big groups, she mixed with all of us who did the role play. So, there was the off chance, as you were hanging out and playing the role, that maybe one of the others was actually her. She got a kick out of the dress-up and sometimes if there was a particularly good double or she liked something about your outfit, she might offer a personal item."

"Had that happened to you?" I asked. "Did she give you something?"

"She did." Marsha lit up. "This bracelet."

She held out her wrist so I could see the delicate circle of silver studded with purple stones.

"Very pretty." I admired the bracelet. "I guess that would add an element of competition to it."

"Right." She nodded. "But all in good fun."

Believe me I know a lot about competition and there usually comes a time when it's no longer good fun.

CHAPTER FOURTEEN

As Marsha left, I watched her walk across the lobby, again wondering at the difference between her body language when dressed as Purple and when she was herself. It was more than body language. It was demeanor or, I'd even say, attitude. Interesting.

She'd seemed overly concerned about money a couple of times. She'd mentioned reimbursing the hotel and then she'd also seemed worried about paying me. I supposed the Purple costuming didn't come cheap. Nor the travel and hotel stays involved in following the star from venue to venue.

I wished I'd asked what she did for a living. It had to be expensive to support her habit as a Purple Poser.

Since I had the list from Rufus, I ran through it again. I noted a problem with Shar Summer's dressing room assignment. It wasn't where we'd agreed.

I couldn't believe I hadn't spotted that when we did the walk-through. If there was a good reason for the change I'm sure she'd be okay, but Rufus had perhaps not understood the number of sparkly items Shar and Babycakes brought to bear. I'd better check it out before things got started so if we needed to make changes we could. Before things, in Marsha's words, got "bonkers." I couldn't remember if Rufus had used a key card to get us to the backstage area or not. I decided to take my chances.

I retraced my steps and soon found my way to the hotel auditorium. The Ocean Mark had done a great job of labeling rooms and providing maps of exits so it made it easy.

The auditorium was no longer deserted. A crew was beginning some set-up work. More equipment, more cords. A grand piano, some props. There were three guys discussing some problem with the scrim, the big screen that would be used for the photos and videos. I was glad it was Rufus in charge of the dress rehearsal tomorrow night and not me.

"I'm with the event," I explained, although they hadn't challenged why I was there. "I just need to look at some dressing room locations."

They nodded and went back to their discussion.

Pulling up the list in Rufus's email, I walked the hallway. The change to Shar's room assignment was a problem as she'd already dropped off some things in the room she'd originally had. I emailed him quickly in order to give him time to take a look.

I rechecked some of the other room assignments. I'd be willing to bet he had signs ready to go for tomorrow night, but I wanted to have an idea of how I would need to time my own check-ins. Once I'd walked through the timeline, I went to tell the stage folks I was leaving, but they had already gone. They'd turned off all but a few lights so I took my time and stepped carefully. I didn't want to trip on all those ropes and cords.

Sheesh! It would have been nice for them to let me know they were turning off lights.

I had started one step at a time down the stairs to go back to the service hallway when I realized there were people in the shadows of the auditorium. I could hear low voices, and I stopped to let my eyes adjust to the darkness.

It was Drake Owen and Trevor Lang.

I started to call out, but then stopped myself.

Drake wasn't even supposed to be in town. At least he'd told Sunny, Diana, and me that he didn't plan to be. And how did he know Trevor?

I was in a deserted auditorium with two guys who had been close to Purple. One of whom I believed had lied to me. And the other, who had argued with Mandy, and then had avoided talking to me.

Malone's warning echoed in the back of my mind. They had not yet been able to identify any motive. Everyone was still a potential suspect.

Probably not my best option to reveal myself at this point. I quietly eased down the steps, glad I'd gone for the low canvas shoes. I could hear a little bit of the conversation now.

"I can't believe you did what you did." I thought that voice was Trevor. His tone was a little higher than Drake's.

"You were done wrong." That was definitely Drake, the twang was evident. "And now we're fixin' to set things right."

". . . no legal standing . . . don't have the cash to hire a lawyer and take this through the courts." I'd missed the first part but could hear the last. Trevor's demeanor was certainly different from the threatening stance he'd taken with Mandy.

"That'd be a long haul and now you may not need . . ." The voice I believed to be Drake's trailed off into nothing.

What the heck?

I couldn't hear well to begin with from where I stood, and now they were walking toward the back.

"You think about that opening." Drake turned to look at the stage and I could clearly see his face now. I hoped to heck he couldn't see me. I pressed myself against the wall.

"I will." Trevor held out his hand and Drake shook it and then they disappeared out the doors to the public area.

Two guys making a deal? Or maybe one or the other, tying up the loose ends of a murder?

I stood in the dark a while before moving.

Making sure they were gone.

And trying to decide what to do with the incomplete pieces of information I'd overheard.

CHAPTER FIFTEEN

Once I finally got myself together and made my way back to the lobby, I immediately called Malone. The call went right to voicemail. I left a message.

Holy Secrets and Lies, Batman.

I need you to call me back, Malone.

I gave the valet my ticket and waited for my car. Lines of fans continued down the walkway to where the Purple tribute area had been set up. It still seemed to be working out. I hoped Jamie and his grounds crew were able to keep up.

Maybe I'd just go by the police station and see if I could catch Malone there. The trouble was when I caught up with him, I didn't even know where I would start.

The conversation with Sheron was more about people insights than hard facts Malone would be interested in. But my talk with Lew Simpson had told me he had the skills to hack the cameras. Malone might or might not know that. But Lew had also shared his potential for a clash with Purple over signing his purple vinyl record. Had she really agreed to do it and then forgotten to give it back to him? Or more likely forgotten to ask Mandy to give it back to him. Did he own it, or was he up to some sort of scam and they'd figured it out?

And then Marsha and her mention that sometimes Purple mixed with the Posers. Perhaps she had the night she died and that's why they were having so much trouble nailing down her whereabouts. Without the cameras, they knew when people had gone into the room, but they didn't know who might have gone in with her. And don't even get me started on the unreliability of eyewitness reports.

And then finally, there was the overheard conversation between Purple's fiancé and a guy she apparently had a history with. A guy who had some sort of dispute. Business dealings, Sheron had said. But then there had also been Sheron's very odd reaction when I'd asked about Trevor. I didn't know how I was going to explain that to Malone.

I tipped the valet and dropped my bag in the front of my car. As I slid into the driver's seat, a black SUV pulled up. Geoffrey got out and handed his keys to another of the valets, and then walked around to the passenger side. Holding the door open, he offered a hand to his female companion.

I waited. No sting anymore, just curiosity.

Mandy Barton accepted his assist and stepped down from the big vehicle. It seemed an odd combination, the personal assistant and the murder suspect. She looked good in a strappy tank and an asymmetric turquoise skirt that showed a bit of leg. Nice but a big change from her usual blend-into-the-background Girl Friday look. She carried a tan Fendi bag — I knew what it cost because I had just looked at the same bag in red.

Not that there was any reason to think that she couldn't have afforded a high-end purse before. I was pretty sure assistants to superstars made decent money. Buy-several-designer-handbags kind of money. It was just that she hadn't seemed to care before.

Her hair color also was slightly different. The drab blond was replaced with shiny highlights. Maybe she hadn't had the time when dealing with all the chaos of being assistant to a celebrity like Purple. Maybe she hadn't had time to date.

But seriously? Geoffrey Carlisle? Mandy, you have awful taste in men.

They hadn't spotted me although I was

sure Geoffrey would at least recognize my car. I glanced back as I put the Mercedes in gear. He was straightening his tie in the SUV's rearview mirror. He hadn't even noticed my car.

I pulled away and added one more odd happening, aka clue, to my mental list of things to share when Malone called me back.

Parking my car in the garage, I grabbed my stuff and opened the door into the kitchen. I was glad to be home, and my menagerie was glad to see me. I took Dogbert out quickly, looking around the neighborhood. I hated to feel like a prisoner in my own home, and I hadn't thought the note was threatening, but the fact that whoever had penned it had been careful to not leave prints made it seem a little creepier.

Food for the felines could not come fast enough, at least according to them. I refilled bowls, gave out rubs, and rummaged for something for myself. Too bad I hadn't really been at the grocery store when I'd given Malone the impression that's where I was. And what *was* I going to do about Mr. Swanson and Grandma Tillie's brooch.

I had tried Googling him. No luck. I'm usually pretty good at different types of searches, but I didn't know the man's first name. Unfortunately, I'd been a little too quick to walk out of the Bow Wow Boutique when he'd first offered the brooch, otherwise I would probably have better information. I had to think Mel was also not cooperating in the way he'd hoped or he wouldn't still be interested in talking to me.

I found the makings for a salad, threw in some almonds, and settled at my computer to do some further searching while I ate.

What did I know about him? Betty and Mel had met him when they were "glamping" in the Laguna Hills. He didn't really look like the glamorous camping type. Maybe his participation had been encouraged by a wife or girlfriend. The glamping had been an exclusive pet-themed outing where you brought your dog, so that's why Mel and Betty had gotten involved. There'd also been a murder and Betty had hinted at Mel's near arrest, but I wasn't sure I'd ever gotten the straight story on exactly what had happened.

I made a quick note to myself that I needed to check in with Betty and see how she and Raider were faring. I hadn't seen her around since the day at the police station. I really was concerned about her and her St. Bernard, but I also thought maybe she'd let slip some intel if I got her talking.

A quick search of the online news told me that Sunny had made the announcement about a new headliner for the Warriors for the Paws fundraiser. One of the Hollywood news outlets had pulled out an archived story in which Nora talked about her own dog and her efforts to help shelters. She was going to be a fabulous spokesperson for the fundraiser. And what a champion to step in with such an awful situation.

My cell phone beeped from the kitchen where I'd left it. I could use a laugh, so I kind of hoped it was another of the silly texts from Diana switching her and her pets' faces. She had quite an assortment of animals at her house, so there was a lot of potential.

Instead, it was a text from Malone letting me know he was tied up with something and probably wouldn't call me back until morning. Unless it was an emergency, he'd added with a question mark.

It wasn't. My insights and the new information weren't urgent. In fact, though some of the intel was new to me, it was quite possible Malone already knew most of it. I texted back that morning was fine.

When Malone called the next morning, he

suggested meeting at the Koffee Klatch again and that was perfect for me. I had cleared the next couple of days of any appointments. The only thing on my list for the day was getting to the hotel and going over final details. It was sure to be a really long day.

I showered and pulled out newly purchased Rag and Bone blue-and-white-checkered ankle pants. I've found it's good to have a pattern in the event you need to camouflage drools or spills. I added a favorite sleeveless navy shirt and slipped on some flat serviceable sandals. A nice cool outfit that would work well with all the running to and fro at the hotel. My mama would have thought that I'd reached a new low for dressing to leave the house.

I heard her voice in my head saying, "Carolina, you could at least put on some lipstick." And so I dug out an Estee Lauder lipstick and swiped it on. It was a nice coral that had been in the Neiman Marcus care package Mama Kat had sent a month ago. There's no use arguing with her and telling her we have department stores here in California. Like the helicopter mom of a teenager who's gone off to camp, she keeps sending me care packages.

When I arrived at the Koffee Klatch,

Malone was already at a table in the breeze-way with two coffee cups. He looked like he'd had a long night.

"One for me?" I had assumed he had no idea what I drank.

"Yep." He pushed one of the cups my direction. "Not sure what it is but the burgundy-haired barista claims it's your usual."

"So, Verdi is working?" I inhaled the smooth, nutty aroma as I took my first taste.

"She is." He picked up his cup and leaned in. "Sounded like you had information to share."

I started with my dropping off the bill at Purple's house.

"Which you could have mailed," he noted.

"I could have, but I wasn't certain what would be happening with the house and whether it would be the same mailing address."

"And it gave you the opportunity to snoop."

"Well, yes, there was that added benefit." I met his blue gaze.

Dropping any pretense that I'd gone there innocently, I shared Sheron's take on whether Drake and Purple would have ended up actually getting married. And also, her reaction when I'd asked about Trevor and his argument with Mandy.

"She stands to gain as much as anyone from Purple's death so probably has more motive than any of the others." Malone looked thoughtful.

"Who, Mandy? I'd wondered about that."

"No, Sheron."

"What?" I couldn't imagine the tea-drinking, dog-mothering Sheron could be a murderer. "She doesn't seem to care anything about the money. Sheron is all about the dog."

"Could she and Purple have argued about the dog?" he asked. "Was Purple ever abusive to the dog?" He rubbed his chin. I could tell he was remembering the incessant barking the day of the murder.

"Not that I ever saw. She wasn't always as attentive as she could have been. I often felt like Lavender was part of her accessories. Part of the 'look.' " I did air-quotes with my fingers. "I only met Sheron after Purple's death, but I hadn't been working with Purple for very long. She hadn't been in town more than a couple of weeks."

"Okay, just a thought. Go on." He leaned back in his chair.

All right. On to Lew Simpson and his collecting. From Malone's reaction, it was clear that he knew about the vinyl record Lew claimed he had dropped off for Purple to sign.

"What would something like that sell for?" he mused. "Do you have any idea?"

"I did an online search last night and the highest priced collectible records can run into the tens of thousands of dollars," I told him. "Those were mostly big names, but signed increases the price."

"I'll bet so does deceased." He shifted in the metal chair. "By a lot."

"You're right about that." My poking around on the Internet had yielded an amazing appetite for vinyl records. Even unsigned, a popular and rare record could bring ten to twenty-five thousand dollars, and a signature and a provenance, as Lew had explained, added value. Which reminded me of my second Lew insight. "Lew, the collector, also mentioned that in his day job he's a . . . just a minute." I had to find the note where I'd written it down. "Here it is. He's an application developer of internal apps for FinZone."

"He gave us his employer but he just said he worked in their IT department." Malone stared off toward the front of the coffee shop. "He wasn't very specific."

"And then I had a chat with one of the Purple Posers. You know the people that dress up like Purple."

"Oh, yeah." He grinned. "Your pal, Officer Hostas, was not happy about having to deal with all of them."

"I'll bet." I hoped the experience put into perspective all of the times Officer Hostas had dealt with me in unusual circumstances. At least I wasn't dressed in costume any of those times. Wait, there was the one time, but Malone had drawn that straw.

"What did the Poser have to say?"

"Marsha was the fan who'd asked the two fan club presidents for my contact info and she's a very believable Purple role play actor." I continued to be fascinated with the whole cosplay world, and the psychologist in me wanted to know more. "She mentioned that sometimes Purple herself sort of infiltrated the group. Joining in on their events undercover, and that occasionally, if she were particularly impressed with a costume or the player, she might gift them with something of hers."

"Hmmm." Malone clearly wasn't seeing any tie to his murder investigation with this one.

"Okay, moving on." I took a big drink of my latte to prepare for this one. "I was backstage checking out a dressing room issue and overheard a conversation between

Drake Owen and Trevor Lang." I waited for his reaction.

"You were backstage alone?" Not the reaction I'd hoped for.

"Not at first. There were workers, but then they left without saying anything. And they turned off most of the lights which was why Drake and Trevor didn't see me."

"Go on." He did seem to be interested in this one.

I repeated word for word what I'd been able to catch of the cryptic comments between the two guys.

"I didn't think Drake Owen was in town. He'd told us when he came by to ask about us releasing the body that he wasn't sticking around." Someone or something behind me had caught Malone's attention.

"Apparently changed his mind." I took a sip of coffee and casually glanced over my shoulder to see what Malone was staring at.

Ohmigosh! I very nearly spit out my coffee. It was Betty and she had Mr. Swanson cornered by the pastry case.

The octogenarian sported a nice bright two-piece lounge set with sailboats today, and I couldn't see her eyebrows from my angle but I was sure they were coordinated with her outfit. What I could see was Mr. Swanson's face, and from his expression she might as well have been wearing a gorilla suit. He was backed up against the dessert case and looked as if he was about ready to climb in with the tiramisu.

I couldn't feel bad for him. After all, he'd brought this on himself.

Malone noticed my gaze. "Do you think I need to step in?"

"Oh, no." Was he serious? "I think Betty can hold her own."

"I meant, to save the guy." Malone raised a brow.

I laughed. "That's a possibility."

Mr. Swanson had eased away from Betty and started out of the coffee shop when he spotted me and made a quick turn in my direction.

"Ms. Lamont." He stopped beside the table.

"Good morning, Mr. Swanson," I greeted him. "I'd like you to meet, my *friend,* Detective Judd Malone."

Malone eyed the man in his best taking-the-measure-of-someone visual inventory. I swear I could actually see the bravado go out of Swanson. He went from puffed and flying high to deflated in seconds.

"Oh, okay." Swanson blanched. "I've got to go. Got to see — uh — got an appointment." And off he hurried, his short legs on a mission to carry him as far away from us as possible.

"What was that about?" Malone pushed aside his cup. "And why do I suddenly feel like I've been used?"

"Hmmm." I took one last sip and picked up my bag.

"My *friend,* Detective Malone, huh?" He stood. "Glad to know we're friends."

I stood also.

"Listen, Caro, I appreciate the intel about the fans and the people involved with Purple. But remember someone killed Purple and we don't know who. Don't take any chances whether it's with your ex or seemingly innocent fanatics. Okay?"

"Okay." We headed out together just as Betty picked up her to-go order and walked through the propped open door.

"Hey there, you two." The sailboat getup was even more colorful up close, and she'd added a bright-yellow scarf as an accent.

"Want to tell me what Mr. Swanson had to say?" I asked.

"We were just talking RVs," she said. "You know, campers and stuff."

Right.

For once Betty was not chatty. She wasn't even interested in feeling Malone's muscles. She scurried in the direction of the Bow

Wow Boutique without another word.

"Oh, man," Malone said under his breath. "This cannot be good. You, Betty, a strange man, and I'm sure your cousin is involved somehow." He turned and walked with purpose down the street in the other direction. I'm sure, mentally measuring the distance he was putting between him and our hijinks.

I slid on my sunglasses and walked to my car which I'd parked on a side street. Betty was already halfway down the block. There was no point in following her. I really didn't have time for any brooch drama right now. Just a couple more days and this would all be wrapped up. What would the police do about all the fans who were leaving after the weekend? It wasn't like movies or books where they could say no one could leave town. Unless they had a reason to detain someone, I imagined they had to let them go.

My cell phone rang just as I reached my car. It was Diana.

"Hi, hon." I put the phone to my ear and unlocked my car.

"Oh, Lord." She paused for breath.

"Are you all right?"

"No." She took a big breath. "I'm not."

"What's going on?"

"Our new star, Nora, is stuck in Singapore and can't get a flight out."

"On, no. Why?" I supposed someone as important as Nora Worthington flew on a private jet. It wasn't like me getting bumped or missing a connection.

"There's some problem with her plane and the commercial flights are backed up because of tropical storm Nuri. There's worry the storm could become a typhoon." She stopped. "I don't know all the details but I know Sunny is still working on trying other ways to get her here, but it doesn't look good."

"What can I do?" I couldn't imagine what else could happen to derail this fundraiser.

"Nothing really, hon." Diana slowed down a bit. "I guess I just needed to have myself a mini-meltdown." She chuckled. "Tell you what you can do, the next time I want to get involved in something like this, I want you to tell me to write a big check and walk away."

"You've got it," I responded. After all that had happened with this event, she was probably serious.

CHAPTER SIXTEEN

I pulled out onto PCH and turned south toward the Ocean Mark P. What would we do now?

As I drove down Pacific Coast and passed the Bow Wow Boutique, I reminded myself that Melinda's shop had done well in spite of some negative press she'd dealt with early on from a disgruntled customer. My business would survive Geoffrey's interference. And Warriors for the Paws would make it through this latest crisis. When you go big, you don't go home. We would weather this.

In less than ten minutes, I pulled into the circle drive at the hotel. The parking attendants and I were almost on a first-name basis now. I'd been in and out of the hotel so many times in the past two weeks that they'd probably driven my car more than I had.

The lobby was packed today with the Purple Posers out in full force. I watched a group waiting for coffees and realized that though I'd spent some time with Marsha and knew what she looked like in real life, I probably wouldn't be able to pick her out of the group.

Tania stood near the registration desk and I waved at her as I passed. It would be a long weekend for the hotel staff, but that was nothing new for Tania. My phone buzzed; it was a text from Rufus. He wanted to know if I'd arrived and I texted back that I had.

Joining him backstage, I helped tack up signs on the rooms. I didn't know how to help with the lack of a headliner, but I could fill in assisting Rufus.

Diana and Sunny arrived shortly after that and pulled Rufus into a confab, I assumed to talk about options. When he came back to where I was working to finishing up the signage, he was as subdued as I'd ever seen him.

"Good grief, Caro." He jabbed at his tablet. "When this is all over we all deserve a vacation or at least a spa day or something."

"Or something." I put an arm around his shoulders and gave him a squeeze. "I'm with you there, hon."

Celebrities were beginning to arrive with

their dogs. The noise grew as more celebrities and the canines arrived and checked in. The hallways echoed with chatter and woofs and a few whines. And I can tell you the whines were not the dogs.

I helped direct the stars and their pooches to the right rooms. The noise level continued to grow as more people came. Shar and Babycakes not only had a luggage cart packed with who knew what, but also had brought a makeup artist. I'd figured that many of the stars would have staff and stylists the day-of but hadn't realized that would also include dress rehearsal.

As I had expected, the sounds and the tension translated to nervous dogs and so there was a couple of close calls with a bit of snarling. But thankfully no biting. Only a few minor accidents, but hotel staff had planned for that and had a clean-up crew standing by.

I had just offered to check on the arrival of the veterans and therapy dogs when Mandy pushed through the crowd, followed by Drake Owen. I was surprised to see him as, I was sure, were most of the others in the vicinity. He walked through quickly and spotted Rufus who pointed him to the room where Diana and Sunny were holed up.

Well, well. What was up?

Mandy turned in the other direction. Had they been together or was it just coincidental that they'd arrived at the same time. I looked around for Geoffrey, whom I would have expected to be with Mandy based on last night.

I wasn't sure after hearing that Sheron had fired him, where that left the handling of Lavender for the event. If it were up to me, I'd have Sheron do that handling, as the dog seemed most comfortable with her. But no one was asking me.

After confirming the veterans had not yet arrived, I went to make sure Shar and Babycakes had gotten settled. They seemed to be doing fine. The others on my list were also in their dressing rooms.

Rufus stepped out of the way as a rolling rack of equipment came through.

"Anything I can do?" I asked. "My stars and their pooches are all settled."

"Pray," he deadpanned.

"Been doing that, sugar," I answered. And I had.

Sunny stepped out of what I'd now come to think of as the war room. Her arm was hooked with Drake's and she waited while those in the backstage area let them through.

"If we could have everyone out front for a

few minutes," she requested, "we won't take up too much of your time."

Though not everyone had heard her request, the word got passed. I helped Rufus knock on dressing room doors, and soon most everyone on site had filled the auditorium. There was still no sign of Geoffrey. Despite being fired by Sheron, he should have been there for his other clients.

"Thank you, all, for being here," Sunny spoke from the stage. Someone handed her a microphone and she continued, "Thank you for your commitment to this cause. And for continuing with us in spite of the terrible tragedy of losing a fellow performer." Her voice broke and she looked over at Diana.

Diana came forward and reached for the microphone.

I'd seen it before but was always impressed. In a matter of minutes, the lady, even with Mr. Wiggles tucked under her arm, suddenly morphed from Diana, my caring friend and stray collector, to larger-than-life big-screen Diana Knight, the Hollywood star.

"Hello." She waited a couple of beats and then flashed the signature Diana Knight smile at the crowd. "We are so thankful you all have continued with us in spite of the tragic circumstances, and we know that you do it to honor those that have served our country."

"What we do," she continued, as she swept an arm toward the crowd, "gives a voice to those who make silent sacrifices. Our soldiers, our veterans. The least we can do is to help continue this program that provides therapy dogs to those who have given so much more than we ever could repay."

I knew it was part of the speech she was going to give during the event and I'd heard it already but I also knew it was sincere.

I swallowed the lump in my throat.

"Yesterday, we announced that Nora Worthington would step in for Purple, graciously filling in at the last minute. This morning we found out that Nora is stranded in Singapore. All planes are grounded due to weather and it's unlikely she will be able to join us for Barking with the Stars."

The crowd gave a collective sigh.

"However, the show must go on." Diana winked and grinned at her use of the cliché then looked over at Sunny who now seemed able to continue.

Sunny took back the microphone. "As of about five minutes ago, we've had an incredible offer. Drake Owen has offered to step in and will do us the honor of performing the final number of the show."

Drake stepped in from the wings to hug both Sunny and Diana.

"My fiancé cared a ton about this cause and this organization," he said, "and, though I'm sure I won't be the draw that either she or Nora would have been, I'm happy to do what I can. Thank you for hanging in there with us." He handed the microphone back to Sunny.

"Thank you." She nodded toward Drake. "And thank you." She bowed to the crowd. "Okay, let's get this rehearsal started."

Rufus stepped up. "We will take it from the beginning. Just like it is on the program."

Everyone filed back to dressing rooms and places. An outside door at the back was open with a crew bringing in instruments. Rufus had said the veterans and their therapy dogs would be coming in that way as well. The group had arrived and they seemed well organized. No surprise there. Between Jonathan Trimble and Rufus, all parties were clear on where they were supposed to be and when.

The flow of people to the stage was orderly and I could hear the soundcheck going on. I poked my head into Shar's dressing room to check on her. She gave me a thumbs-up and then lifted Babycakes' paw to give me a paws-up. I smiled and went on to the next room to check on Plucky and Carson. They were also good.

I didn't know what the plans were for Drake, so I wanted to check with Mandy on whether he was going to have any interaction with Lavender. I'd pass on my tips for keeping the dogs calm on stage to him, and also make sure he understood what Rufus and I had talked about in terms of if anything got too stressful.

The back door seemed clear for the moment so I stepped outside. Rufus had a staging area set up for the therapy dogs, and I have to tell you this was the calmest area I'd found so far.

Jonathan Trimble spotted me and he and Whiskey came over. "Hey, it's good to see you again."

"And you." I was so pleased he was involved. His experience and the time he'd had to work with his dog would be such an asset. The calm assurance they had would spread.

"Is your daughter excited about tomorrow night?" I asked.

"Excited doesn't begin to describe it." He grinned. "She had to have a whole new all-purple outfit to wear. She is definitely counting the hours."

We stood and talked a bit and I watched as people came out through the back door. I was shocked to see Trevor Lang was one of the people.

I didn't try to talk to him, though after overhearing him and Drake talking the other night, I was curious why he was still around. My money was still on him in the pool of suspects.

"Almost ready," Rufus called from the doorway.

"Okay," Jonathan answered. "All right, time to line up," he called to the others.

The men and women who'd been sitting with their dogs or playing catch in the sandy area beside the building, responded.

"I'll talk to you later." I patted his arm. This time Whiskey stood but accepted my being close to his human without a problem.

Back inside, I spotted Mandy ducking into the room next to Shar's that now said "Lavender," which I guess answered my question about whether the dog would still make an appearance.

I followed her. "Lavender doing okay?" I asked.

"Yeah, I didn't bring her. It's not like she needs to rehearse." She opened a drawer and then closed it.

I begged to differ but there wasn't much I could do about it at this late stage. I'd simply have to be alert for any problems tomorrow night.

"How are you doing?" Again today, she looked different than she had while working for Purple. Her outfit was full of color and up-close I noticed the attention to detail. Mandy was attractive but must have felt overshadowed by the very flamboyant Purple. Much like the change in demeanor I'd notice with Marsha, the Purple Poser, when she was role playing, Mandy seemed to have developed a new role for herself. Or perhaps dropped the old one.

"I'm okay." She picked up a hairbrush that had been left on the dressing table and hesitated. "Listen, I know that must have seemed odd seeing me with your ex-husband."

"No worries on my end."

"I didn't want you to think it was a date or anything like that." She ran fingers through her newly highlighted locks. "He'd asked to meet about Lavender and discuss handling her potential issues at the event."

That must have been before Sheron fired him.

"Frankly, it doesn't matter to me who he dates." I waved off her concern. "Still, it's good you're not seeing him. Most people see through him in a very short time."

I hoped she got the not-so-subtle point I was trying to make. If she'd been living in Purple's shadow for a long time, and it seemed she had, the girl could be extremely vulnerable to the attentions of a charmer like my ex.

I didn't want to spend any energy at all discussing Geoffrey. "So, tomorrow night you'll be bringing Lavender?" I asked. "Had you thought about having Sheron come along? She seems to have bonded with the dog and it might be calming."

"She's busy," Mandy dismissed the idea. "Plus, she's bossy."

Well, then.

"Have you discussed with Drake when Lavender will be needed?" I wasn't sure if he was going to pick up all the spots where Purple had been slotted to speak or if he was just doing the finale number.

"I haven't. I guess I'll find out when they tell me." She continued walking the room, picking up things and then putting them down.

"Well, let me know if you need me for anything." I wasn't going to keep trying when clearly she was not interested in my suggestions or my help.

I headed back outside to see how it was going with the therapy dogs. Jonathan and the others had just come back out from walking the stage. They were grouped with Rufus talking and I didn't want to interrupt. I walked to the edge of the fenced area and checked my messages.

I'd had my phone on silent because of the rehearsal and noticed that I had a message. I listened.

It was Sam. He was back in town and wanted to have dinner tonight. I called back and left a message that I was tied up with the rehearsal. Things seemed to be going smoothly thanks mostly to Rufus and his organizing. Once we'd done the run-through, I would dash home to give Dogbert a break and then I'd be back at the hotel most of the evening.

I wasn't avoiding Sam. Really, I wasn't. But right now, my focus was on getting through today and tomorrow. Through this event. One thing at a time.

One thing at a time.

CHAPTER SEVENTEEN

Once home I took Dogbert for a quick walk, grabbed some lunch, and checked my email. I felt pretty good about the dogs and the setup. I still wasn't sure what I thought of Drake Owen, but it was nice of him to step in, and I'm sure Sunny was thankful.

My email contained a couple of responses from clients who'd been out of town when I sent my message about Geoffrey and his misrepresentation. Once this fundraiser was over, I had a number of things to take care of. One was Geoffrey. The other was Mel and the brooch.

I wondered what Betty and Mr. Swanson had been discussing at the Koffee Klatch. It sure-as-shooting had not been campers and RVs. And for that matter, the campers people used for the kind of trip Mel and Betty had gone on weren't your average camping experience. Maybe I could get some intel about Mr. Swanson by following that line of thought.

I hit the search for "glamping rentals" and couldn't believe what popped up. Geeze Louise, some of those things were bigger than my house. I checked out some of the sites. "Easy rental, no fees." One boasted extras like decking with carpet, Wi-Fi, and an outdoor shower with underfloor heating and mood lighting. How much do you suppose it costs to rent something like that? The bigger ones looked like a tour bus for a rock star.

I dialed one of the numbers to a dealer up the road a bit toward Newport Beach. The man who answered seemed very eager to hook me up with an all-inclusive glamping experience.

"There was a recent glamping event nearby where you could bring your pet. Do you know anything about that?"

"Sure. That was the 'Glamping Under the Stars' and it was organized by the Laguna Beach Animal Rescue League."

I slapped my forehead. "Well, I am an idiot."

"Pardon me?" The man was probably in agreement. I thanked him and assured him if I was ever in the market for an RV with a heated outdoor shower with mood lighting, I would be in touch.

I had forgotten it was the Laguna Beach ARL who'd organized the thing. Maybe Geoffrey was right. Maybe I was losing it. The records of who had attended would be in the files at the ARL — a place I volunteered on a regular basis. I'd been making this way too hard.

I immediately dialed Don Furry, my favorite volunteer at the ARL, and asked if he could get me the list of Glamping Under the Stars attendees. Don promised to get back to me soon.

While I waited, I began the preparation for today's dress rehearsal. I had my notebook, my list, and a baggie of pupcakes and doggie treats. I grabbed a handful of dog toys. Finally, I threw in a brush and a lipstick for myself. My mama would be proud.

In a short time, Don called me back with exactly the info I'd been looking for. The Swansons lived in a house in the older part of Laguna not far from downtown. They'd been right under my nose the whole time.

"Have you ever had any dealings with them, Don?" I asked.

"Not much," he said. "They attend most of the fundraisers. Seem nice enough."

Nice wasn't the word I associated with Mr. Swanson.

"Anything you can think of that you remember about them?"

"Well, you're going to think I'm nuts." Don laughed. "But I think the mister has a major gambling problem."

"Why do you think that?"

"They were dropping off a donation of some supplies, and I noticed a whole console in his Range Rover full of California Lotto tickets. Not a few. More like hundreds." Don painted the picture. "Then I saw him throwing them away in the ARL trash. I'm guessing he didn't want the missus to know."

Oh, that explained so much. If he was in trouble with gambling debts, he might think the way out was to tap two Texas girls with money, by auctioning off a piece of jewelry they both wanted. And if he'd heard stories of some of the trickeries we'd resorted to, maybe it wouldn't seem out of line.

Everybody has their own story, don't they? I mean Mel and I were at each other's throats over a family brooch. And Mr. Swanson had a gambling problem. It must have seemed like he'd hit the jackpot when he'd come up with the piece of jewelry.

It was obvious I needed to handle this a little more carefully. I'd see that we got our family brooch back, but I also now knew that Mr. Swanson needed help himself.

I hung up from talking to Don Furry and noted I had a message from Sam. He said he would just plan to join me for dinner at the hotel.

Back in my car and driving toward the Ocean Mark P, I worried if dinner with Sam was a good idea. I was glad he wanted to see me, but I was also a little concerned that meant he wanted to talk. I knew we shouldn't put it off. We needed to clear the air sooner rather than later. But this was not the time. I'd been tempted to beg off with busyness until after the fundraiser, but in the end, I'd agreed to dinner.

I pulled into the hotel and handed my car off to the valet. My first stop was backstage to see what I could do to help Rufus. Several hours later, we had programs unpacked, instructions laid out, and we had checked that the path from dressing rooms to stage was clearly marked.

The hotel staff had been through with a quick cleanup and Rufus had verified water or other refreshments had been ordered for the dressing rooms. There had been a crowd of volunteers earlier helping out, but when the celebrities left, so did they.

Rufus thanked me for hanging in with him. "Sometimes it helps to have a second set of eyes on things."

"No problem." I was happy to make myself useful. "I hope you can take a breath now. We're in the home stretch."

Leaving Rufus, I headed to the hotel restaurant and let the maître d' seat me. I could tell when Sam arrived by the cessation of sound in the restaurant. I was used to the entrance Sam inadvertently made when he crossed a room. The room went quiet and every female in the place from seventeen to seventy drooled like a puppy at chow time. One of the things I loved most about him was that he was completely unaware of having that effect.

He was casually dressed in dark pants and a white shirt, and though I'd started out the day thinking I looked okay, I suddenly realized I now looked like I'd been dragged through a knothole backwards. A quick freshening up would have been wise. I could hear Mama Kat's voice in my head telling me she raised me better.

Sam leaned over and kissed me before he sat down. The waiter appeared immediately with menus and water. Sam also ordered wine, glancing up at me to see if I concurred with his choice. I nodded, but I hadn't really been listening; I was too preoccupied with the things I needed to put on my list for tomorrow.

"You look tired, *cara misu.*" He reached across the table. "How are things going?"

"Well, the headliner is dead, our backup star is stuck in Singapore, the hotel is threatening to eject the crazy fans, and half of our auction items are missing. Other than that, things are going great."

Sam winced. "I'm sorry I haven't been around for you."

"Well, there's that too." I ran my fingers through my hair and came across a random wad of pink glitter, probably from Shar's dressing room.

"Let's get you something to eat." Sam looked around for our waiter.

"Oh no." I could not believe it.

"What?" he asked.

I nodded toward the entrance.

As if this day hadn't been wacky enough. The maître d' was seating Mandy Barton and my ex-husband. Thank goodness no-where near us. But at a table on the open-air patio, so right in my line of sight, and too close for comfort.

Geoffrey looked over and waved.

Asshat.

Mandy looked a little sick. I suppose it didn't look good being caught going to din-ner with the man you'd just claimed you weren't dating. I feared I'd been right and the Geoffrey Carlisle charisma had sucked her in.

Leave her alone, Geoffrey. I don't know what you're up to but I'll bet it's not good.

I took a closer look at him. His face was blotchy and he looked pretty wound up. And a little slapped together for his usual date night attire. Was he drunk? The man never went out in public unless he was perfectly put together. Tonight, it appeared his clothes were a bit askew. I thought about that for a moment. *Oh!* I guess maybe pre-dinner activities must have been pretty physical.

Ass. Hat.

He seated Mandy with a flourish, grinned at the nearby patrons, and then skipped around the table to seat himself. You heard that right. Skipped.

Before sitting down, he plucked a champagne flute off the table and flourished it as if he were a magician on stage. He turned a full circle with a big exaggerated smile at the room and then at Mandy.

What the heck?

The two fan club presidents, Cindy and Yuki, were at a nearby table. I hadn't noticed them when I came in. Cindy spoke to Mandy, but then frowned at something

Geoff said. Suddenly Geoffrey did an odd pirouette and clutched his chest.

His face drained of color.

He collapsed on the floor.

Most people at nearby tables froze. A few stood.

I also stood. Shocked. Unable to breathe.

Sam was on his feet in a flash and hurried to where Geoffrey lay. He knelt beside him, then looked up and made eye contact with me.

"Caro, call 911."

I had my phone out and was already dialing.

An older man hurried into the room. "I'm a doctor," he said. "Let me take a look."

Sam asked people to move back, and the man started CPR. A hotel staffer rushed up with a defibrillator, but the paramedics were there in minutes, surrounded Geoffrey, and began their work. Perhaps there'd been sirens, but, if so, I hadn't heard them.

Sam came back to the table and took me into his arms. I looked up and searched his face. He shook his head slightly. His dark eyes answered my unasked question.

Sam sat with me for more than an hour in the hotel lobby. They had transported Geoffrey to the hospital, but he had been nonresponsive.

Good grief. I had no idea how to feel. I couldn't stand the man, but I hadn't wanted him dead. I was numb.

I sat thinking about the past few months and how awful it had been when Geoffrey showed up in my life again. And then my mind would rewind to the Geoffrey I'd married, or rather the man I'd thought he was. In retrospect, I'd been so young and dumb and innocent. I'd wanted so much to get away from all of my mother's expectations. He'd seemed smart and sophisticated and everything all the Texas boys I'd dated before him hadn't been.

A sound brought me back to the present. I looked around and then focused my gaze on Sam who sat next to me on the wicker bench. Slowly more sounds came through. The whooshing sound of the fountain, snippets of conversation, groups of people coming and going. I noted all the activity, but couldn't rally myself to move.

Tania came by and slipped a bottled water in my hand. I took a drink and let the cool liquid run down my throat.

Sam had taken care of communicating with the paramedics and ultimately the hospital. He'd also arranged for Mandy to be taken home. And then he'd waited.

Steady as a rock.

"Ready to go home?" he asked.

I nodded. I rose and walked to the front. A group of Purple Posers was returning from the tribute site. I wondered vaguely if Marsha was among them.

He handed his ticket to the valet, though I was pretty sure the guy hadn't forgotten which car was Sam's.

"I can drive." I was exhausted, I was numb, but I was okay to drive.

"Indulge me."

I didn't argue. When the Ferrari arrived, Sam held the door and helped me in. The short drive to my place was quiet.

CHAPTER EIGHTEEN

The day after a traumatic event can sometimes have a surreal feel. You wonder, "Did that really happen?"

The day after Geoffrey's death was beyond surreal. I'll admit that I woke up thinking maybe I'd dreamed the whole thing. Then I looked to the chair where I'd dropped my clothes from the day before, and it came back in a rush.

Geoffrey. Dead.

Wow, I couldn't wrap my head around it.

I moved Dogbert, two cats, and the pillows they'd been using, and climbed out of bed. I started coffee and sat down at my kitchen table.

Unable to stay put, I paced. My big back window looks out at a million-dollar view. That's why I'd bought the house. The blue sky, the endless ocean. That and it was far away from Texas and Geoffrey. I'd needed to start over and I'd chosen Laguna Beach to make my own way.

One of the last jumbled thoughts I'd had before I finally fell asleep was that I needed to charge my cell phone. I hadn't had enough energy to get up and take care of it, plus I was pinned in by critters. I should probably find it and plug it in.

I went back to the kitchen. It was plugged in. Either I'd done it on auto-pilot or Sam had done it for me. I was betting on Sam.

I picked it up and checked for messages.

Diana, Sam, Malone, Melinda, Verdi, and a few others I'd also need to call back. The one from Melinda was short and simple.

"Caro, honey, I'm thinking of you."

That one almost broke me.

I poured another cup of coffee, wrapped my robe tighter, and picked up my phone to start the process. Before I could hit re-dial on the first call, my phone rang.

It was Malone.

"Caro, I want to share something before the press gets a hold of it."

"Okay."

"This morning we received an anonymous tip about Geoffrey Carlisle's involvement in Purple's murder. We searched his apartment about an hour ago and found the murder weapon."

"What? Wait. What?" I put my coffee cup

down, my hand shaking. "What was it?"

"A gold statue of Purple," he answered. "It looks like an award. You know, like an Oscar only this is a likeness of her."

"I saw that statue when Betty and I were in her suite." I got up and began pacing again.

"We knew it was something heavy. And we knew it was odd-shaped, but we've been careful not to put any of that information out to the public."

"What happens now?"

"We won't release anything about this until we've had an opportunity to finish our investigation."

"He didn't do it," I blurted out.

"Caro, no one wants to think that some-one they know is capable of murder." Malone used his let's-be-calm voice.

"No," I insisted. "I'm absolutely sure. Geoffrey did not kill Purple."

My doorbell rang, and I spotted my car in the driveway. Sam, bless his heart, was delivering on his promise of getting it home for me.

"You are still going to follow up on Lew Simpson and Trevor Lang, though, right?"

"We will complete the investigation."

That wasn't an affirmative, but probably the best I would get.

"Thank you for the call." I really did appreciate the heads-up. An unexpected thoughtfulness from Mr. Hard-Line Cop.

"You bet."

I had to find a way to convince Malone that Geoffrey was not the killer, but right now I could see why it seemed pretty clear he was. And, I needed to do it before the opportunity was lost and the investigation closed.

I opened the door and Sam came through.

He wore jeans, a black V-neck t-shirt, and sandals. Even with his dark hair mussed, he didn't look disheveled. In fact, he looked like a magazine ad. I wore my ratty, turquoise "The best things in life are furry" robe, yesterday's makeup, and hair that would scare small children. I looked like a train wreck.

I guess, if a guy was worth keeping, you had to see what he was made of when things got real.

He got a cup from the cupboard and helped himself to some coffee.

Dogbert came barreling from the other room when he heard Sam's voice, and Sam knelt to rub the needy pooch's belly.

Some women judge a man by the way he opens a door for her, remembers her birthday, or treats her family. Me? I judge a guy by the way he treats my dog.

"That was Detective Malone on the phone." I flopped down on the couch.

Sam looked up from his play with Dogbert. "And?"

"They found the murder weapon in Geoffrey's apartment."

Sam was silent. He didn't seem surprised.

"He called you first, didn't he?"

He nodded, his dark eyes searching my face.

Suddenly another thought occurred to me. "You've talked to him this whole time you've been gone?"

He looked guilty. "I was worried about you. A murder. A bunch of crazy fans." He stood, picked up his coffee cup, and slid onto one of the breakfast stools at the counter. "We kept missing each other. I needed to know you were safe."

"He didn't do it." I waited for Sam's reaction. "Geoffrey did not kill Purple."

"I agree." He turned on the stool. "I don't think he did either."

"He has a heart attack and then the murder weapon is found in his apartment." Dogbert jumped into my lap and I scratched his ears. "I don't buy it."

"If not him, then who?" Sam shifted from the stool to sit beside me.

"I think there are two very good possibilities." I pulled my knees up and Dogbert jumped down to go check for food. Thelma and Louise, hearing Sam's voice, came out of hiding and made their way across the back of the couch to his lap.

"Who do you suspect?" Sam absently petted each feline in turn.

"Lew Simpson is a collector of memorabilia and had given Purple a very rare album to sign. He claims she never returned it to him. There's big money involved and I think he could have broken into her suite in an attempt to get his property back."

"Wasn't there any security for her suite?"

"There were security cameras but they'd been hacked." Louise shifted to my lap and circled a few times before settling in. "He works in the tech field and I think would have the expertise to disable the cameras."

"But why kill her? Why not simply take what he was after?" Sam had stopped petting Thelma and she batted at his hand to get his attention.

"I think he didn't expect her to be there and maybe panicked and hit her over the head." I drained my coffee cup. "She'd begun staying at the hotel because of remodeling at her house."

"That seems like a possible scenario." Sam

leaned back into the cushions.

"More coffee?" I offered. I was glad to have a someone to talk out my theories. Usually that would be Diana, but she'd been so tied up with all that had gone on with Barking with the Stars, we'd not had a chance to discuss some of things I'd learned.

"Let me get the coffee." Sam set Thelma beside me and took my cup. "You're clearly being held down." He indicated the purring Louise who batted her eyes in response. "You said, two possibilities. Who's the other?"

"A former bandmate, Trevor Lang, who was trying to settle some sort of business dealings with Purple. According to her assistant there were papers Purple had promised to sign."

Sam handed me a full cup of coffee and perched on the arm of the couch with his own cup. "What kind of business dealings?"

"I haven't been able to find out. I hope Malone and company have talked to him."

"I'm sure they have."

"I know." I had spotted the fleeting smile. "I saw Trevor arguing with Mandy — that's the assistant — and I overheard a conversation between him and Drake Owen, Purple's fiancé."

"You've been busy," Sam noted.

"There's something not being said there. Some sort of secret. Mandy isn't saying. Even Drake Owen isn't saying." I shifted to look at Sam, and both cats decided it was time to look for a less antsy sleeping spot. "Call it intuition or whatever, but I think there's something not being shared. Something that might help with the investigation."

"Caro, love, generally when you have a sense about someone or something, it's not guesswork or even intuition. It's your highly tuned people skills working on the problem."

Aww, see this was why I found the guy irresistible.

He got me. He believed in me. *So why couldn't I commit?*

"Thanks for that." I held out a hand and he helped me out of the cushions. "I hope Malone is truly continuing to tie up loose ends and that one of those loose ends leads to the real killer."

I gathered up our coffee cups and took them to the kitchen. Opening the refrigerator and peering in at its lackluster contents, I offered to rustle up some sort of breakfast.

Sam passed. Which was undoubtedly a good thing because I wasn't sure I could have delivered. Unless he was interested in an apple pupcake, I didn't have much to offer.

Sam's ride was there to pick him up. I thanked him again for bringing my car to me. It probably could have waited, but I felt better having it at home. He left to take care of some business he needed to deal with and I started the process of returning calls.

I wondered how many would have already heard about the murder weapon being found at Geoffrey's apartment. Malone had said they wouldn't release the information, but I'd bet within hours it would be out there. In so many ways, Laguna Beach was a small town where everybody knew everybody else's business.

Murder weapon or not, nothing had changed as far as I was concerned. To me the best bets were still Lew Simpson or Trevor Lang. Both had problems with Purple; both had had a lot to lose. And I'd witnessed both lose their temper.

CHAPTER NINETEEN

I really wanted to talk to Mandy about Geoffrey. She was the one who'd been right there and might know something that would help. She would know how much he'd drank and what else he might have taken. Some drugs have odd interactions with alcohol. Or maybe there was something he'd ingested that had caused an allergic reaction. Or could be it was a simple heart attack as they suspected.

I wasn't sure she'd talk to me if I was up front about the reason, but I'd use the excuse of checking in about the event. And in all honesty, I really did need to go over some of the details with all the changes that had occurred. If Mandy loved anything, she loved details. And maybe she had a detail, a piece of information that could help clear Geoffrey and didn't even realize it.

I called her cell phone and she picked up right away.

"Hi, Mandy, it's Caro and I have a couple of items I wanted to confirm with you about tonight." I pulled out my list. "But first, I just wanted to say, I know it must have been awful for you when Geoffrey collapsed."

"Yes, that was scary." She paused. "Still he seems the type to have a heart attack, doesn't he? I mean so intense about everything."

"I don't agree." I hadn't meant to say it quite so sharply.

Geoffrey was a slick charmer, a louse of a husband, and user. But I wouldn't have called him intense. He was more apt to weasel his way out of a problem than fight.

"Well, I guess you would know," Mandy noted.

"Is there anything you can think of that would have brought on his heart attack?" I asked. "Maybe something he ate or drank."

"He'd definitely been drinking before he picked me up." Mandy hesitated. "I wouldn't say he was drunk."

"When I saw you and Geoffrey come into the restaurant, he seemed to be acting a little strange."

"What do you mean by strange?" she asked.

"He was loud and boisterous. He got a little crazy, dancing, talking to people." I

315

detailed what I'd seen. "Anything you noticed?"

"He'd called and said he wanted to meet about the dog," she began.

"I thought he was no longer working with Lavender," I interrupted. That's what I'd understood anyway. Sheron had been pretty clear about it.

"That's right," Mandy agreed. "But he said he had some major concerns about her and I thought I'd better hear him out."

That sounded like the Geoffrey I knew. Using Mandy's worries to wiggle his way back in to working with the pup. Wining and dining her when if he'd truly had concerns they could have been handled with a phone call.

"Anything in particular you noticed when Geoffrey picked you up?" I still wasn't convinced that she hadn't been taken in by his attentions.

"Like I said, he smelled like he'd been hitting the bottle."

"I didn't see him drink anything at the restaurant." I couldn't be sure but I didn't think there had been time for the waiter to even bring a drink.

She thought for a couple of minutes. "He did mention that he'd been at the Cabana with some of the people from the event."

"Do you know who?" Could it have been Trevor or Lew? Could one of them have slipped something into Geoffrey's drink?

"I don't remember that he mentioned names. What are you getting at?"

"I'm not sure. He just didn't seem to be himself." I'd probably probed enough about Geoff. It didn't seem like she knew anything that would convince Malone. Still if the police could talk to others who had been at the Cabana, maybe someone would remember seeing Geoffrey and whom he was with.

"Sorry I can't be of more help." She had tried. And had given me some new information to share with Malone.

"That's okay," I responded. "I'm just still trying to process it all, I guess."

"I understand."

I'm sure she could. I reminded myself that Mandy had lost someone close to her a few days ago. And now, another death right in front of her. I felt bad for pressing so hard.

"Can we talk through a couple of things about tonight? I know Rufus will be there to keep everything moving smoothly." I flipped to the page with the program order. "I'll be backstage to help with any of the pets that need assistance. It can be a little hard on them with so much going on. They're not show dogs, so they're not used to the smells of all the other dogs and the sounds of a production like this."

"I'm sure it will be chaotic."

"Now, you said you'll be bringing Lavender, is that right?" I hoped the dog could stay calm. If we ended up with the endless loop of barking, that could be bad for the other dogs and make the finale a no-go.

"Yes, I'll keep her in the dressing room until just before it's time."

"That's great. And then you'll hand her off to Drake for the finale, right?"

Rufus had clarified that would be the only time they'd need Lavender on stage. She was, in a way, standing in for Purple.

"Right," she confirmed. I sensed a lack of warmth when I mentioned the country star. I guess she wasn't as enamored with him as the majority of the female population. "Is Drake okay with Lavender? I mean has he held her? If they're not used to each other that can cause a problem."

"I think they'll be okay for that short time." Mandy didn't seem at all concerned and she'd probably seen them together.

I hoped she was right but I wasn't so sure. An animal who'd just lost her human, handed off to a strange man in front of a crowd of hundreds. I wished we'd been able to rehearse with Lavender.

"Drake will do the final number while holding Lavender?"

"That's right." I could almost see her multi-tasking with her cell phone on the other end.

For the finale, Drake would sing to Lavender one of his hit songs, "Man's Best Friend." However, for this performance he'd altered the lyrics to say, "woman's best friend, too." It was sure to be emotional for all of Purple's friends and fans.

"Then he'll bring Lavender back to you." Another worry for me that Drake was able to handle the dog. "Will you be there to take the dog at that point?"

"I will."

"Okay, sounds like we're good." I still thought having Sheron there would have been a good idea. Maybe I'd see if she was available as a backup.

I had a thought. I'd bet Sheron would love to see the show. I'd call and let her know I'd leave a ticket for her at the front desk. I made a note to myself.

"Thanks for indulging me." I tucked my list away. "I'm afraid I'm a little frazzled with all that's happened."

There was a pause.

"I'm sure you are too," I continued. "By the way, I saw your friend Trevor at the rehearsal. Someone said he's playing backup for Drake Owen."

"Not my friend, but good for him." Her voice had hardened.

"His issue with Purple, it got resolved?" I pressed.

"Trevor had business with Purple. It's been taken care of."

That sounded like an echo of the conversation between Drake Owen and Trevor. Motive. What motive could Geoffrey have possibly had? None, that I could tell. But it sounded like Trevor may have.

"Taken care of?" I said. "In what way?"

"What's this? An interrogation?" Much like Sheron had when I talked to her about Trevor, Mandy bristled when I brought him up. Neither seemed to want to talk about the details of Trevor's problem with Purple.

"No, of course not. I'm sorry." I needed to back off and quit badgering the girl. "You know, I guess I'm just still in shock."

"I understand." I could hear her take a deep breath. "I'm sure it will all be sorted out soon."

Oh, Mandy, if only you knew.

After talking to Mandy, I returned the other calls. It was comforting to talk to Diana. I think she understood more than anyone else

320

how I could despise the man and still mourn the loss.

"I know it won't do any good because you're going to be there anyway, but truly if you're not up to tonight, it's okay." I could hear barks in the background and Bella, her housekeeper, shouting at the dogs to be quiet. It was comfortingly familiar. "You've done plenty already."

"I want to be there." I knew the show could go on without me, but couldn't imagine not seeing this through.

"I know you do." I could hear the smile in her voice. "But I had to say it."

"Fine, you've said it." I loved her honest straightforward way. "Now, I've got to get dressed. I'll see you there."

CHAPTER TWENTY

Let's get this show on the road. It was time, I was ready, and I was dressed to the nines. More like the tens, if the price tag on my outfit was any indicator. Pink Valentino crepe trousers and a long, floral silk tunic suited the tropical décor, and seemed perfect for the night and the venue. Though it was to be a star-studded evening, I still needed the freedom of movement to get nose to nose with our furry friends.

Sam left his Ferrari with the parking valet who all but drooled over the flashy blue sports car. I'm sure Sam was used to it by now. Even in a part of California where flashy sports cars are plentiful, it stood out. We locked arms and entered the hotel.

I'd talked to Malone before leaving home. He'd promised to follow up with the information Mandy had shared about where Geoff had been prior to coming to the hotel with her. While it seemed pretty clear that

Geoffrey had died from a heart attack, they had planned an autopsy because of the circumstances. But there wasn't any indication it had been anything else. I knew in my heart of hearts there was something more. If they could just find it.

The hotel lobby was lined with the best of the Hollywood press corps. Cameras flashed. We stopped for a photo op.

Mama Kat would be so pleased if I actually made the news in something unrelated to a murder. And on the arm of a handsome eligible bachelor? Well, she would be beyond thrilled. I might not be exactly back to good daughter status, but it was definitely something she could brag about at the club. It didn't matter that my ex-husband, an accused killer, had just died of a heart attack right before my very eyes the night before.

It doesn't matter how you feel, it's how you look. A frequent quote from the Mama Kat book of "You-Better-Get-It-Together-Girl Rules of Life."

Sam squeezed my hand and smiled. "You okay?"

I nodded and smiled back.

Click. *There's your photo, Mama.*

We slipped off to the side.

"I'm going to have to miss the pre-show refreshments," I told Sam. "I need to head

323

backstage and make sure everything's hunky dory." I was still concerned about the potential for day-of nervousness of both celebs and dogs.

"I'll mingle with Diana and Dino." He waved at them across the room. "And then Dino and I will save you and Diana seats down front in the reserved area." He lifted my hand and kissed it. A gesture that would have seemed overdone by anyone else, but was so much a part of who he was it seemed natural. "If you can get away to see some of the show, great. If not, I'll see you right after."

I made my way through the back hallways again to the dressing rooms. Earlier I'd confirmed arrangements, and I knew Rufus had everything under control. But I'd promised my clients that I'd be available through the show and I wanted to do one last walk-through.

Rufus stood by the backstage entrance resplendent in his black tux, purple vest, and perfectly tied bow tie. His ever-present tablet was polished and at the ready. He seemed amazingly calm. In fact, calmer than I'd seen him through the whole thing. When he saw me, he stopped.

"You look gorgeous," he said.

"Thanks, hon." I joined him. "You don't

look too bad yourself."

"You don't have to do this," he said, his voice thick with emotion.

"Yes, I do." I patted his arm. "But I appreciate the thought."

I first checked in on Shar. There were pink sparkles everywhere. And I mean everywhere. The hotel would be cleaning up sparkles for the next six months. Babycakes had a new gown. And what a gown it was. I swear my fancy Texas cotillion party dress would have seemed drab in comparison to the Chinese Crested's latest frock.

"She looks best-in-show tonight and so do you." I gave Shar a thumbs-up.

"Thanks, Caro." The little actress seemed in control of Babycakes, a situation that would never have happened when we'd first met. I felt good about the difference.

I moved on to Armand and Elizabeth Watts and their little Skye Terrier, Plucky. Again, everything under control. Next stop, Carson. I also poked my head in and checked on Kristen Karmania and Scamp, her teacup chihuahua. Given the circumstances it seemed like the right thing to do.

The dressing room was packed with KK and her posse. She came forward when I asked if they needed anything and air-kissed my cheek. "I was sorry to hear about your ex."

What can I say? She made an effort.

I moved down the hall looking for any issues. Finding none, I checked the entrance where they'd be bringing in the veterans and therapy dogs.

Jonathan Trimble stood just outside with Whiskey by his side. Like Rufus, he had a sense of calm about him. No fancy notebook computer for him, but I was sure, nonetheless, that the details he'd been charged with had all been covered.

He offered me his arm as I stepped through the doorway, and I appreciated it. I would have probably been better served with more practical shoes for the night, but with the reception right after, I'd opted for not having to change. It was a short program and would move quickly. The idea was to raise awareness, and the number of big stars participating would certainly accomplish that.

All donations were welcome, but it was the reception where Warriors for the Paws hoped to connect with the big donors. Those big donations would make a marked difference.

I walked through the lineup of veterans with their dogs. They were the real stars tonight. Bringing them on stage in person was a fantastic way of making it real and bringing everything together.

I chatted with a few of the veterans, met their dogs, thanked them for coming.

I glanced at the time. Better head back inside.

"Well, I think we're ready," I said to Jonathan who still stood near the exit.

He offered me his arm, and again I was glad for the assist. But he held me back for a second. "We veterans so often feel alone or like no one remembers." He swallowed hard and took a deep breath. "I hope you and the others know how much this means."

I had no words. This time I couldn't resist giving the big guy a hug.

I looked at Whiskey for permission. The Lab not only allowed the hug, the look in his brown eyes said he approved.

When we got back to the staging area, the show had started. Sunny was onstage talking about Warriors for the Paws, explaining the program and why it was so essential. Pictures of success stories played on the screen behind her, and then the sobering numbers. The suicides. The numbers that had shocked me to the core when I'd learned about them.

That's what had tugged at Purple's heart

as well. In spite of the ego, in spite of the problems she might have had, she'd wanted to make a difference. How great that Mandy and Drake, the people closest to her, pitched in to see it through. I felt my throat tighten and turned away to regain my composure.

In doing so I ran smack dab into Trevor Lang. His spiky hair reminded me of Shar's Babycakes when she used gel on the little pup's top knot. I didn't think Trevor would appreciate the comparison to the funny little pup. He appeared to be going for the tough, rock-and-roll-guy look with his ripped jeans and worn leather jacket. A guitar was slung over his back.

"Oh, sorry." He steadied me. "I didn't see you."

"You're Trevor." Up close, I could see he wasn't very tall. Was he tall enough to have struck Purple if she were standing? "I tried to talk to you a couple of days ago."

He looked confused.

"On the street," I reminded him. "I yelled your name. You took off."

"Yeah, sorry." He looked sheepish. "I guess I was a little spooked by everything going on. Pan and everything."

"There was history between you, right? I guess you were angry with her? That's so hard now." I wasn't going to pass up this opportunity to ask. Malone wouldn't be happy, but we were surrounded by people. How much risk could there be?

"Nah. That's ancient history." He moved to leave, but I stepped in front of him. "Once upon a time Mandy and I were an item. And I had a fling with . . . uh . . . Pan. And I . . . let's just say I was young and stupid."

Young and stupid? I could sure relate to that.

"So, you and Mandy. You and Purple?" I tried to put it together in my head. Had Mandy known that?

How awful.

"Yeah, like I said, it was stupid and a long time ago. It only came up again because I found out Purple had been passing off one of my early songs as her own."

"That must have made you angry."

"I guess." He shifted nervously and ran a hand through his spiky blond hair. "At first, but she agreed to make it right. Unfortunately, she didn't get all the papers signed before she died. But Drake's the executor and will be able to move forward with what we'd agreed on."

"Did Mandy know?" I couldn't get over how she could have continued to work for Purple all this time, but she had.

"I'm sorry, why are you so interested in

my business?" Trevor glanced around.

"Did Mandy know?" I repeated.

"Not until Pan told her." He stared at me. "Why?"

"That's what you and Mandy were arguing about? When you were at the house?" Wow, I had interrupted that exchange all wrong.

"Yeah, it turns out fifteen years isn't long enough. Hell hath no fury and all that." He shrugged. "She went a little crazy on me."

I stood still, trying to digest what I'd just learned, adjusting the lens on my thinking. The backstage din eddied around us. I glanced up to see Rufus frowning in our direction.

"Lady, I've got to go." Trevor righted his guitar. "Drake is about to go on and I'm his new backup guitar player."

So much to sort out in what Trevor had just said.

Details that explained the conversation I'd overheard between him and Drake. And the reaction from both Mandy and Sheron when I'd mentioned his name.

But if Drake was about to go on, that meant they were also going to be bringing the veterans on, and then Lavender needed to be ready. I raced back to the dressing rooms.

CHAPTER TWENTY-ONE

I knocked on the door marked "Lavender" and entered. Mandy had the dog on the dressing table in front of the mirror putting on the finishing touches.

"Can I help with anything?" I asked.

Mandy jumped at the sound of my voice.

"You both look great." I was careful to keep my voice clam. It calms anxious dogs and humans in stressful situations.

Mandy looked festive in a soft-lavender chiffon skirt. Lavender looked a little confused by everything but she wasn't barking so that was good. Mandy had her back to me, but I could see she was digging in the big duffle bag that had all of Lavender's accessories.

She pulled a bow out of the duffle bag, settled it on Lavender's head, and clipped it in place.

"That's not the right bow." I reached for the bag to help, but she pulled it back.

This bow was purple and a very nice bow, but it was definitely not the bow Betty Foxx had delivered.

"Yes, it is," Mandy insisted.

"No, the bow Lavender is supposed to be wearing for the finale is the one from the Bow Wow Boutique. Remember? It has Purple's grandfather's military bar worked into it." I hated to be a pain, and I knew it was just a bow, but it was the wrong bow. Purple had gone to a lot of trouble and it seemed wrong to disregard her wishes.

"It doesn't matter." She zipped the bag closed.

"Here." I held out my hand. "Give me the bag and I'll look for it."

"Never mind," she snapped. "This is fine."

"But —"

Mandy slung the bag over her shoulder and opened the door. "I'll bring the dog back here, and since Sheron is here at your invitation, after I bring her back she can take her."

"Wait." Drake hadn't started yet. We still had time to get the right bow on the dog.

Mandy didn't stop. I followed her out. Sheron was in the wings and I wondered why Mandy hadn't simply let Sheron handle getting the bow on Lavender. She was so good with the dog, and clearly Mandy was stressed out.

Then I heard Drake on stage.

"And this song is for our star in the heavens, Purple, or Pandora as I called her. She believed so much in this cause. She was raised by her granddaddy, a World War II Purple Heart recipient."

Yes, she was and she'd had that bow made so a piece of her grandfather's history was part of this event.

I couldn't fathom why Mandy didn't see the importance.

The veterans and their dogs began to fill the scene behind Drake. I could see Jonathan and Whiskey across the stage on the other side making sure everyone got on.

Mandy stood stage left, just a few feet from me, holding Lavender. The dog's bag was slung over her shoulder. I crept closer and got another frown from Rufus. When Mandy walked forward onto the stage to hand the dog to Drake, Rufus snagged the duffle. He was not about to let her ruin the look of the production with a clunky bag.

She gave him a glare but kept going.

There was applause as the fans recognized Lavender, and I'm sure many of the Purple fans also recognized Mandy. Drake linked her arm with his as he took the dog.

I snatched the purple duffle bag from

Rufus and opened it.

Well, for cryin' in a bucket. The bow was right there. The gold ribbon, however, was splattered with dark stains. Why hadn't Mandy just said so? When Betty Foxx had spilled the pomegranate juice it must have stained the bow.

I felt my face get hot as I remembered. Betty and her lunge forward, the juice flying all over, Purple's shock.

Oh, man, if we'd known, the bow could have been replaced. I'm sure whoever Mel had used could have made another bow.

Wait a minute.

I pictured the scene in my head again. Purple, Betty, the bright-red pomegranate juice. The juice on Purple's wig, Betty's head, and the poor dog. But the bow hadn't been on Lavender when the juice spilled, it had been over on the desk. If this wasn't juice then it had to be something else. I rubbed my finger across the dark stain.

Blood?

I stuffed the bow back in the bag and zipped it shut.

With a click, all the final pieces of the puzzle suddenly fell into place. I knew who had killed Purple and thanks to my earlier chat with Trevor I knew why.

It *had* been a crime of passion and the

killer had been right under our noses the whole time. Taking care of details.

I stepped away from the stage area, and pulled my cell phone out to call Detective Malone. Just as I did, my phone vibrated with an incoming call.

"Caro, you were right," he said. "I just had a call, we did a rush tox screen and there was a drug in Geoffrey Carlisle's bloodstream. One that wouldn't mix well with alcohol. It appears to be methylphenidate hydrochloride or Ritalin. We didn't find any at his apartment. Do you know if he was on that?"

Oh, wow.

I really wanted to focus on the "Caro, you were right" statement but the drug was truly the other missing piece of the puzzle.

"Geoffrey was *not* on methylphenidate. However, Purple was and ordered large amounts at a time because she was on the road." The bag Betty had accidently taken from Purple's room had been Ritalin.

"So, that means —"

"I don't know all of the whys, but I know for sure who killed both Purple and Geoffrey." I looked back at the stage. Drake was holding Lavender and singing the closing number, but where was Mandy?

"Caro?"

"Just a minute, I've lost sight of her."

I spotted Mandy as she exited stage right instead of coming off stage left as we'd rehearsed.

"Mandy!" I shouted.

She glanced back at me and then slipped through the crew toward the back exit.

"Stop her," I yelled as I tried to push through the crowd lining up to go on for the final thank-yous. The chatter was so loud no one even reacted.

I circumvented the crowd taking a path behind the backdrop, but I wasn't going to make it in time; she was almost to the door.

"Stop her," I yelled again.

Suddenly Mandy was head over heels in a flurry of lavender skirts, and then like a rag doll she was sprawled on the floor.

As I got closer I saw the reason, Sheron held the end of a cord she'd yanked just as Mandy was getting away. Mandy scrambled to her feet and dashed for the back exit, but it was blocked by Whiskey's growl and Jonathan Trimble's bulk.

"I think you need to stay put, miss." He pulled out a folding chair and sat her on it. Trimble and Whiskey stood guard, their eyes on Mandy.

I didn't think she would be going anywhere.

With a nod to Jonathan, I hurried back to stand in the wings where I'd been before. As Drake Owen came off the stage, he handed me Lavender and then headed back to be there for the final acknowledgements with the larger group. I gave the dog a cuddle and handed her off to Sheron. She cradled the dog and whispered something to her.

Malone must have already been onsite when he'd called as he was there within minutes, followed by two uniformed officers. Neither of which was Officer Hostas, I'm happy to say. Malone had the uniforms take Mandy out the back. I'm sure Sunny and the others appreciated the effort to minimize the media furor.

Applause sounded from the auditorium and Drake and the others surged off the stage, oblivious to all the excitement that had just happened backstage.

The stars and their pets all deserved a pat on the head. I checked in with each and congratulated them on a job well done. I picked up a few lost dog toys to return later, including a fluffy pink pig that I was sure belonged to Babycakes.

I popped my head into Lavender's dressing room. I'd given Malone the bag containing the bloody bow, but wasn't sure what else Mandy might have brought along. Sheron stood by the mirror lost in thought, Lavender still in her arms. She turned as I came in.

"Are you okay?" I couldn't believe how quickly she'd acted.

Sheron nodded. "I can't believe it was Mandy all along."

"Hard to believe," I agreed. The clues had been there, but none of us had seen them. "You're welcome to come to the reception."

She shook her head. "Thanks, but I'm just going to take her home."

"Do you want one of the officers to go with you?" She was clearly shaken by learning Mandy was the one who had taken Purple's life.

"I'm okay." She hugged Lavender to her.

I gave the pup a scratch behind the ears. "I'll look in on you two tomorrow."

In the end, barking with the Stars had come off successfully. But that myth about there being no such thing as bad publicity? I think we'd all agree — not true.

Tomorrow there would be plenty of time for announcements about caught killers. Tonight, we'd celebrate the silent heroes and try to do some good to help them.

Diana had joined Sunny on stage for the

final remarks. Nora Worthington had joined them for the closing. She had arrived in LA and been driven straight to the venue so that she could add her support.

Rufus, Diana, and Sunny knew something had gone on backstage during the finale. I waited until the majority had left for the reception before I filled them in.

Then I went down front to explain things to Sam and Dino.

The after-party was in full swing as we made our way to the ballroom. There was still work to be done, and Sunny and Diana were in their element, schmoozing the rich and famous, explaining the work, asking for support.

Some of the veterans had stayed. I was sure Jonathan had not, but I looked around for him. Rufus still worked at making sure everyone was taken care of. I hoped he had a major rest planned for tomorrow. All of next week for that matter.

Sam and I talked with a few people. I introduced him to Tania whom I'd grown attached to. Several of the Purple Posers stopped by to speak to me, mostly to drool over Sam.

I thought I recognized Marsha in the group based on how she handled her dog. I took a chance. "Is this Periwinkle?" I reached in and petted the pooch's head.

She nodded and gave a big grin holding the dog close.

Of course, with the wig, her grin was the only part of her face I could see.

"She seems to be doing great."

"Yes," she said, her voice clear. "Much better. Do you have a moment?" The self-assurance was evident; she wore it like she wore the garb.

"Certainly." I stepped off to the side. "More issues with Peri?"

"No," she whispered. "I should have told you before. The note was from me."

"The one asking me to call?"

"Yes." She bit her lip. "And then when you called there were people close by who might be involved. I panicked. I'm sorry about that. I hope they catch whoever took those things from Purple's suite. I've been seeing them online so someone is selling them and that's not right. She gave them for this. For them." She waved a hand at the room. "Here's a list of the places I've seen them." She handed me a note written on the same type of paper.

"I'll see the detective gets this," I said. "Thank you."

"You're welcome." For the first time it was Marsha's normal voice and not the strong

Purple role.

I tucked the note in my bag and Marsha rejoined the other Posers.

I looked around for Sam.

Reality had caught up with me. I was more than ready to call it a night.

Once back at my place, I slipped off my shoes and accepted the glass of wine Sam had poured for me. He settled beside me on the couch.

"Caro," he began.

"I can't —"

Boy, I hoped he realized I wasn't up to the Big Discussion right now.

"Don't put me off." He shifted to face me. "You don't need to say anything. No pressure. You don't need to respond. Just listen. Okay?"

I nodded.

"The last week while I was in New York I realized something. Maybe because I was there to sort out a problem a family member was having with his fiancé."

"A family member?"

"Ah, yes. My cousin, Dmitri. High flier. Probably in way over his head this time." He chuckled. "But I don't want to talk about my crazy family."

The man did not know crazy. If Mama Kat

341

ever got him to Texas for that barbeque he would meet full-blown crazy.

He took my hand and turned me so I had to look at him. "What I want to say to you is this." He paused. "You, Caro Lamont, are the woman for me. That will never change. There is no expiration date. There is no rush. Whatever time you need is the time you need. I will be here."

The doorbell rang.

And thank the Good Lord for that because my heart was so full, I was about to fall to pieces.

He didn't move right away, but continued to look at me. "We will take this one step at a time. We will take as long as you need."

The doorbell rang again.

He didn't move for a full minute. "You understand?"

I nodded, unable to speak.

He released my hand and went to answer the door.

"It's the police," he called.

How many guys can declare their love, and then answer the door to a homicide detective without breaking stride?

Not many I'm thinking. Not many.

Malone filled in the gaps on what had transpired between Mandy and Purple.

She'd lawyered up but not before a tirade about her frenemy, Purple. Malone felt like there was enough evidence for a jury to send her away for a very long time.

"She admitted to making up the stalker. She'd done it to rattle her boss, but then it turned into good publicity so she continued. She also admitted to the note on your car hoping to rattle you," Malone said. "She was just a fount of information. Until her lawyer arrived and put an end to that."

"How on earth did you get the blood work done on the tox screen so quickly?" I knew it usually took weeks if not longer.

"I called in a few favors." Malone grinned. "Now, I owe a few."

"So, Mandy hadn't known Purple was the reason Trevor dumped her way back when?" Sam asked.

"Not until he showed up wanting Purple to acknowledge she'd not given him credit for one of her big songs." Malone took the coffee Sam offered him. "When the truth came out and Purple told her to get over it, Mandy lost it. Bashed the singer over the head with a statue of herself."

"And Geoffrey?" I asked. "The Ritalin mixed with alcohol made Geoffrey act crazy and then stopped his heart." I still had the awful visual of him grabbing his chest. "But why kill him?"

"It looks like from some of the emails we were able to recover, he was engaging in a bit of blackmail."

"Now that I can believe." I hadn't thought Geoffrey was capable of murder. But blackmail? Yeah, I could see that.

"We'll need you to come down and sign a statement about tonight." Malone drained his cup and went to put it in the sink.

"Oh, I almost forgot." I grabbed my bag and pulled out my notebook, the pupcakes, dog treats, my makeup bag, several dog toys, and finally the list that Marsha had given me.

Sam and Malone looked at each other and shrugged.

"This is from one the Purple Posers." I handed the note to Malone. "She says you'll find several of the missing memorabilia items on these sites."

"Two different crimes. Same crime scene." Malone took the note.

"Before Purple was killed?" I'd wondered about the timing.

"Most likely before she was even in the room." He tucked the paper in his pocket. "By disabling the cameras so he could break in, our thief really complicated the murder investigation. We'll follow-up."

Sam walked Malone out and then refilled our wineglasses and settled in beside me on the couch.

"I know what," I said.

"What?" He smiled.

"Let's talk about something other than murder."

He held out his glass to clink it with mine. "I can toast to that."

CHAPTER TWENTY-TWO

The next day, I finally got my run on the beach. Not to be too dramatic about it, but I felt like I'd been caged. I'd needed so badly to get out and feel the sand beneath my feet.

Sam and his hugely handsome Border Collie Mac, joined me, which brought the day up another notch on the best days list. We played in the surf, soaked in the warmth, and as the sun melted into the horizon, ran along the beach until we were flat exhausted.

Exactly what I needed.

Sam, Mac, and I had just crossed PCH and started down the block to top off the perfect evening with a dark-chocolate hazelnut gelato, when I spotted Mr. Swanson a half block away. A quick sprint, and I had him by the arm. I could see his Range Rover parked on the street and wasn't going to lose track of him this time.

I'd convince him to give me Grandma Tillie's brooch back and then I would call Melinda and we'd sort this thing out once and for all. It was time to mend fences. Enough was enough.

I held on.

"Let go of me." Swanson twisted to get loose.

"When you hand over my brooch, I will." I didn't let go. "I know you want the money for gambling debts."

"How do you know that?" He stopped twisting and stared at me.

"I have my ways." I looked him in the eye. "You know, something like that can be awful, but you need to realize that you have a problem."

"What I need is to get the money back in our retirement account before my wife finds out," he muttered.

"The money won't really solve your problem though, will it?" I knew there was a pattern with a gambling addiction, and he'd be right back at it if he didn't get help. "I have a colleague who works with gamblers. Let me give you his information. Okay?"

He nodded.

I reached in my cross-body for Dr. Hille's card.

When I let go of him, the little gnome immediately took off for his vehicle. Who knew he could move that fast?

My legs were longer than his, though, and I was motivated. I caught him just as he reached for the car door.

"Not nice." I latched on to his wrist. "Okay, if you don't want help, you don't want help. Just hand over the brooch, and I won't have you arrested as a jewel thief."

"Arrgh." He clenched his teeth in frustration, but I wasn't giving up so easily.

Ooof!

I staggered forward as I was suddenly smacked on the backside with what felt like a fifty-pound bag of dog food.

"Let go of my husband." The petite woman reared back to hit me again with a purse the size of a suitcase. I think she was probably aiming for my head, but I was so much taller than she was, all she could reach was a lot lower.

"Stop!" I let go of Swanson and put up my hands to defend myself.

"Get in the car, Otis," the little spitfire yelled. "Quick before she grabs you again."

"Okay, fine." I let go of Mr. Swanson who did apparently have a first name and it was Otis. "I'll just call the police and report you as a jewel thief. We'll let Detective Malone sort things out." I whipped out my cell phone.

Of course, I wouldn't call a homicide detective. Heck, I wouldn't even call the police, but I thought throwing out Malone's name gave my threat more credibility.

"A jewel thief?" The Mrs. stopped hitting me with her handbag long enough to ask.

"Okay, okay," Mr. Swanson said. "I'll give you the ugly brooch."

"Let's go get it right now." I put my cell phone away. "I don't trust that you'll give it to me otherwise."

"Okay," he confirmed. "Come on then."

He moved to get into the car, but Mrs. Swanson didn't move. Still as a statue she stood, her mouth left open mid-comment.

"What's the matter, dear?" Mr. Swanson asked.

"Are you talking about that ugly brooch you had hidden in the sugar canister?"

"You knew about it?" he asked.

"Of course, I knew about it," she scoffed. "I just didn't know what you were up to with it."

"That doesn't matter now." He opened the door to the car. "I need to go get it and give it to this lady."

"Well, you can't." She frowned at him.

"Why not?" He turned to look at her.

"Because I gave it to that funny-looking lady."

"What funny-looking lady?" he asked.

I had a bad feeling.

I was pretty sure Melinda was not the funny-looking lady.

"You remember her. The one with lipstick for eyebrows. We met her at the glamping thing we went to."

I'd been *this* close to getting the Grandma Tillie's brooch back and Mrs. Swanson had gone and given it to Betty Foxx.

Unbelievable.

I stuffed the counseling referral card I still held in Mr. Swanson's shirt pocket. "Buddy, I'm afraid you've got some explaining to do, and I think you're probably going to need this."

I left Mr. and Mrs. Swanson standing there and walked back to where Sam and Mac stood on the sidewalk waiting for me.

Unbelievable.

CARO'S APPLE PUPCAKES

Ingredients
2-3/4 cups water
1/4 cup applesauce (unsweetened)
2 teaspoons of honey
1/4 tablespoon of vanilla extract
1 medium egg
4 cups whole wheat flour
1 cup dried apple chips (unsweetened)
1 tablespoon of baking powder

Directions
1. Preheat oven to 350 degrees
2. Mix water, applesauce, honey, egg, and vanilla together in a bowl
3. Add remaining ingredients and mix until well blended
4. Pour into lightly greased muffin pans
5. Bake 35 minutes

Let cool before frosting. For frosting I use plain yogurt or cottage cheese that I've run through the blender until creamy.

Please note: I always clear my clients for allergies before giving any of my homemade treats. And then I make a notation of any allergies on their charts.

ACKNOWLEDGEMENTS

First, a huge thank-you to the whole team at Bell Bridge Books and especially to our editor extraordinaire, Debra Dixon. We continue to learn and improve because of you, and we thank you for sharing your expertise and insight. Also, special tip of the hat to Niki and Kendal, BBB's marketing mavens. We can't thank you enough for all you do for us.

We are also grateful to Christine Witthohn, our agent, at Book Cents Literary Agency for her ongoing guidance, encouragement, and support.

A special shout-out to Justin, Candice, Joshua, Kelli, and Aaron on this book. It takes a special family to talk plot twists, clues, and murder methods at a family gathering.

And, as always, Tami, Cindy, and Christine

— it couldn't happen without you.

Finally, a heartfelt thank-you to our readers. We feel incredibly blessed by your messages, posts, and emails. We love how you love our stories and how you care about what happens with Caro, Mel, and the rest of the crew. We'd hug you in person if we could. And if we see you in person, look out, because we probably will.

Don't forget to sign up for updates so we can keep in touch!

Mary Lee and Anita aka Sparkle Abbey

www.SparkleAbbey.com

ABOUT THE AUTHORS

Sparkle Abbey is the pseudonym of two mystery authors (Mary Lee Woods and Anita Carter). They are friends and neighbors as well as co-writers of the Pampered Pets Mystery Series. The pen name was created by combining the names of their rescue pets — Sparkle (Mary Lee's cat) and Abbey (Anita's dog). They reside in central Iowa, but if they could write anywhere, you would find them on the beach with their laptops and, depending on the time of day, with either an iced tea or a margarita.

Mary Lee Salsbury Woods is the "**Sparkle**" half of Sparkle Abbey. She is past-president of Sisters in Crime–Iowa and a member of Mystery Writers of America, Romance Writers of America, Kiss of Death, the RWA Mystery Suspense Chapter, Sisters in Crime National, and the SinC Internet group Guppies.

Prior to publishing the Pampered Pets Mystery Series with Bell Bridge Books, Mary Lee won first place in the Daphne du Maurier contest, sponsored by the Kiss of Death chapter of RWA, and was a finalist in Murder in the Grove's mystery contest, as well as Killer Nashville's Claymore Dagger contest.

Mary Lee is an avid reader and supporter of public libraries. She lives in Central Iowa with her husband, Tim, and Sparkle, the rescue cat namesake of Sparkle Abbey. In her day job, she is the non-techie in the IT Department. Any spare time she spends reading and enjoying her sons, daughters-in-law, and six grandchildren.

Anita Carter is the "**Abbey**" half of Sparkle Abbey. She is a member of Mystery Writers of America, Romance Writers of America, Kiss of Death, the RWA Mystery Suspense chapter, and Sisters in Crime.

She grew up reading Trixie Belden, Nancy Drew, and the Margo Mystery series by Jerry B. Jenkins (years before his popular *Left Behind* series). Her family is grateful all the years of "fending for yourself" dinners of spaghetti and frozen pizza have finally paid off, even though they haven't exactly stopped.

In Anita's day job, she works for a fitness company. She also lives in Central Iowa with her husband and four children, son-in-law, grandchild, and two rescue dogs, Chewy and Sophie.